Alun Richards was born in Pontypridd in 1929. He was educated at Pontypridd Grammar School and then undertook teacher training in Caerleon before spending time as a Lieutenant Instructor in the Royal Navy. After a long period of serious illness as a tubercular patient, he studied at Swansea University and subsequently worked as a Probation Officer in London. Thereafter, although he had periods of employment as a secondary school teacher and, late in life, an enjoyable spell as an Adult Education Tutor in Literature at Swansea University, in essence from the 1960s he was, and successfully so, a full-time writer. He lived with his wife Helen and their four children near the Mumbles, close to the sea which, coupled with the hills of the South Wales Valleys, was the landscape of his fiction.

His output was prodigious. It included six novels between 1962 and 1979, and two collections of short stories, *Dai Country* (1973) and *The Former Miss Merthyr Tydfil* (1976). Plays for stage and radio were complemented by original screenplays and adaptations for television, including BBC's *Onedin Line*. As editor, he produced best-selling editions of Welsh short stories and tales of the sea for Penguin. His sensitive biography of his close friend, Carwyn James, appeared in 1984 and his own entrancing memoir *Days of Absence* in 1986.

Alun Richards died in 2004.

HOME TO AN EMPTY HOUSE

ALUN RICHARDS

PARTHIAN

LIBRARY OF WALES

Parthian
The Old Surgery
Napier Street
Cardigan
SA43 1ED
www.parthianbooks.co.uk

The Library of Wales is a Welsh Assembly Government initiative which highlights and celebrates Wales' literary heritage in the English language.

The publisher acknowledges the financial support of the Welsh Books Council.

The Library of Wales publishing project is based at Trinity College, Carmarthen, SA31 3EP.
www.libraryofwales.org

Series Editor: Dai Smith

First published in 1973
© Alun Richards 1973
Library of Wales edition published 2006
Foreword © Rachel Trezise 2006
All Rights Reserved

ISBN 1-902638-85-9
    978-1-902638-85-0
Cover design by Lucy Llewellyn
Cover painting Ernest Zobole (1927-99)
About a House no 2 (1987-88) oil on canvas, 153 x 183cm
Copyright: Estate of Ernest Zobole
Reproduction: University of Glamorgan

Printed and bound by Gwasg Gomer, Llandysul, Wales
Typeset by logodædaly

British Library Cataloguing in Publication Data

A cataloguing record for this book is available from the British Library.

LIBRARY OF WALES

FOREWORD

When I first read *Home to an Empty House* in autumn 2005, I was living with my fiancé in a basement flat beneath his parents' house, impatiently awaiting the renovation of our own home. It was a box; one kitchen/lounge, a hotel bathroom with a mini-tub, the plug pulled free of its chain, and a bedroom below the family kitchen. Each morning I was woken by the ceiling creaking; my soon-to-be mother-in-law pounding across it in her relentless quest to prepare a nutritional breakfast and delicately wash everyone's clothes, and make real tea with a real teapot; a matronal domestic goddess.

Ironic then, that this book is set in a basement flat, that of Walter the wise-cracking paranoiac and Connie, teacher of the 'backward class', a couple who know much about sex but little about each other, locked in a marriage doomed to fail. The relative upstairs here is Connie's Auntie Rachel and they hear her in the mornings too, gargling salt water. I would like to think that is where the similarities of our situations begin *and* end, but if I'm honest I must admit that I see myself in Connie. By the time I discovered this character, she'd been thirty-two years on the page. It's not an exceptionally long time really, but sufficient enough for a few changes in the attitudes and expectations of women, given the recent speed of our alleged evolution. In many ways we have surpassed equality – we are chairmen, chief executives, Prime Ministers and mothers. We cherry pick the life experiences that we want: smile genially over our hand-baked flans at the weekend, demand cunnilingus in the bedroom and then on Monday, turn sour-faced in the boardroom. I thought this was a relatively new occurrence but Connie has always been a precocious dominatrix, lacking in sentiment. Why else, while waiting to have sex with Walter for the first time, would she have said this:

> What he could never understand was that I wanted it as much as he did. I don't know where he got his ideas about women from. He professed to be knowledgeable about whores, but that was all. Perhaps he wanted me in a whore's get up. I didn't mind if it would help him.

Surely for a woman of the early Seventies (the same age as my mother), she has a particularly modern outlook. Or maybe I'm being naive. It's the Millennium after all and even reality television allows footage of masturbation with the aid of a wine bottle. It must have started somewhere. Moreover, it's probably not a question of timing at all. Alun Richards wrote in his 1986 memoir *Days of Absence* about his deep disliking of 'the exclusivity of the immensely unattractive world of men'. In much of his work, male characters are unreliable, often useless, losers, while females are outstanding truth-tellers: the realists who describe life, as is. Perhaps it's because Richards's father abandoned his mother three days after his birth, and never returned. Whatever the reason, *Home to an Empty House* is no exception. Connie is one thing but Auntie Rachel is the keen surveyor who sees through all, including her niece's extra-marital affair.

> It is the oldest story in the world, the older man and younger woman, the one seeking what he has lost, the other finding out what is in front of her... Soft, I call it, like all wishful thinking. They snatch at each other's bodies in the dark and think it is important.

It was in fact Richards himself who had a particularly modern outlook. He would have grimaced at a suggestion that his work was confined by his being Welsh, although Welsh he was, born and christened Alun in Pontypridd. Richards' Wales was the South Wales valleys, outward-looking, non-Welsh speaking and already rich with the influence of migrants; a place that bred 'champions of the world, not bloody Machynlleth'. The *Bloomsbury Dictionary of English Literature* refers to him as a writer who rejected 'a romanticised Welsh past of myth and anecdote and who was concerned instead with the modern Wales of rugby, beauty queens, television, the language question and the industrial and spiritual decline in the South Wales valleys'. They are subjects that I, a 'new writer', am still dealing with today.

In order to faithfully tell of this new world, Richards relied on many of his own experiences. Serious writing, he suggested, should not misrepresent the scenery of its creator's mind. A writer was at his best when he was 'up his favourite alley'. In an essay called *The Art of Narrative*, Richards says, 'It seems to me that there is what an

American critic once identified as "a psychological burn" in human lives, a very clumsy expression but one which indicates that the pain of loss, or the intensity of experience can create the most complete revelations'. It is not wayward therefore to suggest Walter's bout of tuberculosis, the very thing that allows Connie time and privacy to stray, is based on Richards's own experience of the infection. He spent two years in hospital receiving treatment. This is Walter at the onset of the illness and opening of the work:

> You ever been ill? I mean really sick, the sense of rottenness deep down, a feeling of poor quality about every limb you own? Nothing supports you like it should, ashes in the mouth and you haven't even got the puff to do up a shoe, and there's this pallor on you, all cheekbones and eyes, the lines where they shouldn't be, the sweat coming at the wrong times as when you look at an unexpected flight of steps, and you've become a right pedlar of sighs.

Richards's candid approach does not however make his work cold or in any way unattractive. He hated hypocrites, snobs and bullshitters, testimony to which can be found in his 1995 Rhys Davies Memorial Lecture. On the subject of having edited the 1993 *Penguin Book of Welsh Short Stories*, he says, 'few Welsh writers have a discernable body of work.... With one or two exceptions, you would never think that there is a power structure, wealthy families, groups of persons whose lugubrious self-enhancement as they pass from committee to committee is ripe meat for the discerning eye.' This nuance influenced him to expose many of these illusions and snobberies in his work but it invariably pushed him, as a person, towards the edges of society. He worked as both a probation officer and a school teacher, jobs which coloured his writing. I'm reminded of one story about his time at Ely Comprehensive. Taking a class largely made up of black thirteen-year-old boys for physical education on a wet Monday morning, he decided to teach them to play rugby. Standing on the running track, the rain misting his thick spectacles (they'd been a necessity since his illness), he held the ball tightly in the crook of his arm, and said, 'The object of this game is to get the ball, any way you can.'

'Any way, Sir?' one of the boys enquired.

'Yes, any way.' The boy jumped and spat at the lenses of his glasses, grabbing the ball while Richards was blind. And Richards's response? 'I laughed out loud.'

It is this rare warmth of human character that allowed him to write *Home to an Empty House*, a frank tragicomedy about ordinary people living against the backdrop of an industrial Wales that is quickly falling away, never getting what they want, but finally realising what it is they need.

Rachel Trezise

HOME TO AN EMPTY HOUSE

CHAPTER ONE

WALTER

The white spot of the ophthalmoscope moved in close, unblinking like a ferret's eye, an unnatural button brightness moving closer, right in close so I couldn't blink away the tears, but I saw his jowl then, filmy behind the instrument, his smooth, clean-cut, pretty boy's jaw, then smelt his lime aftershave sweet to the nostrils against the antiseptic clinical smell, wincing for a moment as he grasped my forehead with his other cold hand and turned me round to get another angle. I was sweating, icicles trickling under my armpits, my good shirt coating and bowels near emptying with fear, but just managing not to get a knee shake which would have been a giveaway because in order to get in close, his knee was between mine, jammed up close to my crutch as he kept looking down that peeper of his.

You ever been ill? I mean really sick, the sense of rottenness deep down, a feeling of poor quality about every limb you own? Nothing supports you like it should, ashes in the mouth and you haven't even got the puff to do up a shoe, and there's this pallor on you, all cheekbones and eyes, the lines where they shouldn't be, the sweat coming at the wrong times as when you look at an unexpected flight of steps, and you've become a right pedlar of sighs.

Ah... you say. *Ah... Oh... Aw...* And before you know where you are, you're doing it all the time. Everything about you is paper thin, you feel. You'd bite a nun's head off for the sake of not shutting a door, and even when you get a grip of the old alk, lifting the top of the bottle doesn't produce as much as a bubble. A little less of the you-know-what, you say to yourself, whatever your special *what* is, but in your heart you know you're beat.

That was me then, only worse than the bilious squidges in front of my eyes, every time I gave the cough an airing, there was this mystery about my left eye.

'The blip from out there,' I'd reported to the optician when it first appeared. 'A little white spot. I can see it there quite clearly, only it's not there from your point of view if you know what I mean? Left eye, and I can see it with my eye shut if that's any help? No, not your left, my left.'

The optician was a woman, white coat, letterbox lips, chunky eyebrows, grey hair wrapped in a bun like wire, and a prile of lumpy garnet beads swaddling a prime leather neck like a white Bantu sitting behind a pot. She cooked me all right.

4

'Definitely a case of eye strain. I should say reading glasses are a possibility.'

'Glasses?'

'Do you do a lot of close work?'

'Only when the lights are out.'

'It won't be necessary to wear them except for close work.'

'I'll remember that,' I said. 'But can you hurry it up?'

It was still there, a white blip like an unhatched spider's egg in front of me. How did I know that tarantulas don't usually attack in the daylight? They can sit watching their victims for hours until the light goes. And then – bingo! – the shutters are up. I have that kind of melodramatic mind. Which is just as well, the way things turned out.

When I got the reading glasses, it was still there. The lenses didn't alter it either way.

I said, 'It's still there'.

'What is?'

'The blip. In the left eye. The glasses don't make any difference.'

There was only her in the room with me but the blip was like a third presence. It would not go away. I blinked, screwed up my eye, squeezed my eyelids together, then opened them quickly. No difference. It was there in front of me, hanging levelly in limbo like a tiny cocoon. I scowled. If it lived with me much longer, it would require a name. How about Joey, I thought. It was getting like a pet.

'A further point,' I reported. 'The lenses don't even magnify it.'

I could see her examining my nose for drink signs, and she gave me a mouthful of teeth with a sudden horse smile and a pay-now, complain-later, giggle as if we were all chaps together.

'I'm sure you'll find the spectacles a relief, but if you're still seeing things, I should consult your general practitioner.'

'Oh, yes,' I said. All good advice. But I was scared. I had no idea what it could be, my thing. And I had no energy, no resources. I dragged my feet every day. I'd no appetite either, felt guilty about one or two things. In short, I was a customer for whatever was coming. The low spots in your life always hit you with your trousers down, and with me, it was general nick, and going on down in the medical stakes. And my fear never left me.

The white light again. My little blip and his white light.

The GP had sent me to him and now he put the instrument against the other eye, mine.

'There's nothing wrong with that one,' I said.

They don't have to reply, of course, but I didn't like his silence. He was young, uppercrust Irish, all shirt cuffs and gold links beneath the white starch, and that impersonal, waxen, SS look that characterises this speciality of medicine. I had this crazy legend in my mind of wayward, drunken, wild-eyed men of brilliance, surgeons who put raw onions in their children's socks and hated to use the knife. I used to think I was the most naive man I'd ever met, and slightly round the twist, you've gathered? I'd believe anything.

Presently, he said, 'Have you done any heavy manual work lately?'

'Certainly not.'

'Tree felling? Using an axe?'

'Not on your life.'

'Jacking up cars?'

'I couldn't light a jackie jumper.'

He nodded and began to scribble a note.

'I want you to get your chest X-rayed.'

'Oh, that...'

If it's easy to guess, your diagnosis and mine, it alters nothing. The moment I started hearing the mumbo jumbo – cavity upper left ventricle, pains in the chest, marked loss of weight – I had that feeling of passing into other hands, a depersonalisation that prisoners get the moment they go through the gates. Still it wasn't old coffin nails, but pulmonary tuberculosis, such a cliché and so dated. Of course, I was just old enough to remember tales of families going down with it, the street scourge. Galloping consumption, they used to say. I'd met a baker whose girl refused to marry him because of his pallor. He had the sign, her family told her, and for weeks he became a handkerchief watcher, squinting for flecks in the early morning, watching himself for confirmation that flour wasn't the only ruin of his love life. But this was a decade ago, operatic like then. Or so I thought. And I had this eye too, my little white spider, Joey the One.

Only this was another department.

It was, they said when I got there, to this other department, rare. (Hats off, one and all!) A condition of the vitreous known as Eale's disease.

'I don't see more than six cases in a year,' the white coat said.

Charming. I never found out who Eale was, but there was no definite prognosis. They couldn't say, he said. Nobody could say.

'What d'you mean you can't say?' Fear makes you unreasonable and I always sounded anyway like the shop steward the motor companies most wanted to sack. He couldn't say? What the hell was he there for?

He picked up a pen and began to scribble again. Their MD handwriting... Nothing said and just writing away, squinting at the X-ray plate which was up on his private movie projector, a muscle twitching as he crossed a *t* and the clinical finger writ on. Silence.

There are moments in your life when silence hangs in the air like dust. Nothing moves; you can almost see it, the stillness. All these ophthalmic cookies operate in dingy holes like wizards. You'd swear somebody wanted to hide them away. There were corners in his hole where you had to crouch. It was laced with tomes, bulging out of the fireplace, standing on the gas fire, piled up to the ceiling in two corners and here and there, glinting silver discs dotted about like metal eyes. From his squinting apparatus, they were all laid out with an exquisite studied casualness. Genius at work, I tried to kid myself. Except that green was the universal colour in the decor, county council green.

I took out a cigarette and lit it.

A sigh pursed his lips – what was he writing, a thesis? – he looked up, found a tin lid from under a thatch of files, nudged it forward, then got on with his composition.

I gave the John Player a booster, sucking it right down, and flicked the ash neatly on the floor. What did he mean, he couldn't say?

I felt that looseness in the bowels again. Try as I would to make jokes, they were growing sour. Joey and me, we'd been together for nearly six weeks now, and he was still sitting there, a blotch on the target area. I could distinguish light and dark, but he was growing. Oh, not shooting up, not anything like that, but bulging so that I couldn't really see much beyond him. Streamers had appeared, tiny, floating attachments lazily curling and uncurling themselves when I moved my head, at large there in the inner eye like the particles of an amoeba. I kept wanting to rub that eye, had developed a sideways look and a grin like a circus clown's in the hope of permanently drawing down the lower eyelid so that the streamers floated top left as I tried to get a peep at objects with some definition. While Joey was out of the way, so to speak; around the corner of his lodging. But it didn't work. I must have looked like a cross between the leader of the peasant's revolt and a Maltese brothel keeper with a developing hump fattening like a marrow where the shoulder dropped. That smile... My smile... It was the saddest thing you ever saw.

Presently he finished the letter he was writing with a piece of calligraphy like he was Mary Queen of Scots and going down in history. He underlined it too, thick broad strokes of the biro.

'What is your occupation, Mr Lacey?'

I produced the chamber of horrors smile and gave Joey the blink. I'd been touting a well-known dog food but didn't like to say so. 'Market research,' I lied. 'A very hard sell.'

'In that case I shall have to notify your employers. It's most important that you shouldn't come into contact with people for some time.'

Then he handed me the medical certificate. Where it said, Duration of Illness, he had written, *indefinite*.

Oh, the awfulness of awful!

'You'll have to prepare yourself for a long period of hospitalisation. It's all in the letter.'

I gave him the nod, bowed, and beat it down the stairs, heels tapping as I went, stuffing the letter in my suit pocket and bolted for the pub over the road. I went through the traffic, head down, shoulders hunched, hands in pockets, muttering to myself like some screwy academic enraptured with a speciality. Only my speciality was me. A lorry just missed me, an articulated job, air brakes squealing, and out of the corner of my working eye, I saw the driver's purple face framed in the cab window. His rage worked like a whiplash along his lips.

'Why bother, pal?' I said, and wandered on.

I heard him swear but I agreed with him. I could have been under that wheel without thinking of the trouble it would have caused him. I could see his time sheets messed up, his phone call back to wherever he was from, the doubts created in his Governor's mind. Some nut, he'd say to his wife, the bother of me. It took him a minute to restart and I went into the pub without looking back.

I was gathering regrets with every step I took. You could do nothing without affecting other people, but everything that happened to you, hurt you the most. That was a fact of life for me, but before I got to dwell on it, I ordered a pint and took it over to the corner by the dartboard. The bar was almost empty, an old man and a sad labrador dog on one side, the landlord in his shirt-sleeves looking over horses in the paper, and me in the corner, a shaft of light over my left shoulder cutting the room into halves, the dust hanging in it, and rising and turning over and vanishing as it moved from light to dark into the shadows. Dust always does that in gloomy pubs. Dust and silence... They'll be the end of me.

But even as I took the head off the pint, I knew I had to snap out of it. I had Connie to tell, thoughts on the wifely score. Then there was Auntie Rachel, our landlord, protector, and old mother earth. She'd got me the job on the dog food and to jack it in, I had to inform her cousin, Iestyn, our Area Manager. There were complications all round. You couldn't even get ill without Connie's family rattling the hambones. They were a tribe, and Connie had married outside the tribe, spoiled herself in their book. By marrying the wanderer. Meaning me.

The letter in my pocket for my own doctor was beginning to make me itch so I thought instead of Auntie Rachel. I was there when she phoned Iestyn. I could always tune in on that for a scream. I had plenty of corking memories.

'Is that you, Iestyn? Yes? Well, I've got a favour to ask. It's Walter.'

I remember Uncle Iestyn at the wedding, small, gold-toothed, blinking beady eyes rivetted on to Connie's laced-up navel. He was the sort of man who says, 'No daughter of mine, etc...' Somewhere amongst the worshipful masters, the Gods of her tribe, there must have been decent people who were also awful and nice. Like me. But they'd emigrated.

'Yes, Walter, Walter Lacey, Connie's Walter. You came to the wedding,' Auntie Rachel said.

I heard Uncle Iestyn's epiglottis clicking away in an aria of noncommittal glug-glugs. He never swore, or drank or bet, was the inventor of the early morning salt water gargle, and had never had a cold.

'Walter? Ah, yes. Yes...' he sighed, and I sympathised.

We were all packed tight up to the phone, me, Connie and Auntie Rachel, heads together around the earpiece waiting for the signal like Marconi's dutiful inlaws. I couldn't resist a crack.

'Perhaps he's saluting?' I said. 'I mean, as the ship goes down.'

'What was that?' Uncle Iestyn said, coming through with his coroner's voice.

Auntie Rachel flashed me a look. At seventy plus, she ate people. Kindness itself, as she said of herself, she knew when to draw the line. This was the last time, she said. The line was around my neck.

'He's having a little bit of difficulty,' Rachel said.

Connie caught her elbow: 'Tell him there's a slump in the second-hand car business.'

'He wants something better than straight commission,' Auntie Rachel said grimly. 'He doesn't make enough to live on. And he lets her get anaemic.'

That was the family for you. No strangers to disaster, they fed on it like benign sharks with shielded cutting teeth. Bad luck, ill health, a tightening of credit, they had noses like acrobats for the high tensions of overdraft living. And they were medically inclined too. Auntie Rachel reckoned she could spot alcoholics in the pram. By their swallows...

'I think he'd better come up and see you, Iestyn. There's things you can't say over the phone.' Auntie Rachel put the phone down solemnly as if it were a judge's gavel and turned to me. 'You'd better wear your good suit. Take care there's not a hint of anything about your breath. Not a suspicion, mind! Drink, I mean.'

Connie nodded, took a curler out and looked at it reflectively. We were supposed to have gone out, when I'd come home with two-pound-two and the cards.

'Thank you, Auntie Rachel,' Connie said. 'He ought to be more than grateful.'

Two women looking at you in that way they have, the beachcomber's last chance. I must have been ill for longer than anybody knew. I finished the pint, went out to a phone box and got through to Uncle Iestyn after a long delay, looking at myself in the mirror the while. 'He's worn himself to a shadow;' I hoped they'd say, the family. 'Given his *all*!' But I'd been on the pop too. I'd even eaten a tin of the dog food by way of demonstration late one night at The Gutter, our condemned local. Ten pints and through the tin, jelly and all.

'Uncle Iestyn? Is that you?' he didn't like me to call him as family and had pointed it out. 'It's Walter this end. I'm down in Ponty.'

'Is it the car?' I heard his voice ticking off the likely items of dismay, company car written off, samples gone, and his real worm-tunnelling fear, broken glass in the product. A rival firm had got theirs with this miscomputation, a giant botchery on the assembly line that sent insurance inspectors chalk-faced and funeral-voiced along the entire retail outlet of the area, until there wasn't a dustbin licker whose owner hadn't slapped a claim in. *Alleluja to the gumless of our four-legged friends! Change to KKK and build yourselves up again!*

'No, it's not the car, nor the samples, it's me,' I said.

I could hear his aria again, the back of his throat tensile with ahh'd alarm. Poor sod. He suffered from every wind that blew, especially when there was a waft of me in it. Taking me on in the first place must have required an act of courage like Woolworth keeping the prices down.

'My condition is indefinite,' I said, mixing it up. 'I don't know where I got it from, but it's there, see, a doubler, chest and eye, eye and chest. Interrelated,' I explained. 'Eale's disease. D'you want to hear me cough? I can do a trembler.'

He thought I was having him on.

'As a matter of fact, it's dangerous for me to be out at all. They want me to keep away from people. If I do the decent thing, this kiosk will have to be disinfected.'

Did Rachel know?

'No, nor Connie,' I said. I had that to come.

Was I in a fit state to drive?

'Listen, I'm not drunk,' I said. 'I'm ill. Have you got that? Ill.'

Was it mental?

It soon would be, I thought. But something must have communicated itself to him because he offered to come down and drive me home. There was this niceness to all of them, if they'd just forget how hard they'd worked, and what a low opinion they had of me.

I said, 'You can pick up the car later. Better let me get home first.'

He said, 'Look after yourself, Walter, boy. Your health is all you've got.'

Now there was a thing to say.

I picked up the car and drove home, just Joey and me. I held him level like the centre spot of a target, holding steady at 4 o'clock, squinting at the cats' eyes with my other eye as I eased the Mini along. They gave us Minis when we started and worked up to bigger tin from there. I'd offered to do a deal for them, but you can guess the answer to that. I tried to think of something good to tell Connie, but as usual, I had only myself to take home. Got it yet? The universal provider was a tramp.

It was a sunny day, that was the rub, light reflecting along the tarmac surface of the road, beams of light plummeting like silver and reflecting off everything shiny I passed. Ahead of me on the road was a Land Rover and trailer with one of these powder-blue fibreglass speedboats and an eighty-horse Merc engine lumped on the stern, dead sexy. I could see a blazered young burk at the wheel, his bird beside him and water skis sticking out of the back of the Land Rover. Off to the rah-rah-rah. Well, good luck to you, pal. Salt tang and menthol ciggies, sand up your

15

crutch. It occurred to me I hadn't seen anything as healthy for years. I had this woeful capacity for the tarnished view. There was a nail in our wedding cake, I remembered, one of your actual rusty nails, but it was only this last year that things had gone on the slide. It looked as if I was going to have time to think about it. Prolonged hospitalisation, the quack said. His letter fried in my pocket.

We didn't live far from the foot of the valleys, a flat on the perimeter of this industrial estate, halfway from nowhere, but high up, overlooking the ribbon development beside the river. We got winter smoke and summer fog, but there were patches of green, sycamore woods and there were one or two sheep farms still left, rambler's walks if you could ramble, and we had the feeling of being above things. Connie taught backward children in a secondary school on the edge of the estate below, and usually brought home more than me. Whatever happened, she'd manage. It was some consolation.

I stuck close behind this Land Rover and trailer, musing thus. I'd once had to take an advanced course of driving, but now I was back on the slovenly, elbow on the window, a fag on, trying to relax. A power boat for the summer... For some reason, it made me think of professional people. As a group, I mean, the high flyers. Letters after your name, a parchment in the hall, a code to protect you in case anybody split, an assured income, wet or fine. Commission always burned me up. But then I had no skills, no apprenticeship, craft, nothing. It was the penalty for wandering. Always a smart alec, sooner or later I was bound to get mine.

But what the hell? Up off the floor, brother! I thought I'd stop off and take a bottle home and then we could sit around and have our own case conference. Be reasonable, I could hear myself saying. It may not be as bad as we think. What was the word I hated? – Bland! Well, bland we could be. Calm, accepting, the pale figure in the corner, Pelmanised by the trained will. We have to look on the bright side, take stock, just a temporary setback. The trouble was I wanted to scream and scream that age-old cry from the nursery – why me?

You know the feeling? Self pity. It's what you must exorcise first. Burn it right out!

I had a good go right then. I must have put my foot down on the accelerator with a chronic exercise of the will because I suddenly shot forward and rammed this speedboat with such a clunk the propeller of the Merc shot up in the air, cocking itself like a small cannon. We all ground to a halt, Mini, Land Rover, and trailer locked in a love coupling that would need surgery to break. The propeller shaft was stuck up the Mini's jaxi so to speak. I began to laugh.

His bird got out of the Land Rover first, high yellow trouser suit, peach colouring, a fuzzy mass of copper hair. You know? *Homes and Gardens*, swing chairs in the garden, hair done in beer, fragile to the touch.

'Have you any conception of what you're doing? Any conception *at all*?'

'You're very beautiful,' I said gravely. 'If I had to see anything last of all, it's great that it's you.'

She stared at me, niffing for drink. He joined her then,

blazer buttons flashing, super lilac cravat, the both of them staring in at me through the offside window. I didn't move. It occurred to me that now the moment had come, my calmness was something out of the regimental annals, the regiments of me.

'What the hell d'you think you're playing at?' he said. For some reason, he was nervous. Why had she got out first? Perhaps he was another one like me, better with the scabbard than the sword.

'Andrew,' she said. 'He may be in a state of shock.'

I tried to open the driving seat door but it was jammed. I eased across to the farside door, feeling the sweat clammy around my thighs. I'd manufactured a pool of it. I got out, drew myself up and blinked in the sunlight. I was taller than them both, six foot, eleven stone and gaunt with the undertaker's front parlour look, an easy laying-out job. I kept my voice grave and commiserating.

'I am on my way to hospital ultimately,' I said. 'I have a condition of the eye known as Eale's disease. Round these parts we don't see more than six a year and the vitreous may haemorrhage at any minute. It's my fault entirely. I should have insisted on an ambulance.'

'Oh, my God!' she said.

He didn't know what to say.

As I said it, I didn't believe it myself. That it was true was wicked.

'If we leave the trailer, can we run you somewhere?' she said.

He said, 'Perhaps we'd better ring for an ambulance. I don't see anything wrong with him.'

'It's inside the eye,' I said. 'Like a tea bag.'

I could see he didn't believe me and I was on his side.

'I've got TB as well,' I said. 'And I'm very run down.'

'I can see that,' she said.

We stood there in a welter of indecision. A car hooted as it drove past. Out of my good eye, I could see the driver grinning. They'd grin at John Reginald Christie around here. I wouldn't be surprised if there wasn't a Necrophiliacs Anonymous.

'It's just up the hill there,' I said. 'But of course, I could walk.'

That did it.

'Unshackle the boat,' she said to him.

'You're very kind,' I said. I followed her to the Land Rover. I could hear him hammering at the speedboat coupling behind us. Finally, he broke it loose and we all three sat in the cab. Then she put her arm around my neck. I was nodding slightly. My good eye was watering as if it had suddenly woken up to the fact that it was working a single shift. I brushed a tear away.

'How will you manage about the car?' she said.

'I'll ring Uncle Iestyn.' His suspicions would be confirmed, I thought. It would take the Attorney General to make him believe it didn't happen before I phoned. But I was too weary to bother.

When we got home, I asked them to stop away from the house.

'My wife doesn't know,' I said.

I could see the reaction in her eyes and I wanted to dwell on it, but I found a company card and gave it to the bloke.

'All the cars are covered. I'll get in touch. Sorry about the Merc.'

He nodded, another thing I'd messed up.

She said, 'Well, Good Luck.' Damn nice.

I gave her the spot-on sign with curled forefinger and thumb, and my crook's smile again.

'Don't forget to write,' I said. I could see him bristling but I had to say something. I didn't turn to see them off. I found my key, noticed the shudder of the curtain in Auntie Rachel's upstairs flat, opened the door and went in. The whole thing was beginning to burst in on me, and now I had to find the guts.

But as soon as I got myself into the kitchen, steadying myself against the ultimate collapse, I saw Connie sitting at the table marking pastel drawings she'd brought home from her backward class. All very wifely. But what got me was that she was nearly starkers with one of these floppy sun hats pulled over her ears. She had the sun lamp beaming on her from the bread board. She was on the complexion kick again, stuck there cooking like a lush.

I stopped dead and stared at her. She didn't look up. She put a mark on one of the pastels and picked up another, scrutinised it.

I blinked. It could only happen to me, the scene of my life, the real *misère ouvert*, flecks in the handkerchief and all, and stripjacknaked, there she was, her cuddly bum spread all over, legs askew, swingers swinging, her country maid face serene except for her tight-drawn valleys' mouth which had dropped at my entrance as if I were a racial memory of the Great Depression. I say valleys' mouth, but

I don't mean she's the sort who reminds you she'd take food off her plate like her father and his father and his father's father's – but she can cut when she wants. She's got the family tongue. Acid is as acid does.

I leaned weakly against the lintel of the door, taking her in, the other threequarters.

At last she looked up, eyes appraising.

'Don't tell me, cards?'

'Worse.'

She nodded quietly to herself. She was born patient. She had this capacity for acceptance that sometimes made me want to cry. I'd seen her with sick deformed kids I couldn't bear to look at, and she oozed sap like an oak tree. There was something substantial there in that woman. I knew it and loved it and marvelled at it. It was of the earth, earthy, and on the side of the angels, the deep core in her, the strength, the being.

But didn't I have a chance too? The more I thought about it, the more I felt like the guy Queen Victoria wore out. Who was the player in this lousy drama that gets the real kicks, I asked myself. Wouldn't I like to be Joan of Arc now and again? You bet. Here I am, I thought, poxed up to the eyebrows, a mass of cavities, haemorrhages, one of six of your actual cases seen in a year, the outpatient of outpatients, king of the ruptured vitreous, and I was even denied my entrance. I wanted to scream, 'The prognosis is so bad that ophthalmic specialists do not even talk to me!' 'But she just went on cooking, turning to brown below the bra-line and surveying me with that Assistance Board appraisal.

'It's much worse than cards,' I said again. 'The sack is an infinitesimal part of it.'

She must have seen me blinking. 'Well, glasses won't hurt your appearance. Especially if you grow a moustache.'

Lunacy reigns. I'd told her about my eye and the ophthalmic visit but not the X-rays. She'd naturally assumed that the slightest suggestion of me wearing spectacles would drive me straight to the glass grinders. I shook my head, went over to the settee, sat, clasped my hands together, adopted the death cell pose.

'The reprieve has not come through. The Governor has to break the news. Hanging is back.'

'Pardon?'

I said sombrely, 'I want you to put some clothes on and listen very carefully.'

She examined her nails. 'There's an NUT dance on Thursday. I'm going to wear that see-through dress. I thought I'd brown up a bit.'

I stared at her. She nodded benignly like a total stranger in a railway carriage and went on marking the pastel drawings. Shuttle-shuttle, the seconds were going by like trucks.

'I am very seriously ill. Eale's disease,' I said with emphasis.

'Eale's disease? You haven't got worms?'

'Vitreous haemorrhages,' I clenched my teeth.

'What's the vitreous?'

I looked away. I didn't know. The SS man hadn't said. Was it anything to do with china?

'It's inside the eye. That spot I told you about.'

22

'Drink,' she said, dismissing it.

'It's not drink. It's in the eye. And it's bleeding, bleeding all the time.'

It wasn't. But as I said it, I knew it might. 'And I've got TB as well. I've got a letter in my pocket for the quack. They said a long period of hospitalisation. They don't see more than six cases a year. They can't even give me a prognosis and they don't want me to mix with people. I'm poxed.'

There it was at last, the hysteria. I was going to break it gently, the soft voice, whimsical smile, the measured tones of your man in the grey flannel suit, that ordinary dope at the bus stop who measures all things well. But I was near screaming. Under the whip, I always did everything at the top of my voice.

She looked at me steadily for a moment, taking it in. Most of the rubbish I came out with, she could break down sentence by sentence like a trade union negotiator filing away at bullshit clauses. But she didn't say anything immediately, just looked me over, the lines on my forehead – I'd had them since I was ten – the pallor, the stoop, and a visiting gift, a nervous tic I'd recently acquired, the pressures of being me.

She swallowed, gave the faintest shrug of her shoulders, then smiled.

'Well, that's that then.'

'Yes,' I said.

'I wish we'd had a baby.'

'Oh, that.'

'It would have been something we've done.'

'Yes,' I said. 'Something done.' Doing anything real was what eluded me.

'Still,' she said. 'We'll manage.'

That was what our kind of people always did, manage. When you learned to do that, you grew up.

She didn't say any more, turned the sun lamp off and went into the bedroom to put her clothes on. Not another word.

Would it have been different with a pram in the corner? Not for me. I had nothing to perpetuate. But what the hell? The lowest of low is sorry for yourself. I stumped to the cupboard and found the bacardi. The breeding idea stuck with me as I poured a drink. Of all things, I suddenly remembered a sign from a farm near where I lived once. *Nostromo*, it said. *Prize Arab stud. Enquire within.* For a skylark, I did once and you ought to have seen Nostromo. He was so bushed, he would have given the Sheik of Araby rickets, I swear! The only thing to that nag was his sign outside, all done in fine gold script. The farm was mortgaged and they threw it up for appearances or something, or maybe Nostromo'd got the pox too. When I saw him, he couldn't mount a nosebag. I quite understood.

I filled my glass again, recovering slowly now. My attitudes... The trouble I thought, outside of me, was that we knew so much about awful. You turned the telly on, there was a limb in the gutter, somebody's house gone up in smoke, four-figure numbers of dead every week, towns, villages, homes, lives, all expendable somewhere or other. You couldn't invent a dirty trick that wasn't somebody's policy, all high-level stuff. So what did you do but opt out

24

unless you were some kind of crank? Unless it was bread and butter, ordinary people didn't bother any more, just escaped, building private forts against the general dismay. With others it was salary gravy, the things people had always done, only more and bigger and better, and kids just went potty and slammed out at the nearest thing. There was this world and that world, and people like me didn't want to join either. Now why was that, I thought? And why did I feel yet another additional guilt?

I heard the clip of her high-heeled boots on the passage tiles.

'There's coke in the fridge,' she called encouragingly. She stuck her head around the door. 'What are you doing?'

'Thinking,' I said.

That alarmed her. 'What?'

'The lewd thoughts of Chairman Mao.'

'Hey?'

'The relationship of awful,' I said.

'As long as you're not dwelling on it.'

She went away.

Ideas, I thought. I never had any. Books, I never read them nowadays. Nothing moved me. I didn't believe a word I read in the papers, only what I saw for myself. And I was the original non-joiner. Nothing and nobody to recommend me. Well, good, I thought. Splendid... Grand... Super! Well done, sir!

I took another gobble at the bacardi, a hot shot that hit me in the Never Never where I frequently retreated, a comforting habit I'd had since I was a kid. In the Never Never, I was king.

'Mr Headmaster, Chairman of the Board of Governors, Members of the Staff, Ladies and Gentlemen, Boys and Girls, Friends... Our principal speaker today has no education to speak of, and nothing to recommend him. Slovenly, ill-kempt, insolent, of irregular and intemperate habits, his most distinguishing feature, I should say, is that he bears responsibility for nothing... and is by way of being a hard case locally.'

'Hurrah!' I said. 'Hurrah – Hurrah! A toast to the young swab, sirs!'

She must have heard but she didn't say anything when she came in. She'd on this mulberry midi-suit, white stretch boots and a cream-coloured gaucho hat that I called The Miner's Last Goodbye. Prophetic.

'What are you doing?'

'Addressing the public.'

'Is that supposed to be funny?'

'Forget it,' I said. 'You know how it is in the Foreign Legion. What are you dressed up for?'

'Whatever people think about you, I make my own impressions.'

'You can say that again.'

'Oh, come on. Quick,' she said. She softened. 'If you've told Uncle Iestyn, he's bound to have phoned Auntie Rachel. Let's go before she comes downstairs.'

I'd forgotten about the car. 'There's another thing. I wrote off the car.'

She hesitated. 'You're not making this up just to distract me?'

'Distract you? No. But I'll have to tell him.'

26

'Are you sure?'

'Surer than sure.' I took out the letter. 'I don't know why, I haven't opened it.'

'Because it's not addressed to you,' she said simply. 'Come on. If you haven't got the car, we can have a drink afterwards. You used to say it gave you a lift.'

So I did. But that was one more excuse.

She took my arm as we got out on the road. Auntie Rachel's curtain shivered again upstairs, the watcher watching. But we didn't look back. It was dark now and the street lamps were on, the shadows of trees lying like tall men over the road as we walked down the hill to the surgery. There was an unusual nip in the air for a late summer's evening but I could just see the joins in the paving stones, and for a while tried to play the kid's game of not stepping on them. She gripped my arm tightly but we did not say anything. I caught a glimpse of her face under that crazy hat. It was grave and concerned and for the first time I understood what she was really feeling. Seeing me examine her, she wrinkled up her nose and winked affectionately. A little moment then, a true communication. But that wink... It was so brave, it made me want to cry. When we were silent, we were like that, saying meaningful things to each other, our minds not spoiling the strength of feeling there was between us. Whatever happened to me, I knew I always had that, a bridge that led me to another, better self. And I counted on that.

But in the surgery, the world intruded again.

'Mm... now that is interesting. Eale's, eh?'

Our GP was bland. Elderly, tweeded and unhurried, he would look at a broken door latch with sympathy. Women loved him. He robbed practices for miles, attracting the neurotic like a healing disciple whose fame travelled before him. He always gave the impression of having time; in fact, he dealt with his time like a card-sharper dealing a hand. He had all the time in the world, you felt, provided there was nothing much wrong with you. Then he wore out hospital staffs with the cases he referred while he perfected the art of giving you just what you wanted. Auntie Rachel put him on her shopping list just after the ironmonger. She felt him always good for a call, was comforted and reassured, but she seldom took anything, preferring just to chat. He had a small enough practice to get by, a younger partner did all the night calls. I had never had much to do with him, except that he'd once come up with a princely diagnosis for my chest pains, 'Fat on the chest wall'.

I ask you? Eleven stone of raw, exposed nerve, and fat on the chest wall? But the fact that I was back with a real diagnosis only confirmed his wisdom in referring me.

'I thought,' he said knowledgeably, folding the letter. 'But Eale's is one out of the blue.'

'What is it?' I said.

'The vitreous.'

'Of course. But what is it?'

'A condition, old man.'

'Ah...'

''Fraid I can't tell you much. We'll have to leave that to the ophthalmic johnnies.'

Johnnies... You'd think they were a club.

'Now the TB, I can tell you about.'

'Yes?'

'It's not like it was, is it?' Connie said. He'd complimented her on her hat. They were an inch off looking at me together, the fractious subject. It was a feeling I'd get to know well.

'Not at all,' he said. 'We've got rid of the pine tree conception years ago. We'll have you up and about in er... months.'

I'd heard they did surgery now but didn't like to ask.

'The death rate these days is very low. Why, they're even closing down most of the hospitals. The difficulty will be to get a bed.'

I didn't like his smile. 'A bed?'

'Hearts are the things these days. Hearts all the rage.'

Out of fashion again then, I thought. 'Well, the sooner I go in the better,' I said. 'Is there something I can take?'

But he wouldn't give me anything. Very rare for him. I knew at once I was in a different category.

'You'll have to be put somewhere where they can keep an eye on your er... eye.'

'Oh, yes?' I said.

'And of course, they'll want to get stuck into the tubercle as well.'

I didn't like that phrase. Not at all. Get stuck into it? It sounded painful.

'You never hear of it these days,' Connie said. 'TB. It's gone.'

'Get a load of this!' I stuck my chest forward but she wrinkled up her nose with disapproval, and I relapsed into silence. When he said he didn't see any harm in giving me a mild sedative, she thanked him profusely as if he'd done something. He said they'd be in touch. As we went out of the door, I saw him stretching for a tome. He didn't ring the bell for the next patient and I pictured him in there turning up the pages. It was extraordinary but I already had an inkling of the unusualness of it all. Eale's. It lay across the back of my mind like a hangover. Joey hadn't moved.

'It could have been a growth,' Connie said consolingly.

'How do we know it isn't a growth?'

'Because it isn't. He said it was a condition.'

The straws at which the ignorant clutch! There comes a time when you can say nothing. You've got it, and there it is. By now, I was getting used to it. Earlier my frenzy had driven me to the edge of collapse but now I was just tired. Out of the blue, he'd said, and that was me, it seemed. But at least I was walking. A walking case of blues.

We went into our usual corner of The Gutter, our local. As it happened, there was no one there we knew. We had a landlord who'd devoted his life to alcohol and there were days when he fell asleep under the taps in the cellar, but it was his night off too. We sat alone in the snug bar: two bacardis and coke. I looked at the edge of the bar. It was old mahogany, a deep weathered red, chipped by the passage of a thousand escaping coins. It seemed absurd that on a wild night I'd eaten the dog food out of the tin at that very bar a few weeks ago, a high point in after-hours drinking that was already a legend. The things you do to avoid the ordinariness of you.

Connie said, 'Well, that's that. After tonight, I don't

think you ought to drink too much. Before they take you in, I mean.'

'And tonight?'

'You might as well have a last fling.'

I knew what was on her mind. 'It could be dangerous,' I said perversely. Usually, I was the original last fling. There were days when I'd celebrate a fly landing on the wall.

'If we take a bottle home, we could drink it quietly.'

'A bottle of rum?'

She didn't say anything.

'Yo ho ho,' I said.

She still didn't say anything.

'Yo ho ho *and a bottle of rum*?' I said.

Then she said a terrible thing: 'We're just two people for whom things haven't gone very well.'

'And?'

'That's all.'

I knew what she meant and it was suddenly the low point of low. Two people for whom things hadn't gone very well.

'No,' I said. 'It's just me.'

We didn't stay much longer, picked up a bottle, and walked home. Sometimes you feel the weight of the past like an old worn overcoat, coming between you and your present skin. With me, it was always hard to examine, the sum total of things. I blundered on, flitting like a moth before every flame that blew. The salesman has only the present to live in, his only immediate goal, the sucker in front of him. But now the sucker was me. Even the way I

31

spoke gave me away. Everywhere I'd worked, it paid to be smart, the smart crack from the smart alec often made the sale.

For some reason, I thought then of my brother as we walked home in silence. Older than me, he was everything I was not, successful, calm, the Headmaster's dream boy, or The Vicarage Kid as I'd called him once. He was an examination passer, my brother. He'd won a Dartmouth scholarship at the age of thirteen and was now an intelligence ace in the embassy in Moscow. Can you imagine that? A brother of mine, naval attaché! He'd got this gift for languages as well as plenty of the family con. Only he played his cards straight, nose to the grindstone, thumbs to the seams of his trousers, duty-struck, something that had always bothered me. He'd become one of theirs while I was always digging in on the other side. When you heard him speak, you'd think there was one of these corny old war films on and he was Captain (D). You know the voice? A mouthful of plums and spray breaking through the nostrils. Commander Victor Lacey, RN, my actual brother. I wouldn't be surprised if he didn't end up bigger than the Greek that married the boss's daughter. As Auntie Rachel pointedly said, 'There are some grubby people about.' Perhaps it was my mistake that I had not gone his way and become a gentleman.

'What are you thinking of?' Connie said.

'Victor.'

'Oh, him? He's about due for leave, isn't he?'

I didn't know. I couldn't stand it if he was. The great thing I had in common with almost everybody I knew was no future, and it comforted me. The successful should mix only with the successful, and besides, I always had a yen for the arabs of this world, Allah's children, my kind of people. But I checked myself. If I started on this train of thought, I knew I'd end up on the old lady, and before we knew where we were, I'd find reasons to be sorry for myself. Murder!

Auntie Rachel must have gone to bed when we got in because the tell-tale curtain was quite still in the upstairs window. Fumbling for the key, I felt Connie beside me, her breathing quickening in the darkness. I knew at once what she was thinking. She was a great one for last times, the last time she wore a dress, the last day of my twenties, and now I suppose, it was the last time I'd return early from The Gutter. Myself, I was always glad of any last time and perversely, her moment cheered me up. I gave the milk bottles a kick, putting my knee in hard between her legs, buckling the midi and feeling the old troop comforter as I kissed her. Then I swung her in with the door, holding her tight against it and bit her on the neck.

'Poxed he may be,' I commented, 'the old bastard still has life!'

'Don't,' she said, a whisper.

I winced, crumpled over against the wall. 'Shot be Christ!' I said. 'They got me in the back.'

'Auntie Rachel…'

'Gassed,' I said. 'Gassed, raped and silenced. The uprising has come at last.'

'In the kitchen,' she hissed.

'Don't you live here then?'

'I don't mind. But in the kitchen.'

She didn't mind in the kitchen! Who was she kidding?

We crept through the passage like Fanny the Maid and the unclean coalman, but in the kitchen I took the cork out of the bottle and poured two stiff ones.

'Music,' I said. 'And you can keep your boots on.'

But she had taken all her discs to school.

'All of them?'

'They use them in the staffroom lunchtime.'

'What d'you mean, use them?'

'Well, they tape them and things. For drama.'

'Drama...'

I spied a record sleeve and went towards it. It was one she'd brought home for Auntie Rachel, a recording of hymns sung in the presence of Royalty.

'Shit,' I said. 'The Bowes-Lyons are at us again. As if they'd ever done anything for us.'

She frowned.

'How would you feel?' I said. 'No music on the last goodnight.'

'What d'you mean last?'

'Oh, get your bloody clothes off, smother yourself in love potions, sing to me with the crackle of patent leather.'

'Stretch elastic,' she said. 'I got them in a sale.'

In the end, we had *Late Night Line Up* for company on the telly, all very aeriated in the head, the swansong of NW1, and finally dying music and a film clip, moon on the Norfolk Broads. Education, goodnight. Now it was our show.

Later, she said hoarsely: 'Always be violent, always like that. Hard.'

34

I smiled. I felt very sleepy suddenly, bushed.

'Don't worry,' I said. 'One eye, one lung, I'll fall on one foot any old how.'

But as I rolled over and drew her with me and against me so that I could feel her heart beating and her sweat congealing with mine, I saw that the telly had retreated into a white blip alone in the centre of the screen. It seemed to stare menacingly at me and I stared back. The effort had brought Joey to life again and the streamers washed all over my eye, floating before me like weed in a tiny aquarium, tentacles curling and uncurling again and slowly the colour below them became obvious, one colour and nothing else, the deep red of an artist's paint box, only it was blood. You couldn't kid your way out of that, I thought. Nobody could.

'Are you all right?' she said anxiously.

'Great,' I said.

From then on, I knew I had to lie to her. Wouldn't you?

CHAPTER TWO

WALTER

Sometimes she liked to be woken in the early morning as we had a list of pleasurable things to do then, but this morning I awoke early, sweating again. I could hear a train in the distance, a new diesel rattling away on the low line beside the river, and nearer home, milk bottles clunking in their crates on a lorry. There was a rime on my lips, last night's fags, and as I put my arm out for a new packet, I tried to remember when I had last woken up with that yip-feeling of a new day. Not since I was a kid, I thought. I held the packet away and finally put it down without taking one. It was dark in the room and I could see the glint of the cigarette lighter beside the bed, my clothes forming an untidy pile where I'd dropped them. I wasn't coughing but I had a dead feeling and lay there as fragile and still as an old pale, pyjama'd leaf.

She'd nothing on and the stretch boots were crumpled over on the floor beside my clothes, their uppers corrugated and flopped sadly to one side. We must have come to bed in a stupor. I couldn't remember. Love making always tired me but that had to be hasty too, in case I died on the spot. What had she said? Be violent. Another month, I'd need a rocking chair and neat rhinoceros horn.

She stirred in her sleep, the roughened skin of her heel brushing against my leg like sandpaper. She was unaware of me yet and the sweat was beginning to dry on me. I still felt weak and feverish but the freedom from coughing was a luxury. You got so you didn't know you were doing it, hack-hacking away in a minor key. But what to do now? She always slept in peace like a child and often I used to stare at her if I woke first. Human beings are a mystery and there are none stranger than those we know.

She stirred again and I turned over on my side. The heat was coming off her body and I could smell her, that curious mixture of talc and mint on her breath. Her mouth was open, full ripe lips, babyish and bubbling.

I couldn't remember her getting into bed and it bothered me, but then I couldn't remember leaving the kitchen myself. She had a habit of putting the milk bottles out when naked, a practice that I discouraged in case it would require me to come and defend her from passing firemen. It was simply doing what she'd forgotten to do the moment she thought of it. It could be anything, like reaching up from the bath to fix a light bulb or checking there were sixpences in her purse at the beginning of the act if I didn't have a good grip of her. She had a gift for distractions and even in her sleep, I had a half-suspicion that her mind was labouring over something totally disconnected with either of us.

But perhaps it was just that I couldn't leave her alone at any time I was with her, least of all now. I slipped my palm between her legs and began a skilful pressure upwards with my knuckle to wake her.

'Time for school,' I said. 'Hi ho, chocolate time.'

But she didn't stir.

I eased my way down in the bed putting my mouth to her breast and working my tongue in the way she liked, the stubble on my chin purposeful and useful in this direction.

'Time we turned out the stock cupboard, Mrs L?'

She came to slowly, stretching herself cat-like and raising one knee as she turned towards me. The skin on the inside of her thighs was always something special and as I got her going slowly and lazily with my harpist's fingers, she began to croon in the back of her throat. It was the way she liked being woken up best and I used to award myself diplomas in this subject. We all have our uses and none more than the sexually-obsessed, dear friends in the clinic.

But even now I couldn't keep my mouth shut.

'The next time, you'll have to wear a mask.'

'Oh, come on...'

I obliged. Insanely, I felt I should be wearing a red cross armband, or some kind of orange warning apparel.

'Hammer – hammer – hammer!' I groaned. 'It's you that's killing me.'

After, I just lay there, my head over her shoulder pressed into the pillow and her hair piled up into my face as coarse as wet sacking. My mind never went blank like they say.

I could have done with a crane now, and I had one of my lunatic pictures of workmen in yellow helmets beckoning a chain brace and pulley into the bedroom as they did a haulage job on me and slung me down to a waiting ambulance below.

'Mad as a coot. Wouldn't leave it alone. All right, lads, your end a bit, Jim. To you... Stand by below! Easy now. Steady.'

Even then, she'd be fussing about making them tea.

Presently, I sighed. I still didn't move. 'This has got to stop.'

She didn't say anything. Her legs were still crossed.

Then we heard Auntie Rachel get out of bed upstairs. This was a performance of which we knew every sound. First, there was the creak of an old feather mattress which expelled her upon the command, then her feet found her slippers, then she bumped herself into them and finally scuffled to the bathroom where she began the salt water gargle, a habit she'd acquired from Iestyn. It was natural, bottled sea water and she'd perfected the trick of passing it down her nostrils, ensuring that the world did not reach her there, a noisy process that we had grown used to like the arrival of the milkman or the postman.

Connie said; 'There she goes.'

'Legs,' I said. 'Unshackle.'

She gurgled, held me tighter.

'Give in,' I said. When we were single, I used to fight her for it. She liked that.

'I know what you want,' I said. 'I know all that. Turn me over, or I'll decompose.'

'Don't,' she said.

'What?'

'Talk.'

I felt too tired. In public, this would be thought obscene, I thought, but I wanted the entire WVS there suddenly, all in their bottle green. They could cluckcluck as they filed past the corpse and publicly arraign her. Married sex had done for me as much as anything else. I could see me addressing the whiskered ladies that wanted to ban things. "Madam Chairman, once they get the ring on their finger, anything goes..."

'Applause, applause,' I said. 'What are you trying to do – catch it?'

Presently, she let me go. I tried to go back to sleep but couldn't. I couldn't see at all now out of Joey's eye, but I'd stopped thinking about that, the way you do. I watched her dressing, squinting out of my good eye. She picked up the gaucho hat she'd worn to the doctor's and hung it on the wall.

'What's that up there for?'

'I'm not going to wear it again. I'm fed up with it.'

'Oh, Christ.'

She paused in the act of putting on her tights and looked at me gravely.

'When you went to bed last night, I rang the doctor.'

'Rang him?'

'Yes, at home. I said you were in no condition mentally to be left lying about. I had to work, I said, and the sooner you went in the better. Today, if he could manage it.'

'Today?'

'He said he didn't think it would be possible but Auntie Rachel's rung Iestyn and he's going to speak to someone, use his influence.'

I sat up weakly.

'When did you speak to Rachel?'

'Last night. When you were asleep.'

'After… after…?'

'After I rang the doctor.'

For some reason, the thought occurred to me that she must have been naked when she rang him, except for the stretch boots. I could see them both on either end of the phone, him in his folksy old suit and her staring gravely at her notch as she spoke.

She nodded and struggled on with the tights.

'You staggered to bed, I tucked you in, rang him, and then went up to Auntie Rachel. She was asleep but she didn't mind. You know what she is. "In the circumstances," she said.'

'Can't I do anything for myself then? – Anything at all?'

'I hope you have,' she said. She blushed, looked down at herself.

'*Nostromo*,' I said weakly.

'Pardon?'

'Prize stud. Enquire within.'

She nodded uncomprehendingly. 'I'm going to get myself inoculated this morning and the district nurse is coming. There's no risk of contamination, anything like that, I asked.'

'Asked who?'

'Doctor. I mentioned it specifically.'

I still couldn't take it in. 'You rang up last night and...'

'After,' she said slyly. 'I told you I'd made up my mind.'

Then she put on her slippers and scuffed out of the room to make breakfast.

I lay back weakly. I didn't know where she got that serenity from, any more than I knew where I'd got me from, but I already had that sense of being used. One minute you're counting your chickens, you're trying to pull yourself together and lying like a legionnaire for the sake of the morale, and the next you're seen through, right to the core. *And used*! That was what got me. Weak as I was, poxed as I was, I was beginning to get a new sense of things and exactly how I fitted in. I'd been so busy making excuses about myself to myself, it didn't occur to me that I was exactly what they wanted. I shook my head, scratched it. I had so few new thoughts that when I got one, it hit me like a dumb-bell.

'And what did Rachel say?' I said when she came back.

'She's seen it coming.'

'What coming?'

'You... This...'

'But...'

'She says it's nothing to do with any of us. You're just not very good stock, that's all.'

'What?'

'And you live like a lunatic. But the thing now is, to get you in. She said – perhaps I shouldn't say this?'

'Go ahead and say it.'

'It's a pity we didn't have you insured.'

I could feel the sweat breaking out again. On the blink,

my good eye was taking snapshots of her impassive face like a police photographer. So now we come to the motive, hey?

'What did you say?'

'She said, it would be a tidy sum. Oh, you know what she is. She's got a thing about insurance. The important thing is, Iestyn will help you get into hospital quicker. The rest is up to the drugs and things.'

I stared at her.

'One day, I'll leave,' I said. 'I will. It'll be me, or them.'

'Fine,' she shrugged her shoulders. 'But that'll be a long time, won't it?'

She sat down at the dressing table to do her face. Beat, I thought, dead beat, me. Bum, I thought, bum, bum, the lowest form of low, me. In it again. Right in it. Family life, I thought, her family life. Their faces flashed before me like cartoon figures. They should have WANTED plastered over them. I knew where she got her serenity from. It was from the protective comfort of their rule. Between them, her Iestyn, Rachel, and several others whose names I'd forgotten, they had drawn their own frontiers and created their own kingdom, and within its tiny confines, they strutted like turkey cocks the moment the door was closed, kings of the rent, fixers the lot of them. They were omnipresent in her life, and because of my inadequacies, in mine too, and now that I was on my knees, further down nearer the floor than I had ever been before, now I saw it, just a glimpse of the reality of it, their power. Only a mug like me would have taken that long to see it and now that I had seen it, of course, it was too late to do anything. For the time being, I literally couldn't move.

But it nagged. Ever since I'd married her, I'd been a part of it though, even got used to it. I'd acquiesced. But now I saw that I was like a child who'd been given crutches the first day he tried to walk. There was evidence of this, stretching back, right back from the time we'd met, but I didn't go into it, just stared at her as she began to touch up her hair.

Nostromo, I thought again, that poor old nag. But I took heart suddenly. There's nothing like knowing even the truth about yourself.

'So,' I said. 'Now we really know where we stand.'

She didn't even turn around from the mirror.

'She didn't mean that about the insurance,' she said, hairclips in mouth. 'She just meant sick pay and things. You won't get any, will you?'

'Exactly,' I said. 'And are we to be graced with a visit from the Monarch upstairs? And the Court?'

'There's no need to be sarcastic. They'll do everything they can. As usual.'

'Exactly,' I said again.

'You know very well they will.'

'Quite. As good as gold.'

She gave me a sideways look.

'You should be grateful.'

'I'm full up to here with it.'

'Well, there then...' she smiled, mushed some lipstick into her lips, then stood up to examine the lay of her tights. 'And there's no need to worry about money or anything. She said especially to tell you. She didn't like to herself.'

'A fitting diffidence,' I said. I sounded just like my brother for once.

She turned and looked at me, pulled down her sweater as if she was giving me an eyeful.

'We're very lucky.'

'Correction. You're very lucky.'

She found a stiff leather belt with a large brass buckle which Auntie Rachel had got from a horse, and put it on, straining the leather to fasten it, so now I got the full cup measurement.

'I'd rather you were frenetic than nasty, darling.'

That did it. Darling... We never had any endearments. 'Allow me the consequences of my condition,' I said.

She hurried towards me and sat on the bed.

'What's the matter with you? We're not going to quarrel, are we?'

'No. Definitely not.'

'No? Go on, I know you. You've turned cold.'

'Perhaps I should always have been colder. They had no problem in handling me ever, did they?'

'What d'you mean?'

'What are you going to call the baby? I can't say Iestyn thrills me.'

She stood up angrily. 'I can take anything except sarcasm, even your whining.'

'That just ended,' I said. It had. 'The moment I get out of this, I'm going to be the Lord Chief Scout somewhere and you're coming with me.'

That fooled her.

'Scout?'

'If I have to go to Basutoland, I'll go. You can please yourself.'

'We'll go where it's reasonable.'

'No,' I said. 'Wherever it is, it's got to be unreasonable.'

She gave me the Rowton House look as if it wouldn't be long before the Salvation Army was the only thing left. In her eyes, I wasn't responsible for anything I did or said any more. It was that obvious, like the duly authorised stare of the Duly Authorised Officer, the man that came with the van. I sighed and said nothing, then we both heard the Frankenstein steps on the stairs denoting Auntie Rachel's confidential entry into the flat. I groaned and turned over but she went hurrying out into the passage, closing the door behind her and I just heard Rachel's sepulchral hiss, old venom lips drawing her into the kitchen. Jabber-jabber-jabber, I thought, a further viperous case conference on the anatomy of me. But I was too tired to bother and lay back on the pillows. It was just like it used to be.

There was just a crack in the curtains and not much natural light filtering into the room. She'd done her hair by the extension light I'd fitted to the dressing table mirror and I lay there in the shadows thinking. In a curious way, we were both orphans. Both our fathers had died when we were small, my mother had remarried and moved away and so had hers, only her mother had other children and made the cardinal mistake of marrying a poor man, hence Auntie Rachel's omnipresent influence. She'd weaned Connie away, increasing her influence year by year until she was both mother and father to her. More than that, she had the spinster's over-possessiveness and that hawk-eye for misconduct which had left Connie a bag of nerves until I'd got hold of her. You'd never think so now, but the girl I married needed me. Or so I was led to believe, as the constable said in the perjury case.

She was fat then, a bulging dumpling, the drab on a blind date, apprehensive about getting into the college hostel late, always looking over her shoulder for people talking. She had Rachel's Welsh thing about this then. The ruling phrases were, 'What will people say?' or 'There are eyes everywhere,' but I soon cured her of that. She was like that, and then she wasn't – suddenly. I mistakenly took it to be me, my influence. And I'd run away from home myself, been on my own since I was seventeen. I'd been around too, a spell in the Merchant Navy after National Service, a lunatic trip across Kenya driving a Willy's Overlander from Mombasa to Nairobi for a customer, and I had only come home to the valleys when a job folded and an uncle of mine died, leaving my brother and me a house. I'd sold it, taken my split and was busy pissing the proceeds up against the wall when I met her and from then on, the opposition of her family was such, I couldn't resist the fight.

And nor could she. She had this knack of appearing a total innocent and making me feel that I was the most independent thing she'd ever done. The scenes with Rachel and Co. were vintage.

'Everything I've done for you over all these years and he hasn't even got a degree! No qualifications whatsoever!' Then there was a pearler, 'In the name of our Lord, I beg of you, no intercourse until you've got your Teacher's Certificate, please...' Later, they got the family spy ring working. I'd failed the eleven plus, and Mama, with the new-found loot of her second husband, had put me in the cheapest boarding school in Western Europe. It's true, I swear. Half the kids couldn't afford the uniform, and all the school turned out, as far as I could see, were car salesmen and male hairdressers. I stuck it, miserable and alone, until puberty because I had nowhere else to go, but then there was the first of many telephone conversations.

'Headmaster here... It's Walter. I'm afraid so, a rather ticklish matter this time. Is his stepfather there? It's confidential, I'm afraid.'

He knew what he could do as far as I was concerned, but years later, Auntie Rachel found out. How, God knows, but she'd found out. I'd put a face on it.

'A young lady with a little bit of difficulty, Auntie R.'

'One of the maids... *Pregnant*!'

'She had a moustache too.'

'Walter!' Connie said. 'He's not like that really, Auntie. And he explained it to me.'

'Explained? What explanation is there?'

I was lonely really, lonely, desperate, that was all. Nowadays, oddballs, beats, freakouts and lie-ins are all the rage. That I was among the first, practically the founder-member, as it were, never occurred to anybody. Only I'd had to work, being on my own, a painful distraction with no virtue in it, and it had brought me to where I was now. I was thirty-two and old, for God's sakes. In the daylight, I looked even forty, and was on the way down, as I'd known for a long time. On the slide, as they say, and it was too late to make threats. As far as I knew, the only thing that would rise out of the ashes was a death certificate anyway, the way I felt. I'd had secret RIP thoughts as I moved from one job to another, and whatever I did, the matrimonial bed was a slaughterhouse of valour. It had given birth to Joey, old friend now, and as for TB, it was impossible, absurd. For some reason, I couldn't get it out of my head that it didn't exist any more. And yet I had it, and two jumps since the diagnosis, by Jukes. Was that not one for the Sex Honours on the birthday parade?

Connie brought the breakfast in. Her face was tense, unbending, that valleys' mouth had reappeared, coming on sentry duty, as straight as a file of stiff soldiers. I didn't doubt the orders had come from the intelligence agency in the kitchen. Only they wouldn't be intelligent, you could bet that. First there was a gruesome beaker, the witch-doctor's raw egg in milk.

'What the hell is this?' It smelled like last year's chemistry set.

'It's what they have.'

'What who have?'

'The Tee Bees. You've got to be built up, Auntie said. She's coming down to talk to you in a minute. I didn't know but she lost two cousins when she was small, and five of the family next door in Telelkebir Street died of it. She only escaped herself through keeping chickens.'

'For Christ's sake?'

'She says they get very difficult. Very aggressive and self-pitying. She remembers it going through whole households. Galloping consumption, it was called then, the White Killer. She says you must have been mixing with Pakistanis and all your underclothes have got to be burnt.'

50

I stared at her. Joey nearly came out of his hole. She put the tray down firmly on the bed. Now, she stood well back and addressed me.

'It's much more serious than I thought. Have you had any relations with Pakistanis?'

I couldn't speak. Not a syllable, not even a glug of protest. It warmed her suspicion. She accused:

'You're always in these places?'

'What places?' At last, I got words out.

'Late night places – clubs. Have you?'

'Have I *what*?'

'Had relations?'

She was deadly serious and continued to stare at me with those stranger's eyes. A chilling thought was that we had gone back years to when we first met. I'd had no effect whatsoever. Five minutes in that kitchen had worked on her in a moment of panic with the effectiveness of napalm, and it was her feeling for me that fried. That I'd never forget.

'No,' I said. I knew she wanted an answer and I was too choked to say more. That she knew I knew black was beautiful goes without saying since there was nothing we didn't talk about, from my Kikuyu adventures to her music master's smelly forefinger. But now reason went out of the window like a curtain blowing in the wind.

She moved away from me, then turned, advanced again.

'You always wanted me to get a sari.'

('They undo more easily,' I'd said. Speedy Gonzalez, me.)

'What?'

'Nothing,' she said icily.

51

I looked for a smile, a wink, a sign that she was having me on, but there was none. There was no reason to what she said, but the effort of concentrating was beginning to fog me.

'What the hell have Pakistanis to do with it?' I shouted suddenly.

'Immigrants,' she said tartly. 'It's all very well to be liberal and educated, the intelligentsia don't have to mix with them.'

'But what has it got to do with me?'

'They're Tee Bee carriers, aren't they? They get here under false pretences and some of them must be rotten with it. That's why I'm asking. We've had smallpox, what next?'

I couldn't answer. All my prejudices were against the powerful, the rich, the urbane and the privileged. I'd seen a few of them and knew how they stuck together, but to hear her go on in this vein was like listening to your mother urging you to go on the knock. I wanted to give her a lecture. It hadn't occurred to me that I'd caught anything from anybody. For as long as I could remember, whenever there was an inquiry or blame to be cast in anything that had ever happened, I always stepped forward automatically because I had a knack of becoming officially deaf to every reprimand. It wouldn't occur to me to accuse, outside the family, that is. I looked at her again, stuck there with her legs together and that Little Miss Muffet expression that she must have kept up her sleeve just for the occasion. It was incredible that I hadn't seen it before. Every day you learn, I thought. Now she sounded like the head girl who sat on the hockey stick. There was that unctious tone, danger to the gels, leaving things like that upturned. Might make a permanent impression on Joanna's.

'When I rang the doctor last night, he said there was no danger to me, but Rachel says quite differently.'

'Ah,' I said. The pipe, Sherlock, I thought. Hand me the match.

'Don't you see? If you've been with Pakistanis, it might be a particularly virulent and incurable form they've brought over with them.'

'What a load of cock!' I said.

'That's what I'm afraid of. Only it's not you I'm thinking of, it's myself,' she stared at me, then blinked as if surprised it had come out.

'Ah,' I said. 'Now that is true.' But curiously I suddenly felt very warmly disposed towards her again. It was all so understandable, her fear for herself. Strangely, I felt reassured and it relieved me, that cry. She'd begun the day all woman, eager and welcoming like the Sultan's first choice after Ramadan, but the moment the fear occurred, she was back in the Headmistress's study, gym-slipped and hysterical as on the day her father died. One's emotions grow in leaps and bounds, following the path of events when events intrude so violently. So she'd had a touch of that again. I looked at her and smiled. I could see the fear in her eyes, the flush of her face, the way her mouth hung open, her breath just controlled. Even as she stood there, she was sorry for what she said, I knew, but it was a true feeling and I understood it. I had been through that self-concern on so many occasions that I was beyond it, case-hardened by failures, and now I felt my calmness as a strength. For the first time in years, it was my turn to comfort. I didn't feel on the run any more. If anybody had the equipment to face disillusion it was me, another thing I was discovering about myself as every second went by. Perhaps my time had finally come and whatever there was for me to bear, I had a sudden confidence. She'd cracked for a moment, but I remained, skulking mentally in my denims, the corporal of the shithouse party, immune to the stench, an old sweat in these fear-making situations. My khaki mind, I thought, but miracle of miracles, I was coming alive too, lying stoutly on my own two buttocks. How typical that I hadn't even got out of bed! Stick it chaps! The Colonel will never leave you! Pass his talc, there's a dear.

'Oh, nuts,' I said. 'Who wouldn't think about themselves? Anybody would. But why should you worry? You look about as ill as a Cheddar cheese.'

She didn't say anything again, but blinked shamefacedly.

'The moment they get me in, you'll have nothing to do. I expect they'll X-ray you for safety's sake, but as for catching anything, you've got to be pretty run down first.'

She half-believed me, but she was still half-indoctrinated. You never escaped from your past, I thought. It was just like it was when Rachel really cast the blight on her. She must have just come out with this propaganda, having slept on it all night, and now it was a recurrence of the ancient theme, her precious niece and me, the gipsy with the cough. No doubt Rachel believed it, every word. She was an avid collector of prejudices and hoarded homely pieces of folklore like an avaricious jackdaw. Now the Pakistanis were getting the stick, years ago it had been the Poles. (In the war she'd heard of a casualty ward full of women with bitten off nipples – the Warsaw touch, according to her!) And, even before that, it was north Walians and their catarrhal money-changers' aaarghs! In her heart, she had a peasant's veneration for the traditional and the unchanging. She didn't mind spiders provided they were her own, but she welcomed strangers like pneumonia. Even people from the next street had mentally to be frisked, held upside-down and looked at through a microscope for about ten years before she gave them the nod. She exaggerated her fears and used them as a life-giving force to preserve herself.

But there was another side of it too, I thought. I'd no doubt she did know a thing or two about the tubercle. And I'd find out. The irony was that the decimated family next door to her childhood home, the ones who galloped away with the consumption, couldn't have had a better neighbour. I was sure she'd been fearless, ready with a bucket or a blanket at the merest knock on the wall. She was a born hot-water boiler, an ever-present attendant on the newly born and the dying. I knew she'd been a layer-out, the heftiest of despatch clerks to the other side. Perhaps of all of us, her experience of life was such that its enormity demanded the absolute clarity of simple prejudices, otherwise she'd never have got by. Now that *was* a new thought, a charitable one for me. I grinned at Connie, who still stood there sheepishly.

'Oh, snap out of it. I can't remember when you had a cold even, and as for me, well...'

'Well, what?' she was still tense, half-convinced.

'However awful it is, it's expected. I'll manage.'

She began to cry then, a limp sniffling that was the worst thing yet.

'Come off it. This isn't you. This is Me!'

I stretched forward and took her hand, drawing her to the bed. She sat down unprotesting.

'I'm a coward.' She kept her face averted.

Somehow I didn't quite believe her, but I said:

'Everybody's a coward. You weren't this morning?'

'I forget splendidly.'

'The poor bloody Pakis,' I said. I remembered an awful corny joke. 'Darling, d'you want to know a good port? Felixstowe, before or after dinner!'

'It could be true, couldn't it?'

'No,' I said. 'But why think about it at all?'

'Auntie's so often right. There's no reason for it, but she is.'

'She's like a bookie who lays off bets all day. Some of them are bound to come up.'

I put my arm around her and she lay against my shoulder, her face still averted.

'I hate sounding stupid,' she said.

'Me too. But doesn't that make everything else so much more interesting?'

She didn't answer, but there was a knock on the door, and Rachel took a step into the room, drawing herself up and sizing up the situation – me close to hers – with that tumbril-watcher's expression I'd come to know so well. She was stout, matronly with immense hams of arms, a small purse of a mouth set in a cake-shop face, her hair coiled behind in a bun, altogether something of a disappointment to look at if you had heard about her first. She had a small head and a large body, bright eyes with a fresh complexion and a habit of standing unobtrusively on the edge of a carpet in the corner of a room, always ready to move to the centre of attention but never seeking it. She could look mild at times, but more than anything, she was *in attendance* always. It was her thing, being at your elbow, her head obsequiously averted like a faithful retainer's.

Now she went to Connie, her hands clasped together, holding ten fingers carefully, like banknotes.

'Is that wise, dear?' she said in her lowered sick-room voice. 'I mean, within range?'

Connie looked up wearily. She didn't have much resistance to Rachel in my presence.

'Germs?' I said. I wasn't going to annoy her – yet.

'You never know,' Rachel said. 'Never.'

Especially with the Calcutta variety, I thought.

'Yes, prudence in all things,' I said.

She looked at me, an eyelid flickering.

'You've seen reason then? At last?'

'It's your duty to protect yourselves,' I said. I found a cough at the back of my throat and gave it an airing, a minor warble compared to some I'd been getting lately.

'It'll get worse than that,' Rachel said to Connie. 'You'll have to bear up.'

Connie didn't look as if she could move. I buttoned my

lip, withdrew my hand from her shoulder and held both my hands together, clasped in front of me. It didn't occur to me I had the same clasp as Rachel's but she noticed, flicked the lizard's eye and again, dared me to say one word.

I didn't, but I twiddled my thumbs, looked away. A moment's pause as if no one was sure the will had been signed. Rachel went over to the window to pull the curtains, giving Connie a pat on the shoulder as she went. I tried to make a face, but Connie was staring past me, looking anywhere. Rachel opened the window wide with such force that the sash cords rattled.

'Fresh air,' I said.

'You haven't had enough of it.'

'Never,' I said. She was sparring for an opening, I could see, but I wasn't going to give her one. Even now, her mind was at work, taking in Connie's folded nightdress at the foot of the bed. She'd folded it yesterday and knew it hadn't been worn. There'd be words about that when they were on their own. Then her eye passed to my clothes on the chair. They lay where they'd been dropped.

'From now on, you'll have to take a hold on yourself, Walter.'

'Clearly,' I said.

'Of course, we'll manage as best we can here.'

Connie stood up. The butter had congealed on the toast and the bacon had dried on the breakfast plate.

'He doesn't seem very keen on the egg and milk?' she said. Now they both stood looking down at me, as if I'd deliberately walked under a bus. The beginning of things to come, I thought.

'Egg and milk is the oldest remedy known to man,' Rachel said sombrely in that small deliberate voice. 'It has saved thousands.'

'Please take it...' Connie said, bewitched again in the presence.

'Thora-Cop-Plasty,' Rachel said to me. 'Ever heard of it?'

'No,' I said. I stared at her.

She gave an informed little nod. 'You will, I'm afraid.'

'What is it?' Connie said nervously.

Rachel ignored Connie and concentrated on me.

'D'you find anything in your handkerchief in the mornings?'

'What d'you mean?'

'Has he got thin ankles?' Rachel said to Connie. 'I can't remember.'

'Well,' Connie said. 'Thin, I don't know.'

'There's not much of him, tall but not much else.'

'I don't see where this is getting us,' I said.

'Thora-Cop-Plasty,' Rachel said again with relish. 'When my cousin had it, they tried to save a few ribs.'

'Now look here,' I said.

'Eggs and milk,' she said. 'Oh, I know what a low opinion you have of me, don't worry. I know, always have known, *but...*'

'Yes?' I said.

'You've got to build yourself up to give them something to work on.'

'Work on?' I didn't like the sound of that.

'It's changed now,' Connie said uncertainly. 'Everything's changed since the drugs. It has, hasn't it?'

Ignorance was present in the bedroom like a fourth person.

'Of course, it has,' I said.

'If he doesn't cooperate,' Rachel said; 'he could *go* overnight.'

That was it. 'For crying out loud,' I said. I laughed. 'Now then, Auntie Rachel. Wishful thinking won't kill the golden goose, ha ha.'

She shook her head. 'I won't say any more.'

'At this stage?' I said. That went home. But Connie looked at the egg and milk in that poisoner's beaker.

'Will you drink it if I warm it up?'

I sighed. All our threesomes became ridiculous. I couldn't even work up a temper unless a crisis happened. But Connie was uncertain and anxious, that was real. I knew I'd have to drink it even if it meant putting a clothes peg over my nose. All my acts of heroism were small like this, small and comic.

'All right,' I said. I thought of Scott's last words in that old movie. 'But for God's sake look after our people.'

She gave a relieved smile but before I could say anything, Rachel opened the bedroom door like a matron ushering out a probationer. Connie took the breakfast tray and went out. I determined to keep the peace.

'Thank you, Auntie Rachel,' I said.

But she just looked at me with that patient, eyeball-shrinking stare, said nothing, allowed herself a slow shake of the head, then drew the door over her face and left without another word. I was beyond, in her phrase. I'd heard it so many times. Beyond. As it happened, I was tired and no sooner did I lay back on the pillow than I was asleep. I reckoned I had it coming, the merest nap. But in the state I was in, my condition as they say, I had got used to nightmares of the most lurid kind. I'd had the luck to travel more than most and had been in some bizarre spots, the reason-defying circumstances that the wandering poor always encounter. The consequence was that my dreams were often in technicolour, large-scale Roman productions with no expense spared on the extras. And now, when Connie for some reason did not return with the beaker full of Rachel's life-giving poison, I passed into the first of the twilight comas that became part of me later. You nod off at first, sinking into weakness, a reverie begins, and your tired old mind plays with a phrase, the phrase takes life, scenes sprout like hairs on a gooseberry. Part of my trouble was that I was a picture thinker. Images ruled me, and since the last thing I'd seen was Rachel's death-rattle shake of the head, it reappeared as I went into limbo. She could convey a world in a glance and, in front of that departing nod I saw, straight-grained and rent-free, the final lodging, its purse-proud brass handles gleaming against the pine walls of the only detached residence I would ever own – a coffin.

For some reason, death had never bothered me, but I'd often thought cheerfully of my own funeral, whiling away many an idle hour in some layby or other. For preference, I would choose a male voice choir to put me under, one of those bellowing groups of short, squat, scrubbed, barrel-chested men in Burton's suits whose extraordinary, spine-chilling sound I had to conduct as well. I saw them all in my mind's eye, ranged obediently above me as I raised an imaginary baton and drew forth sound after sound, composing a nonsense lyric in my mind.

'*Oh, this man... this man... this man... He died of dog food!*'

They could sing even that as if it were the pronouncement of the angelic host, and indulging myself, I had worked my way through a full oratorio in complete command, when I felt something cold on my forehead. It was hard and unfamiliar. I opened an eye. Rachel was pressing a gigantic iron key against my neck. I was sweating again and feverish, although now there was a familiar taste. I blinked, tried to push it from my lips, stared up at her. She removed the key and stood back to look at me gravely.

'Is...'

'Don't talk! Imperative!'

'Is... that... a... key?' My voice was weak, unrecognisable.

She nodded but gave no explanation. Now her face was concerned, the web of lines under her eyes, drawn and heavy. She offered no explanation immediately and I thought I might still be dreaming.

It was hard to get the words out. 'You're not... not opening me up, are you?'

Connie came into the room wearing an apron and they both looked at me. Why was I suddenly so weak? But then I had been singing, had I not? You try the tonic sol-fa for a hundred voices and see where that gets you. Even the shows I put on for myself demanded my all, a real trouper me.

'You'd better lie very still,' Connie said quietly. She seemed faraway and out of focus, her voice coming distantly as if from behind some invisible barrier.

'And you mustn't talk,' Rachel said. 'Talking is fatal, the slightest movement.'

Somehow, I didn't object and regarded them faintly, two blurring faces close to mine, and in Rachel's hand, that jailer's key. It was big and cumbersome, heavy enough to be regarded as an offensive weapon. I looked at it again, but politely said nothing.

But then I turned my head upon the pillow and froze. There it was, brother, a part of me, gout to eyeball, the blood of the lamb on display. I'd had a haemorrhage in my sleep and the counterpane was soaking. I moved my head slowly away like an old round ball. Strangely, I had no fear. It wasn't just that it was one more thing, another – what? – card from the bottom of the deck? But rather, it confirmed my suspicion of the awfulness of things. Beaten to a standstill, I thought; it couldn't come much worse. Custer got his from the Indians, Geronimo died of drink; with me, it was the Treorchy Male Voice Choir. Why did I have to conduct as well?

'We've rung,' Rachel said sombrely.

'We said it was an emergency,' Connie said. 'But you musn't move or talk.'

I turned my head to look at them. The dream lingered at the edges of my mind. Conditioned by lousy movies, now I was waiting for another choir, butterfly wings of song, a sugar plum exit to a sugar plum world. But that was ridiculous. My sense of smell told me that. Pardon me.

'There's a bit of a niff in here,' I said. I sounded aged. 'How about a vodka?'

'Please...' Connie said tearfully. 'Not even jokes.'

So it was as bad as that. Hanging on a thread, I thought, batman ding-donging on a slender gossamer. No wonder they wanted me on the egg and milk. It was a gargantuan clog, Auntie Rachel's life-preserving constipator; wisdom to the old herblore after all. But what was the key for? It bothered me.

'The key? I must know about...'

'Something cold, for the back of your neck,' Rachel said.

'At first, we thought it was a nosebleed,' Connie said.

'Haem-opt-ys-is,' Rachel said deliberately. 'I knew. You must have lost a pint at least and if you open your mouth once more, I shan't be responsible.'

My mind kept on working like a rusty old cuckoo clock, half-formed ideas uncurling lazily like broken springs spilling into space. Their air of gravity was faintly hilarious. Perhaps I was always indifferent to people's concern for me, a fatalist in the face of everything that happened. Somewhere along the line, I'd lost the sense of controlling my own destiny. Was this an illness, this impotence? If it was, it did not concern me any more, I suppose, than footrot bothered an infantry soldier in the trenches. Tomorrow was limping towards me, not billowing clouds and a sunrise full of promise, but an ugly stillness, light fading and rumblings under the earth, threat once more in the air. I tried to belittle it, this sense of doom. Red in the eye, salesman's warning, I said to myself. You have to say something even to yourself, even if it's only nonsense. The important thing is to keep talking, maintaining your dialogue with any kind of life.

The front door bell rang. Connie tip-toed to the door. It was Uncle Iestyn.

'He's done his usual with the car.'

'He's very ill.'

'That's what I've come about. I've been on to the Chairman. Yes, the Hospital Board. Everything's fixed. I went to see him personally.'

Magnificent nepotist; action! But I didn't hear any more and Rachel went out, brandishing the key like a witch's wand and closed the door behind her. Alone again. Everything took time. They were so alarmed, looking at me like spectators at a street accident. Move nothing, touch nothing; it was safer. They must have gone into the kitchen because I heard raised voices, then quiet, then the kitchen door opened, and finally Uncle Iestyn appeared, holding a black homburg across his chest. He wore his black pinstripe, stiff collar, Rotarian sticker, and on his ancient watchchain, a medallion indicating his presidency of some grocers' organisation. He did the dog food as an extra while his wife managed the shop.

'Walter bach... you're not to speak, not a word!'

I didn't even nod.

He eyed the victim and gulped. How did I know he had an Iberian head? And a curved forehead like a melon, sucked-in cheeks and a whistler's mouth.

'I got on to Bowcott Jones, the Chairman. You're going in today. It's arranged.'

65

I nodded, a Herculean process of bringing my chin down an inch.

He did his whistle in reverse, a short intake of breath.

'Pity you're not a mason. We'd have had the best man in London for you. Never mind.'

I signalled an acknowledgment to that too. Live with nepotists, you must acknowledge their Gods at every level.

'However,' he said breezily, 'with this complaint, worry is the killer. You take it from me.'

'What about the tomato sauce on the bed-cover?' I thought. But what I'd forgotten was that they'd seen it all before. Our elders, the extent of their lifespan, I thought. Nobody ever sings the praises of our valley people, only folksy ghosts.

'Have you got a dressing-gown?'

I shook my head. He looked at me, measuring me up.

I wanted to laugh again. He and Rachel had the complete answer for everything. Nothing really bothered them because there was always something for them to do. They were always busy, always helping, worrying away at details I never even thought of. A dressing-gown... I knew he'd go straight out and get one at cost.

'And as for anything else, Walter, boy, put it right out of your mind.'

I risked a word: 'Ta,' I said.

He looked up as we heard the sound of the ambulance siren down the road. Connie must have rung the emergency service, Iestyn went to the bedroom window and stared down at the road outside. The back of his neck flushed and he turned away irritably.

Connie came in; 'They're here.'

I could see he wanted to say something, but not in front of me. He went out to the passage to find Rachel, strutting as he went.

Connie put a spare pair of pyjamas into a grip. She already had a wash bag.

'I'm coming with you, but for God's sake, don't move. Let them lift you – everything.'

I grinned. Relief: now I was everybody else's problem.

Rachel showed in the ambulance men. They had one of these dinky trolley stretchers with snapdown wheels.

'He didn't have time to shave,' Rachel said apologetically.

They didn't pay any attention. They put the stretcher down, folded a stiff blanket and slipped it under me. I might have been broken glass.

'All right, mate? Ready, Fred?'

'To you.'

I was tucked up like a baby and out of the house in seconds.

'Take your good coat,' Rachel called to Connie, but she came with me, just herself, handbag, and my grip. Then they closed the door of the ambulance. The windows were made of blue glass and restful. I felt utterly relieved. She held my hand.

'Don't say anything – anything at all.'

I didn't. Later, I found out what irritated Iestyn. He'd ordered another ambulance through his connections. It passed ours as we turned off into the main road.

'Two ambulances,' Rachel said. The other arrived as she was preparing to burn the bed sheets. '*Two!*'

I felt it was my due, but being me, I had a preference for the one with the siren. It seemed a more fitting exit. After all, there were two of us, Joey and me.

CHAPTER THREE

CONNIE

On the way to the hospital, for once, he said very little. I wanted to look at his eye, but whatever was there, he said it was no use looking. I couldn't see it, he said. Nobody could see it, except him. It was inside the eye. Eale's Disease... I'd never heard of it.

The ambulance driver patted my arm as we got in the back of the ambulance. Very comforting and fatherly. They had a snap-down seat for relatives to sit on and they pulled it down. I didn't say anything, just looked out of the window. I could see out, but other people couldn't see me. Ideal. They didn't use the siren and they didn't seem to hurry. It was our emergency, not theirs.

He closed his eyes as they slid the trolley in. When I held his hand, he smiled but did not open his eyes. His hand was hot and limp as he rested it in mine. Poor Walter. He always looked strained and wore his tenseness like a protective armour as if to say, upset me and you never know what might happen. There was supposed to be danger in it, this tautness. But now his pallor put a different complexion on everything. Perhaps it was the light filtering in from the windows, which were tinted and gave his face that blueness over the pallor that seemed especially unnatural. Middle-aged men sometimes have that colour around the edge of their five o'clock shadow. Someone had told me once that it was the cells beginning to die, first the tiny hair follicles turn grey, and when they shaved, the blue note was the beginning of decomposition. At about the same age, the backs of their heels turn grey. Nature's warning, dead hair and dying skin.

I kept on holding his hand. His eyes remained closed. I felt my elbow getting stiff, but when I took it away, he moaned so I kept it there. Really, the eye was too much. One in six cases a year... It was another lie, I was sure. He said he needed glasses. He didn't say anything about the ophthalmic specialist before he went. If there was something wrong with his eye, surely, it would be visible? The TB I could understand. 'Run down,' Rachel had said, 'he's always looked run down.' But when something is permanent, you learn to live with it. What did she expect me to do?

He moaned again.

'We're nearly there,' I said. 'But you mustn't talk.'

I was afraid of another haemorrhage. And I'd had enough of his talking. I couldn't understand where the haemorrhage had come from. Was it his lungs? If it was an ulcer, I could understand. I'd only met his mother once. The first thing she said stuck: 'He lives on his nerves.' And mine now. Anything to do with the nervous condition was believable. But not the eye. Could it have been something to do with syphillis, some bug that stayed lurking in the bloodstream? He was just the sort to have had a dose. I could see him being sorry for good-hearted whores, sentimental in his beer about any face that happened to be next to his. We'd discussed it once. We discussed everything to do with sex. He seemed frankly amazed that I was as interested as he was. I didn't show I was more knowledgeable and experienced. They don't like that, lovers or husbands. But you couldn't say the strain was due to me. He'd always had it. I never said no to him, anyway. Whatever he wanted, he had. And some inventions of my own. His illness came from inside him, not from me. All that.

Or so I liked to think.

One of the ambulance men slid back the partition window.

'We're taking it easy because of the haemorrhage.'

'Thank you.'

'Won't be long.'

I nodded, smiled as he slid the window back. Poor Walter, I thought again. Everybody who knew him said that if they liked him, which most people did, although he'd swear the world was against him. It was just they wouldn't trust him with any part of it. Poor Walter... Good old Walter. Everybody said that too and looked at me as if I were doing social work. But if we'd had a child, I would have had what I wanted.

71

Two porters came out to meet the ambulance at Casualty. The driver opened the door. They had a casual conversation.

'What's this then? Run over?'

'Haemorrhage.'

'Heart, is it?'

'Haemorrhage.'

'In the street, was it?'

'Haemorrhage.'

'He's not bleeding now?'

'It's internal.'

I followed them up the covered way. The corridors of hospitals… White tiles, the smell of paint, rain dripping on covered ways, a small boy with a fracture crying miserably, relatives gazing like sheep, a bad-tempered sister looking for something in a drawer. Why is there always this rush?

'Name?' someone said. 'Age, date of birth, occupation?'

'Gentleman,' Walter said with a grin. He was beginning to enjoy it.

'You musn't talk,' I said again. There were suddenly so many people, I couldn't see who to begin with.

'We'll have to have the stretcher, Mrs', the ambulance man said apologetically.

'Just let me get his particulars first,' this other person said.

An orderly brought another trolley. It had no pillow or blanket.

'He is not going on to that,' I said.

'Doctor-What-is-it? And his religion?'

'You get his head,' the ambulance driver said to his helper.

'*He's not going to be moved,*' I said.

The Sister arrived holding what she'd been looking for: a magnet. Legs like bottles.

'For goodness sake...' she said. I'd raised my voice. 'This is a hospital not a cinema queue. Move him on to the trolley.'

'No,' I said.

'Wheel him in there,' the Sister pointed to a side ward. 'Quickly. And take the trolley with you.'

'I'll put down C of E,' the person bending down said.

For once, he'd said nothing.

'If you'll just wait here, Madam,' the Sister said to me. 'Doctor'll be along in a minute. He's having coffee.'

'What is the name of your local doctor?' the enquiring person said. 'Mrs What-is-it?'

'Lacey,' I said. I'd allowed myself to be sidetracked already. Obviously they'd taken him out of my sight to move him. I didn't feel weepy, just annoyed.

'And your local doctor's name is?'

'Can't this wait?'

'No.'

'Well, it will have to.'

The Sister came back, even more annoyed.

'He's had a haemoptysis. You didn't say it was tubercle?'

'Diagnosis isn't my function,' I said.

She flushed.

'There's also an associated condition of the eye,' I said. 'Eale's Disease. I understand my Uncle has spoken to the Chairman of the Hospital Management Committee.'

'I haven't heard anything...' she hesitated. That went home. Who you know is the important thing in Wales. Always.

'No doubt you will,' I said flatly.

Bitchy, bitchiness, ice. You have to know what you're capable of, live with it, and use it. Dealing with her, I was glad he wasn't there. 'The haemorrhage has come quite unexpectedly. In the normal course of events, he would have come in as a matter of routine.'

She didn't know what to do.

'If you'll excuse me, I'll ring up, Mrs... Mrs...?'

'Lacey.'

She went away. The enquiring person came back.

'Would you like to sit down, Mrs Lacey?'

Nepotism works.

'Doctor will be along in a minute.'

'I'll wait just here,' I said. The important thing is not to be over-awed. People suffer for their ignorance, are pushed about. Not me.

The doctor was a Pakistani. I thought of what Rachel had said earlier, my own fear, what he might have passed on to me. Self again. I'd got over that for the moment. I was as ashamed of my prejudices as anybody.

'This is Dr Quereshi,' the Sister said. 'I'm afraid your husband will have to be moved again.'

'Again?'

'He should have been admitted to the sanatorium.'

'Is he in a condition to be moved?'

'Dr Quereshi's going to have a look at him. I'm sure it'll be all right.'

She wanted to get him off her hands, I knew. I quite understood. I had the same feeling.

While they were in the side ward, the second ambulance came. By now, they'd begun to look at me curiously as I stood there fixedly on the same spot. People had begun to walk around me. Now they brought him out on the trolley, another change of stretchers.

'It's like draughts,' he said. 'They're playing me.'

'We won't be long,' I said. 'They'll know what to do in the sanatorium.'

I saw the Sister flush. I dared her to say anything. Three stretchers in three minutes.

'Don't change the level of his head,' I said to the ambulance man.

They were crisply efficient. It was just another Walter incident. Eventually, we got moving and I sat beside him again, and again he held my hand. I could feel his weakness through that hand. He was beginning to perspire freely. I wiped his forehead but he nodded my other hand away, and lay there like a child in its cot. The fact that he was silent was alarming, but as we drove along, my own thoughts were worse. Later, he'd recall this ride like some cinema clip, a passage between hero and heroine. He had this picture of me that was totally erroneous; and not only of me, but Rachel, all of us. You couldn't tell him anything. Nor argue. Sometimes he could be sidetracked and distracted like a child, but he remained Walter. I'd done everything I could, supported him, housed him, earned for him, collaborated in all the affections which he supposed he induced in people, but the moment had come when

75

something had snapped in me. If I couldn't have a child by him, I didn't want him.

He opened his eyes suddenly: 'Sorry.'

You couldn't keep on saying, 'Don't talk.'

But I said, 'Don't talk.'

'I wouldn't look at anybody else,' he said.

I know what it was, Rachel's prejudice which I'd passed on in a panic, thinking he'd picked something up from some immigrant girl, a dose or the TB. He'd romanticise even that.

'Forget I ever said it,' I said.

'You didn't really think...'

'Of course not.'

I did though for a moment, that's the point. What you have to learn, even about the men you marry, is that they can say what they like with such conviction that they'd convince themselves. The fact was, I could just see him with his bar-room charm, half-cut in some pub. The slightest bit of egging-on and any foreign tart would set him off like a tap. It was all he wanted. Sex without responsibility, sex without the politics of seduction, sex on the bus stop, sex without speaking, all as natural as tea after meals provided he was far enough away and there was no chance of me knowing. I don't say he did it all the time, once was enough to catch anything. Don't call me hard, just a realist.

'Why didn't you come into the side ward?' he said quietly.

'I was dealing with the Sister.'

'Ah, the dealer...'

'Sh...'

I looked at his eye again and still couldn't see anything. Why was I so bitchy to that Sister? Panic. I could scream at him and freeze her, and still show nothing on my face. The difference between us, I thought, Walter and me, was that he showed everything and felt nothing real, I showed nothing real and felt everything. But no, that was too simple. What then? We had only one thing in common. We knew everything there was to know about sex, and nothing about each other. We had exhausted the instinct and had nothing to say in the silence that followed. And now he was ill. Which brought us back to where we started. Poor Walter.

He said, 'It's hard to find the guts, isn't it?'

'Energy, you'll get it back.'

I was glad he closed his eyes then. If he knew what I really thought, it would kill him. How? Why? When? I thought. Pointless questions. I couldn't understand how any human being could be so ignorant. All these picture thinkers give the impression of intelligence. They are never short of anything to say, but nothing happens. They communicate nothing, their noises die down and they're short-term, amusing people, passing acquaintances, that's all. Unless you marry them. Why did I do that? Because no one else ever asked me actually to marry him, that's why. Anything else, all the action, with and without, but marriage, no. And when I was single, I'd got so I preferred married men, taking time over it, being used. Nobody ever cried over me except Walter. Nobody ever needed me like he did. In a strange way that nobody'd believe, I had to marry him to conceal my power to hurt him. And my vanity. He thought me beautiful when I was plain. I dressed carefully but my hips were too big. I had this frankly sensual face that connoisseurs didn't mistake. ('This might hurt,' he said the first time. He'd ripped my dress and jammed his own trousers in a coat hanger!) Still, it was nice to be thought nice, nice to be liked, nice to have presents, nice to be wanted all the time. The hell was not to feel like he did and still be married to him. That's what I should have known, should have been myself the male partner while he fizzed like a dizzy blonde, hopeless, inept, his dreams racing beyond his capabilities, and now his body. Without that, I didn't give us much chance. Now he'd wrecked his body, while mine had stayed the way it always had been, ready and waiting. Declare yourself always, I thought bitterly. That was important.

The sanatorium was a misnomer. They'd built it before the war in the days when TB meant something but now it was mostly hearts and cancers, quite a modern building near the coast with grounds that only the state can keep up, pine trees, long drives and gardens laid out in a geometrical pattern. They kept a small ward going for the Tee Bees though. Why did I keep saying that? Rachel's phrase, I expect. I did listen to her, dismissing half she said, remembering the rest. I thought her a shrewd woman in some ways. She usually got what she wanted.

Walter opened his eyes as we slowed down and the ambulance backed into another covered way. The nice thing about him was that he wasn't frightened for himself ever. If only he wouldn't keep seeing me now as some kind of pastiche heroine and himself as the fallen warrior.

'Christ!' he said suddenly. 'I shall have to write to you.'

'If you like.'

'Well, of course.'

I knew he had difficulty spelling, another consequence of his ghastly education, which irritated him when I had to correct things, but I didn't say anything. I just wanted him in there, under care. I could decide what to do afterwards.

The ambulance driver got out and gave a cheery rat-tat-tat on the side of the ambulance, then opened the doors noisily.

'There's nothing to this complaint these days,' he said knowledgeably. No doubt he also thought us a young couple for whom things hadn't gone very well.

This time they brought a stretcher from the hospital. It was altogether a more modern building. The staff were casual and unhurried. The ambulance driver looked up my legs as I got out of the ambulance. Knowing men, I supposed he thought I was going to go to waste for a few months.

They took us to the examination room, laid Walter on a couch. A registrar came, calm and accepting, with a soft New Zealand accent. He twigged at once that I wanted to talk to him on my own. Without the child, as it were. He'd had X-rays sent him and a letter: communication. I explained about the haemorrhage. He was unworried.

'We're going to put you on bed rest, Mr Lacey,' he smiled at Walter. 'The extent of the tubercle is confined to one lung and when we see how you react to chemotherapy, we hope it'll clear up the eye.'

'Hope?' Walter said sharply. He had that comic, hoarse catch to his voice; 'What the hell is chemotherapy?'

'Walter,' I said. I felt like a mum. 'They're only doing their best.'

'It's an allergic condition, your eye, an allergy to the tubercle. We can only suppose it will clear up as the drugs clear up the infection.'

'Chemotherapy means drugs,' I said.

'Hi ho,' Walter said. He gave me a stare.

There was another Sister, a white tunic, red belt, high heels. She had the letter, an ageing blonde still looking after herself.

'There's a note here about drops.'

'Ah, yes,' the Registrar said.

'Drops?' Walter said. 'Oh, yes, I've had them before.'

He hadn't told me.

'They are eye drops to keep the pupil dilated,' the Registrar said. 'You'll find it difficult to read.'

Walter gave me another alarmed glance as if to say, stop them!

'Anything else?' he said to the doctor.

'You'll have to be very patient, Mr Lacey.'

'Charming,' Walter said. But he was resigning himself.

'I'll take him to the ward now,' the Sister said. 'You can come and say goodbye.'

It was strange to keep on seeing him handled by other people. I did not feel guilty about my sense of relief. He was their problem now.

The Sister called an orderly and they took him out. When they opened the door, I could hear a man coughing in the distance. It was deep in his throat, ending in a lubricated wheeze like a leaky accordion expelling air. I knew it was a man because he spat expertly.

'Oh, Christ,' Walter said as they took him out. 'Listen to that.'

When he'd gone, the Registrar pointed to a chair. I sat down and crossed my legs.

'I don't understand about the eye,' I said. 'You can't see anything surely? I can't.'

'You can with an ophthalmoscope, but we don't know very much about it, I'm afraid.'

I struggled for the word. 'Is there a ... prognosis?'

He smiled. 'I can't tell you anything definite. I've never seen a case before. But I've looked it up. Vitreous haemorrhages. The tissue is weakened and the haemorrhages occur within the eye.'

I had to say it. 'Will he lose his sight?' I said quickly.

He considered his answer. 'It's impossible for me to say. The best thing he can hope for is that he responds to chemotherapy, and that the allergy will disappear as a consequence. He'll have to be immobilised for a considerable time.'

I couldn't stand it if he went blind, I thought. I just couldn't. I had a vision of him with a white stick, smiling bravely, tapping along behind me wherever I went. That he was likely to be feeling schoolgirls as they helped him across the road didn't matter. Blind, he would be tied to me forever and I couldn't bear it. Even children grow up and leave you, but not husbands like Walter.

'Oh,' I said. Then I said it again. '*Do you* think he'll lose his sight?'

'I just don't know.'

I was sorry he didn't find any phoney words of comfort. So it was bad then. Walter hadn't lied. For once, he couldn't exaggerate enough. And now I knew.

'But how did he get it?' I said. 'Is it infectious?'

'I know it must sound very irritating, but we don't know very much about it at all. As far as I know, it occurs in young men but the ophthalmic people don't see many cases. It's impossible for them to be authoritative with that kind of incidence.'

Now I was glad that he was talking to me as an intelligent person and being frank. It was better than Walter's silent screaming and frenzy. But now I had to be frank myself.

'No doubt you'll give him all sorts of tests?'

'We'll X-ray him, naturally.'

He was looking at me curiously, sensing my discomfiture.

Perhaps he understood something about Walter, or read my moistened lips.

'How long have you been married?'

'Six years. But I would like him to have a Wasserman test.'

'Is there any likelihood of...'

'No,' I said sarcastically. 'That's why I'm asking.'

He didn't say anything immediately. It occurred to me that he might suppose I had reason to fear. But I had not.

'It has to be said, my husband isn't as stable as he might be.

82

He's been under strain.' The strain of being his bloody self, I thought bitterly.

He smiled. 'We'll do everything that's necessary.'

Suddenly, I could see that for an instant he was looking at me now as bed potential. The clinical pose slipped a notch. I don't know what it is about me that makes certain men realise immediately. Lips, hips, the way my nostrils flare? I'll never know. I'd asked and got no response. In the past it had made things easy but now, suddenly, inexplicably, I felt disgusted, sick and ashamed for the first time. You coiled yourself up and kept an even pace, you learned to cope, you said nothing, you lived with yourself daily, and suddenly, like a paper bag bursting, a flood of feeling enveloped you for no reason at all. I looked away miserably. This is what it had come to, my marriage, these grubby thoughts in a clinic, mistrust and reason to fear, and Walter even more helpless than when I married him. That irked me. If anybody had failed, I had. You cannot help your thoughts or the demands of your body and in my case, it was demands from the word go. But your actions were your own responsibility. He must have been ill for months without me noticing. All very well for me to say I couldn't stand this or that. Now he couldn't stand on his feet. If I was going to leave him, I couldn't do it unless he was well.

The Sister came. 'I'll take you to him, Mrs Lacey.'

I nodded to the doctor, who was still looking at me curiously. Perhaps it would be better if I cried more often, I thought. But then I hadn't cried, only felt like crying.

They'd put him in the end bed of a four-bedded ward.

He was near the window looking out at the sea. There were screens around the bed. The sister parted them, but then stayed with us.

'Oh, Christ,' he said. 'Did they tell you anything?'

'Only that you'll have to be very patient.'

'What a lark!'

I wished he wouldn't talk like that. I bent forward to kiss him. 'If you don't mind,' the Sister said. 'Not with this complaint.'

'Be wire mesh soon,' Walter said. He'd found a grin from somewhere. It looked awful against that pallor. I'd never noticed his thinness so much. The knobs of his collar bone stood out under his opened pyjama jacket.

'Visiting days Wednesdays and weekends,' the Sister said, 'If you come down to the office, I'll give you a card.'

Suddenly, I didn't want to leave him. None of us is wholly awful. For six years I'd been married to him. I was more sorry for him now than ever. It was what we existed on, his illusions and my sorrow. Nothing changed, only grew more intense.

'You can ring tonight to see if he's settled in,' the Sister said impatiently.

'After prep,' Walter said, still grinning. 'You must never ring during prep.'

So I was crying when I left, hurrying down the ward past the other patients, salt tears, looking such a nice girl, you know, moved and all, the strong one in the partnership for whom things hadn't gone very well. I kept coming back to that. My phrase and my mistake.

We never said goodbye.

'Well?' Rachel said when I got home.

'It's as bad as he said. It's true about his eye. Serious. They don't know, but he could lose his sight.'

'And the TB?'

'They don't seem to be worried about that.'

She'd made a cup of tea, stirred sugar in my cup, handed it to me gravely.

'You'll have to look after yourself as well. Relatives can crack up, you know?'

'Yes,' I said.

'Iestyn went out and bought a dressing-gown. You'd better let me post it.'

'Yes.'

'And slippers.'

'Yes, slippers.' Why did I never think of these things?

'There's one good thing, he's in qualified hands.'

'Yes,' I said again. I couldn't get over my tears coming out of the ward. The extent of my feeling still.

'We can only hope and pray,' Rachel said. She did the praying.

'Yes.'

'Did they give you any indication of how long it's likely to be?'

'No, they don't know.' I explained about the allergy. The allergy and the eye, I thought. It sounded like the two of us from his point of view, my allergy to him. Only he didn't know about that either.

'Well, you'll just have to go on living your normal life and not let yourself go,' Rachel said.

'Yes,' I said again. I'd been saying it all my life, I thought. I felt weary suddenly.

'He's a fool to himself, of course. He always has been, but there'll be less opportunity for him to damage himself in hospital.'

'Yes,' I said. All true, all obvious, all meaningless. It was what I felt that counted. *Me-me-me*! I didn't think of him.

She couldn't see that I didn't want to talk.

'I'll get you a Marie biscuit,' she said.

I watched her waddle into the pantry, the ribs of her corsets showing through her skirt. She did all the housework and most of the cooking, except at weekends when I did my bit of arty tarty on occasions, and even then she'd go up the back garden for mint if it was raining. Because of her, it was possible for me to live my tiny, joke professional life. Because of her, I was more independent than most, and because of me, she had an interest in life, a love object on which she doted, and it suited me very well. Between us, we could cope with Walter effortlessly. We had everything arranged, and although he occasionally moaned, it suited him too. He could fail all the time, and we were still there, the providers. He never really objected. If he had, I don't know what I would have done, but now it occurred to me that perhaps I'd done more than provide him with a world. It was very obvious how much I did. It was very obvious how little he did. That it could have had consequences on his morale had occurred to me and I'd thought a good deal about it when we were first married.

When he went from job to job, there didn't seem much alternative, and his laziness in accepting everything didn't help. His problems always seemed to be outside the house, a manager, a client, his cars, people who did him down, credit he wasn't authorised to extend, returns he'd filled in full of illegible alterations, customers going sour, and finally wage deductions to which he objected with his usual unreason. But I'd always thought a man should have another world anyway, and what he did outside the house was his affair. He had to do something. And when he fell in through the front door, well, he was home, I thought. And that was my province. Rachel never bothered us. I didn't see what he could logically object to, unless he provided something better. Managing women induced resentments, I knew, but no one ever told you what to do with men who couldn't manage. You adapted yourself the best you could. Or so I thought.

Why then did I feel guilty?

Perhaps because that was his expertise, making me feel guilty. And when I thought about it, I was sure no one ever fired him without regret either. But they still fired him. And would always buy him a drink. He never parted on bad terms. But he always parted. Why?

Rachel came in with the plate of biscuits.

'We never think, do we? What other people have to go through.'

Her chat. There was a Christmas card motto in every other sentence. Oh, other people's lives! I didn't answer. Then I thought; stuffing! That's what he lacked. He had guts, but only like a sail in constant exposure to the wind.

He was always taking it. If he wasn't in trouble, he'd invent it, create it, that was his artistry. He always stirred up a patchwork of minor things that added up to a maximum accretion of hurt, until finally, he became the permanent and permanently self-inflicting wound. And unwittingly, I'd been a conspirator, I thought. Those who do good create charity when the need for it shouldn't exist at all. I'd have to leave him. Have to.

So my guilt soon vanished. I didn't even have the need to go around asking anybody to look at my side of things. I didn't care for long enough, and when I did, I usually kept it inside. Without getting tense and twisted. It was just private. And I wasn't going to talk to Rachel about it. I knew she wanted to. She would have fed on us if I'd let her. He didn't think I knew that either, but I did. The truth was, I only wanted her involvement as long and as much as it suited me. If you're selfish, be selfish, I thought. You make your own life, all that. Walter, Walter, Walter. I was sick of Walter

'Poor Walter,' Rachel said. She could grieve for anybody and now she was settling down for a morning of it. I'd soon be sick of her too.

She'd telephoned the school to explain my absence. They said I could take the day off if I wanted to. But I didn't want to. Dull kids, my expertise. My whole life was a conundrum. I usually kept the two separate, classroom and outside. I could manage them because I gave them order and expertise. I couldn't manage Walter because I couldn't give him order and he had no expertise. Brute truth. So leave him. The thought kept recurring in my mind as if it was an animate thing trying to grow up into a decision.

'I'll have to get back to school,' I said to Rachel.

'They said you could take the day off.'

'I don't want to.' Other people needed me.

'I'll post the dressing-gown and slippers express post then?'

'Thanks,' I said. Oh, see to him for Christ's sake, I thought, he's killing me.

But he wasn't. He was just in a more serious Walter-situation than usual. Except for his eye. Always a reservation.

I went to school. I taught in a hut. Literally. It was a pre-fab building at the edge of the school yard, a post-war construction that had had to last. We had a coke stove, intense winter heat, a huge china sink and our own lavatories around the corner next to the woodwork store. We were completely isolated from the main building, me and my little lot, 4c. It was Bryn's idea to get a woman installed with the odds and sods. Bryn was headmaster of this ancient secondary modern that the comprehensives didn't want to include. Any day now we were supposed to be joining up in the grand pattern of education for the area, but the fact that we catered for a sedimentary population tucked away on the edge of an old industrial area meant that we were not awfully welcome. The neighbourhood had a reputation, the council estate was mostly prefabs which the better tenants avoided and passed on to more permanent buildings. The whole area was a kind of mistake, originally a munition workers' settlement that developed the wrong way, leaving a half-built village on the mountain side of the factories. We came under the urban area education authority but all in all, we were forgotten about, which suited us. The children were not the kind to wear blazers, smile at prefects or indulge in house systems. Very few went on to grammar schools from the primary school, and when they came to us, the over-riding ambition was to leave. School was still bloody school after all, but we kept the roof on, were good at minor things like gardening and woodwork, and despite our high delinquency rate, we were old, poky and affectionate. Vandals left us alone, our children offended against others not us, and the easy-going, managing air of the place warmed me.

It was Bryn's doing really, making the best of an ancient nineteenth century building, and coping in spite of the chicken-hearted recalcitrance of the Authority and the pressures of the middle class. But he understood the neighbourhood and the children. He had this bluff tolerance rare in school teachers, and inspired affection and loyalty. He had nous, in short. We always had trouble with the very dull. He preferred the word to retarded or emotionally disturbed, said it was a concept their parents understood, and he attempted to provide simple learning situations so that they could progress slowly. They had to have affection and be understood, which was the idea of my little family home in the shed. Every time they fell, there was me to pick them up. We'd been getting some nasty violence, fights in the playground, windows broken, copper pipes wrenched from walls, when he suggested creating a form for the more backward adolescents. They'd all got reading ages about seven years below their actual age and had few skills. If we put them together, let them go at their own pace educationally, gave them an interest and kept it practical, he thought we might succeed more. So we put in carpentry benches and vices, roasted chestnuts around the stove, made our own furniture, isolated ourselves with an air of privilege, and it worked. The Inspectorate called it an interesting experiment in compensatory education. We called it a home from home. Our delinquency rate dropped, attendance improved, there were even thank-you letters from parents. Bryn said it was all due to me. Very flattering. What I liked was that I had a world of my own, wasn't fussed with a timetable, could live my own life and regulate it.

He was waiting when I got in. In a small way, I was indispensable. My little family depended on me. Anybody else was holding the fort, that's all. Rachel had told him about Walter.

'How is he?' Bryn said, concerned. I'd called in at his room in the main building.

'Oh, ill,' I said. 'TB.'

Bryn was large and untidy, bulging in loose tweeds like a farmer come to the mart. He's the best kind of Welshman, the quiet, gruff, taciturn sort. Never waxes eloquent, doesn't pick his nose in beautiful Welsh, is firm and kind, drinks, has six children of his own, and is married to an ex-barmaid, which is unusual.

He said what everybody else said. 'There's nothing much to TB these days.'

'Unfortunately, he's got it in the eye as well.'

'Oh, no... Poor old Walter.'

'Yes,' I said.

'How the hell did he cop that?'

'You tell me,' I said. I never said much about Walter.

'If you want time off, anything?'

'Visiting's Wednesdays and weekends. I don't know very much at the moment. It'll take them a week to do their tests and things.'

'What a stroke!' Bryn said. 'Poor you, as well?'

'Yes,' I said.

'Anything we can do, let us know.'

'There isn't much I can do,' I said. I bit my lip. I often wondered if Bryn knew about me. He lived this idyllic family life, always going camping, caravanning away across continents on trips with his children. We never talked much, the occasional staff-do, but beneath this jolly farmer's look and the constant involvement with his family, I suspected a very interesting man. He'd been in the Air Force and been a prisoner of war. He was fatherly to me in a gentle way, didn't mind a joke, and was fun too. I never saw him depressed and he always gave the impression it was a joy to be alive. Every morning was a bouquet to him. He'd met Walter, said he liked him, but summed him up, I'd no doubt. Me, he liked, I knew. He was the only man who ever liked me in a non-sexual way. Why did that make me half-afraid he'd find me out?

I said, 'It all happened very suddenly. He said there was something wrong with his eye, but I didn't pay much attention. The optician sent him to the hospital and they told him to get his chest X-rayed.'

'But his eye?'

'Eale's disease. Nobody's ever heard of it.'

'Oh, dear.'

He was full of oh dears, dearie me's, and Duw, duws, the Welsh equivalent. But he couldn't dwell on it. Who could?

'I've got some good news too,' he made a face. 'Your little family have excited the attention of the powers.'

'Excited?'

'There's an Inspector coming tomorrow to spend the day with you.'

'Oh, no.' I hated intruders, even official ones. They talked jargon and got in the way. From the time I went to training college, I never met anybody responsible for education who was any good at actually doing it. They could talk all day, write papers until the ink ran dry, but they couldn't actually stand in a classroom day after day with children and produce results. Give them ideas, they'd manipulate them like fleas and produce paragraph after paragraph, but as to practicalities, the stench of the taught was too much for them. Out of the classroom, I smelled a racket, always. People looking after themselves, not others.

'I'll put him off if you like,' Bryn said.

'Oh, why bother? They have to find something to do.'

He grinned. He agreed with me. We shared a chip about intellectuals. Those who manipulate received ideas finally get strangled by them. It was so much better to have found just one idea of our own.

I took my keys and crossed the yard. We'd painted the outside of the hut with psychedelic paint. It looked like a pop group's headquarters. If anybody came out holding a hypo syringe you wouldn't be surprised. Pot hadn't really hit us, fortunately, and the boys I taught drugged themselves with telly and sport, a hardy, masculine lot around here.

It was the lunch break and the hut was empty save for a boy called Arthur who tidied up and was responsible for the carpentry tools when I wasn't there. I tried to give every boy some responsibility, something personal to do. Everybody should succeed at something, Bryn said. That was the unofficial motto of the school and we'd made it work. There was even a little team in charge of litter and we praised them wildly, the garbage lads. Two things a human being needs, Bryn said. To be wanted, to have a status. It was our business to give everybody a role, a chance of success. In school, I stuck to it dutifully. In school, but not out of it.

Arthur was thin, weedy, lank ginger hair falling over a peaked, spiteful face pitted with acne. He was on probation, lived now with a sister, his mother having skipped. When he saw me, he ran his hand over a row of metal clamps which hung on the wall, his department. He smiled.

'They're all here, Miss.'

'I was sure they would be, Arthur.'

'The Headmaster come in this morning. D'you know what he said to us?'

'No.'

'He said the way to judge us and you...'

'Me?'

94

'By seeing how we behaved when you wasn't here.'

'Oh?' I said. Bryn had this gift of getting across to people. They would understand that, letting me down in my absence, he'd merely reminded them.

'And nobody done nothing, Miss.'

'Didn't you do any work?'

'No, we had silent reading, and then the Headmaster give us talk on the war, bombing and that.'

They'd listen all day to war stories. 'We'll have to make up for it this afternoon then.'

'Was you ill, Miss?'

'No, my husband is.' I knew they'd find out. They find out most things.

I took my coat off and got out the register. We didn't mark it until the end of the day and then it was for the convenience of the authority. Instead of a register, we used a factory time clock that Bryn had scrounged. By making them clock in, we again attempted to produce the work situation. Each boy had a card, punched it himself. It was a simple piece of reasoning and they had a childish pleasure in the method. We had no desks either, benches and chairs, and they could brew tea when they wanted. Our compensatory education was to dispense with everything remotely reminiscent of school.

Presently, they came in, my lot, twenty of them, the underprivileged, the dull, the disturbed, the merely slow. They came in jeans, leather gear, whatever they pleased. They were noisy but friendly, and glad to see me back. Bryn's theme had worked both ways. I too, had a status and was wanted. They would do most things for their Miss and boasted wildly that I could use a chisel better than the woodwork master. Better legs too. They noticed all that.

I said, 'We're going to have a visitor tomorrow, an Inspector of Schools. He's coming here because he's interested in us, what we're doing that's different from other schools. He's been told we're successful. When he's here, I don't want you to be any different, but I don't want him to go away with any false impressions.'

'Bags of swank, Miss?' one of them said.

'Enough,' I said. It was Bryn's phrase. He didn't see any harm in children being put on their best behaviour and had the capacity for extracting the best from everyone. He did from me from the beginning. It was rare for a woman to be left with adolescent boys and I was lucky in being self-contained, favoured, some of the staff thought. But we got results.

I let them work in groups and directed tasks in each group, never stood up and just talked, more like a foreman moving from bench to bench. At first, there was a sex problem. They'd snigger and lean against me, but I soon got them used to that. A boy called Billy Hickey with a mop of blond hair and a body beyond his years used to lie under the bench to look up my skirt. I waited for the moment and trod on his hand.

'No, Billy,' I said. I kept my heel on his hand. 'When you're older some poor girl might give you a chance. But it would have to be dark.'

Their guffaws, his discomfort. They got over my skirts when I became their friend. I never lost my temper, never shouted, didn't give orders but made suggestions. The formal side, reading and numbers, and getting them to write a simple letter, I related to tasks. I made up police notices, betting slips, letters of complaint to neighbours, used a dartboard and a tote – anything to get it away from school. I always worked slowly in the corner with those who wanted to read, spelling out letters with their fingers, their backs to the rest of the class. They could please themselves when they did it. Once I intercepted an obscene letter. Somebody was going to have me down, my tits. I read it to the class. 'Is that what you think of me then?' I said. 'Is that all I am to you?' Nobody did it again. Strange that it was a recurring theme in my life. But, I'd learned most from Bryn, more than any lecture, any book. Teaching is an artisan skill and you pick up tips and wrinkles, once you get the philosophy right. Never insult. Never belittle. Never demean. You have to interest, and work at a communal pace, building from what is known to what is unknown. You have to be patient. More than anything, you have to inspire loyalties, generate warmth. It's a personal business. You have to care. Children are not children, but people.

And I was good at it, good at everything except when my own needs were concerned.

I busied myself for the first part of the afternoon. We were building a scale model of the area, working out a plan of redevelopment ourselves. We'd done the cost of demolition in simple terms, how many lorries, how many shovels, how many men, the difficulties of breaking up non-ferrous materials. I'd made them go out and measure, and kept it practical. Now we were planning the replacement buildings and it would occupy us for a term. I made sure they were all working and went into my own little room after putting the kettle on. There were days when I didn't join the rest of the staff and I was left alone.

I sat down and lit a cigarette, something I rarely did and looked at myself in the mirror. It had been 'won' by the boys and had *Players Please* stamped in the corner. I could see myself full-face, head and shoulders, what other people saw when they saw me.

'Constance,' I said to myself. What a pretentious name! I framed my lips in a disapproving O. I was twenty-seven but didn't look it because of my skin and colouring. When I was forty, I'd be fat, but now I was just rounded, a little too big to be nubile, a little too ordinary to be interesting. If I had any quality, it was freshness and strength, my big bones. And yet the deep-drawn nasal folds of my cheeks and then my lips would have looked well on a whore's face, given other colouring. I once played an O'Casey whore in a College play, and in the make-up, eye-shadow and pallor, I looked just right. 'This is me,' I said to myself in the dressing-room mirror, 'I'm doing what I want, not so much being other people, but looking like that and soliciting.' It was absurd that I'd never been naive like most of the other girls were. Somehow, I always knew things, had a gift for seeing other people's deceits. I didn't know then, but I found I was capable and there was this thing about me that always gave other people the wrong impression unless they were a certain kind of men. In twenty years, I might look like a schoolmistress and although I took care not to now, in some ways it would be better for me to be like that and nothing else now. Everything I knew that worked with children had never seemed applicable to me or Walter. I'd tried and failed and in the end, left him alone.

'Sod Walter,' I said. Who hadn't got the right to be fed up? I was through with him months ago. I didn't want his problems at all. You can lead a horse to water, Bryn would have said, all that. But I'd made a mistake, that was all. Anybody can make mistakes. With my background, it wasn't surprising. You can be as intelligent as you like, your emotions can remain small, barely grown, like greenhouse plants that don't get the sun. I needed someone to take care of me, somebody older and wiser and calmer. What was the phrase? Rapport? Yes, a feeling of playing the same tune.

Bryn came in silently, a Headmaster's trick.

'Caught me smoking,' I said. I didn't get up.

'I thought you'd have the blues,' he said.

'Oh, I've got them all right.'

I called through the door. There was a noisy buzz of interest in the classroom. I knew they were working.

'Arthur,' I called. 'Bring the cups.'

So we had tea in the little stock room, Bryn and I. I knew the rest of the staff didn't like it. Not that he was stuffy with them, but I worked too hard and was too successful. Most teachers are lazy. At about forty, they feel they've had enough and wish they were on expense accounts, moan about the salary and become conscious of their status. But I was happy in school.

99

Arthur poured the tea.

'It's like coming into a family,' Bryn said.

'That was the idea, wasn't it?' My family, father and mother, me.

'This chap that's coming tomorrow,' he said again. 'I can put him off if you like?'

'Walter's not dead,' I said, a little too hard.

'No, no, but if you're upset?'

'It's just one of those things,' I said.

'I don't know if you're interested or not, but they're looking for someone to go on a teachers' panel. It's a schools council project on compensatory education.'

'Oh, no...'

He grinned. 'It's mostly boffins but they're required to have four teachers from all over the country. They'll meet once a month in London.'

'London?' I said.

'Yes. I thought it would give you an interest.'

As soon as he said it, I was hooked but I wondered if he knew why. You never knew anything with Bryn. He had this slow matter-of-factness, the pleasant air of the easy-going schoolmaster, but he was as sharp as a tack. I'd seen him sort out parents, even take the Director of Education's trousers down when he tried to shove some Councillor's unemployable nephew on us. Did he know I'd nearly jumped when he said London? And did he know why? If I needed anything, it was the anonymity of some place where I wasn't known. And London, shows, bars, hotels, different people, different men. Once a month would suit me down to the ground.

'I recommended you because I thought it would do them some good.'

'And me?'

'I thought you'd be interested.'

'Did you?'

'You get expenses and things, time for shopping.'

'Shopping around for what?' I thought. He couldn't possibly know. He was a family man. Lucky him.

'It would do you some good with the Authority too.'

'You're seeing me as a Headmaster,' I said. I crossed my legs. 'It isn't very flattering.'

'I was wondering if Walter'd get paid now he's ill.'

Oh, why bring up Walter? 'No,' I said. That was all.

'It occurred to me, I might get you another allowance from the Authority. Once you've been on this panel it will help.'

Wasn't that nice? More money.

'Thanks,' I said.

Arthur brought the tea in.

'Sir.'

'Ladies first,' Bryn said.

'No, sir,' Arthur said firmly. 'Visitors.'

He liked that. Tiny things were happening, little nuances of feeling passing in the air like electricity and all self-charging. I felt happier, good at my job, appreciated, warm and pleased. And a trip to London every month if I played my cards right. Nice Bryn.

He sipped his tea. 'I don't expect it will be very easy for either of you.'

'Who?' I was wondering who the Inspector was. I'd never met one.

'Walter.'

'Oh, no. No... Poor Walter.'

For the first time ever, I saw him look at me with the faintest glimmer of disapproval. I shrugged my shoulders, I couldn't talk to him about Walter. He might have told me exactly what I should have done. 'The Inspector's name is Evans. He's a senior Inspector.'

'Oh,' I said. 'I hope it'll be nice for him.'

I didn't want to know any more. London, I thought; splendid. And that was all.

I told Rachel. 'They've recommended me to sit on a panel,' I said. 'Of teachers. In London. There's an Inspector coming tomorrow. An advisory committee or something.'

'I've never seen you so excited,' she said.

'Oh, it's just one of those things.'

'I posted the dressing-gown and slippers.'

'Oh, thanks.'

I went into the bedroom to change. There was always Walter even when he wasn't there.

I had a bath, and in the bath I soaped myself luxuriously. There was just time to have my hair done before I saw the Inspector. I began to think of what I'd wear. Everybody in education likes you to be neat; suits, white gloves, cool, deodorised. Well, that's what I would be.

Rachel tapped the door of the bathroom.

'Yes?'

'I wondered if he'd like a magnifying glass. I mean, would it help his eye?'

'No, I don't think so. They've put drops in his eyes and he can't read.'

I sighed. He wouldn't leave me alone and it seemed there was nowhere at all where he couldn't reach me. In an unhappy marriage, there was always infiltration, I thought, the slow destruction of one self by the blight that has crept over another. Who was to blame? What had gone wrong? I didn't know and didn't want to think about it in particular terms, except that it had dawned on me that unhappiness had its own peculiar glow and communicated itself in a thousand different ways. We spent most of our time trying to be happy, trying to look good, passing like shadows in shop windows and the closer we got together, the further we were growing apart until finally, we *were* apart.

I lay in the bath until the water grew cold. Perhaps I had a sense of disaster then, early on. Perhaps, like Walter who always knew there was something waiting for him, I also had a premonition. It was nothing tangible, nothing like his crazy dreams, just a sense of withdrawal from him, the act of not caring, the simple boredom of it. I was never afraid of the dark, or intruders, but now I began to realise that what you fear most, you never really understand. In marriages that went wrong, perhaps it was an awareness of something growing cold inside you, a gradual numbness of feeling that spread itself imperceptibly, stifling the secret, private voice that you felt was really you until it ceased to be your voice and became a stranger's.

But the more I tried to think about it, the less sense I made. Who did I know that was happy anyway? When the chips were down? People managed, that was all. And soldiered on from there.

Walter's phrase. Inadequate people haunt you just as much as Titans. Not that I'd ever met any of those...

CHAPTER FOUR

CONNIE

In the morning, I didn't wear a suit after all, just a midi and granny boots. The Inspector only called in for the morning coffee break. He was in a hurry. They'd already appointed a woman for the working party but she'd gone sick and I was to take her place. It meant travelling on the Friday as they wanted someone immediately. He wasn't so much concerned with me as with getting his forms straight. Bodies had to be there. He needed a Welsh representative in a hurry and someone who could be spared. It wasn't as flattering as I'd thought. Is anything?

I said, 'I don't speak Welsh.' Bilingualism is all the rage now, everywhere except where money or commerce is concerned. Frankly, I wasn't interested in representing anyone.

He said, 'It doesn't seem to me to matter in this

instance. Compensatory education of its nature is a working-class problem.'

I wasn't interested in class either. It was as dated as TB.

He didn't say anything and he looked pained, a tall, thin ascetic in his fifties. He had this immaculate grey hair brushed straight back to cover his bald patch, carefully trimmed sideboards and a little moustache, the kind of whimsical man who tells you English is his subject, then bores you to death. And he'd spent some time in the Sudan. He had to tell you that too. The only interesting thing was his watch, a gold Rolex with a heavy bracelet that must have set him back a few hundred. It meant a certain kind of selfishness, I thought.

'I'd be most grateful if she could be spared,' he said to Bryn.

'Of course,' Bryn said.

So it was up to me. Suddenly it was all very mundane, a school teacher's conversation with a power, as dull as Council offices, plum-duff.

'There's a meeting on Friday,' he said again. 'I shall be attending. Of course, there'll be no difficulty with expenses.'

'All right,' I said. Why not?

'Be careful to travel first class,' Bryn said when he'd left.

'Why?'

'Expenses. And you can stay overnight. See a show or something.'

'You're getting very gay all of a sudden,' I said.

'It'll do you good, girl,' he said.

I liked him saying 'girl' like that. 'On my own?' I said.

'Why not?'

I didn't say any more. The Inspector's name was Evans and he looked like he regretted it. His speech was too clipped and phoney to be natural. If anything, he seemed more ill at ease than I did. The only thing I liked was that watch. He must have gone to some swish jewellers and admired it glittering on his little wrist. I wondered if he was married and what his wife said. But maybe she gave it to him. There was a world of expensive present giving that I knew nothing about.

Rachel was very pleased. 'I always knew you'd get on,' she said. The idea of London impressed her. Whatever the nationalists say, most of the people I know remain impressed with the English.

There was no letter from Walter. I rang the hospital and they said he was settling in as well as could be expected. Everything seemed very flat suddenly. I'd begun to do my nails when the telephone rang. It was the Inspector. He said he was going up by road and could he give me a lift. He must have got my number from Bryn. Cool, I thought. I didn't know what to say. If I went, I wouldn't even have the fun of the restaurant car. I'd forgotten what it was like to order myself a meal and seldom got the chance. But on the phone, his voice was different, low and persuasive. It might have been his son ringing up. He had two accents, our Mr Evans, one for school and one for outside. I pricked up my ears.

'I could pick you up after school,' he said.

He'd made no kind of impression on me, just a tall, grey man whose subject was English, and was in a hurry.

107

'It would be no trouble,' he said. 'Otherwise you'd have to go on the Pullman and it's full of business types.'

I thought him a type myself. All I could think of was the watch, very streamlined, a clear face and four Arabic numerals. I'd watched it glittering as he moved his wrist.

'I don't know about you, Mrs Lacey, but they bore me.'

Perhaps I should have realised then. What did he have to ring me at home for? Usually, I can tell about men but he was over fifty, a non-entity.

'Fine,' I said suddenly. Why not?

'Shall I pick you up in school?'

'Yes, I'll bring a bag,' I said. That would set the tongues wagging.

'Or perhaps it would be better at home?' he said.

Second thoughts, I thought. 'You please yourself, Mr Evans.'

'It would save you having to carry a bag to school,' he said. 'If you like, I'll get my secretary to make the arrangements.'

Well, I wanted fussing over and now I'd got it.

'Fine,' I said.

'About five, Thursday?'

'Right,' I said,

When I put the phone down, I remembered he'd lazy eyes, very light blue in colour, with pale eyelids that flickered slowly over those eyes. For the most part, he'd avoided looking at me directly. But perhaps it was because Bryn was there. I never met a civil servant or a lecturer who didn't pay this obsequious homage to those in the field, as they said. On the phone he sounded much more interesting. But I dismissed him. You don't get that far in education unless all the life has gone out of you. I haven't met many high-ups but the most dominating thought in those I have is pension. At forty, they're already scheming for their old age. Dead men.

'Who was that?' Rachel said.

'The Inspector. They want me to go up by road.'

'Very nice,' Rachel said. 'You never know who you're sitting next to on the train these days.'

I didn't say anything in school and I didn't think any more about it. Until he came with the car to the house. It was an E-type Jag, with a long, powder-blue body like an animal's. It purred, that car, purred and glistened. He was as proud of it as the watch.

'This is my Aunt, Miss Morgan, Mr Evans...'

'What a nice view you have here,' he said straight away.

We were high up and could see the valley hills stretching away in the distance and there was a forest behind us on the side of our hill. There were enough trees and fields to make it country.

Rachel took in the car and said nothing. He came in and admired the dresser in the hall. Then he spoke to her in Welsh. That convinced her, Welsh and an E-type was progress beyond.

He wouldn't take coffee.

'Well then,' he said after a pause. Now I looked at him properly I could see he was very fit, with shrewd lips that smiled too easily. I never liked men who were wonderful with old ladies, but then he was a broiler himself. The watch was glittering again, gold watch, gold cufflinks, a ring with an opal stone, a man of jewellery. When his fingers tapped impatiently on his knee, I noticed they were long and tapered, the nails manicured. He looked dapper in a light-grey suit, a brown silk Foulard tie, more like a man from BEA than anything to do with schools. He kept up his Welsh chat with Rachel, but then she interrupted him suddenly.

'You haven't explained to Walter,' she said to me.

'Oh, I'll tell him when I get back.'

'Her husband is recently afflicted,' she told him. I winced at the phrase. Where does she get them from?

'I'm sorry,' he said, then; 'Well...' again.

'You'll want to miss the Estate traffic,' Rachel said.

If they jabbered away much longer together, I thought he might get off with her!

'I'm ready,' I said.

I kissed her when we left. He took my bag, opened the door for me. You had to lie in the car. I felt the leather cold against the back of my neck. I wondered if he still did it, whether he took the watch off when he did, who had sat in the seat before me, then wished I didn't have a midi on. His angularity, that grey hair, those hands. Yes, I thought, the sooner the better. Not a joke.

'Thank you, Mr Evans,' I said.

I was careful not to say too much too quickly. His age, those courtly manners. Perhaps it was shrivelled up.

He made solicitous enquiries about Walter.

'Eale's disease,' I said. That set everybody off. 'Vitreous haemorrhages, an allergic condition to TB.'

He knew about the TB. His brother had had it.

'Years ago. In the pine-tree days.'

I didn't understand.

'Before streptomycin.'

'You look very fit anyway,' I said.

He liked that.

Before we got on to the motorway, we had to dawdle in traffic. I knew he'd show me what the car could do, given half the chance. He wanted to know if he could do anything for Walter.

'Does he teach?'

'No,' I said. I didn't say any more.

He sensed my reluctance to talk, didn't continue. He was dutifully attentive. Did the window being open bother me, would I like the seat back? And there was barley sugar in the glove compartment.

'Barley sugar?'

He spent a lot of time driving. One tended to get dry. Oh, did one?

What I liked was the death of education as a subject. It always made me frizzle unless it was practical. He didn't mention it once, nor Walter again, Rachel once.

'Your Aunt looks a character?'

'She's one of these matriarchs without children.'

'Mamgu, I know. I had one myself.'

'Where was that then?'

He told me. He was from the valleys too, a scholarship boy, Oxford, the Colonial Service, the War, home to inspect. He'd never taught children. I didn't pursue it, his lack of qualification to inspect. Then, very shyly, he told me his father'd been a miner, and he still had a brother under-ground.

'Poor?' I said.

'Dreadfully,' the accent came back again.

Did that explain the watch? I didn't say anything. He was filling me in quietly. If he was married, he duplicated my silence on that score. Why not? We were having a day away from our normal identities.

On the motorway, he opened the car up. It ticked like a sewing machine, that long bonnet thrusting forward, hitting the ton as we found an open stretch of road. I could see the shape of his long leg through his trousers, his thigh muscles tense.

'You don't mind speed?'

'I don't get enough of it.'

'Good,' he said, very pleased.

Perhaps he got his kicks this way, men and their masturbatory cars. 'I'd have come on a motorcycle,' I said. 'I've always had an urge to drive a Honda, the silver racing one.'

'I'll get one tomorrow,' he said.

'Two,' I said.

'Oh, no you don't. That wouldn't be fun.'

After that, I was certain. The trouble was, I couldn't wait. I didn't want all the pretence leading up to it. I wanted to go out of my mind quickly, right then, and be finished with everything that nagged me. And be done as well. I always used to get sudden urges. It wasn't only sex, I wanted to break out of myself. There was this kind of life and that kind of life, all I knew was I wanted time off from just sitting like a cabbage. I'd been lucky in that I always knew men who didn't like the preliminaries, verbally anyway. Walter was one.

I bit my lip. Memory. Well, he was. I hadn't been out with him five minutes before he started to walk awkwardly.

'What's the matter?' I said.

'Trouble in the butcher's,' Walter said.

'What butcher's?'

'Take a look at this,' he said. 'I've got a joint on offer. Is your shop open?'

He made me laugh then. There's something very attractive about a man who is a shambles. In the short run.

'Would you like some tea or shall we press on and have dinner?' Evans said when we came over the suspension bridge.

'Press on, Mr Evans,' I said.

'Ifor,' he said.

'Pardon?'

'We're moving into England,' he said.

'I never think of these things,' I said. 'One place is like any other.'

'"Mr Evans" makes me feel so old.'

'I feel ageless,' I said. I wasn't going to flatter him.

'You don't look ageless.'

'I don't look as I feel either.'

'How do you feel?'

I took a chance. 'Haven't you guessed by now?'

'I never trust my guesses.'

In a minute, he was going to make some risqué conversation, I could see. 'Perhaps it's just as well,' I said. Let him sweat for a mile or two.

He paid the toll at the end of the bridge. The river was low, acres of mudbanks glistening in the late afternoon sun. Grey, and very depressing. We drove on in silence, passing an Army convoy so he had to concentrate. I looked at the cropped hair of the young soldiers and began to think of Walter again. But I was getting quite detached. It was Walter past tense. The first thing I'd always remember was that, before we were married, he was always trying to get me pregnant. Of course, I concurred, but it got to be a thing with him. After a month or two of nothing happening, he'd lie on top of me for minutes. He knew nothing about the female anatomy. He had a picture of sperm entering like toothpaste, a literal injection that he seemed to want to prolong as if he was using a grease gun. Even then, in those days, he wore himself out at everything he did. The difficulty was finding anywhere to do it since he couldn't come into the college and had changed his digs for a Toc H hostel. Consequently, there were only fields, hedges, the backs of cars or hastily arranged afternoons in borrowed flats where we had to be careful not to disarrange things. Sometimes I fixed it, sometimes he did.

But he couldn't get me pregnant and it began to depress him. His erections went all to pot. I had to use my mouth, teeth, everything I could think of, and his need for me increased all the time. He was always asking me to marry him. He bought four engagement rings, went through all of his savings until finally he was broke. And when he was on his uppers, he finally told me he'd been married before. That was a shock.

It happened one afternoon in a flat I'd borrowed from a girl who'd qualified. I'd met her on teaching practice and she was going home for the weekend. I was going to cook us a meal, had brought a chicken and onions and things to do us a *Coq au vin*. I knew we'd have time to let it simmer. We were going to spend the weekend in bed. Walter'd sold a car and got himself money over the odds on commission and arrived with a crate of flagons and a case of hock he'd got on discount in some warehouse. He always moaned at Iestyn's fiddles but he was just as good himself. It was going to be a debauch if he could help it, and his erections were worrying him so much I didn't care what he brought. But the moment he got into the room, everything went wrong.

First of all the girl who owned the flat didn't drink much and there weren't any suitable glasses. I said cups would do but he wouldn't think of it. He wanted everything to be right. It was pregnancy weekend or he would bust, he said. He'd go out and buy beer mugs, he said, the German kind with lids on them. Why didn't he spend the money on liqueurs, I said. He'd get liqueurs as well as beer mugs, he said, and there was one more thing. What was that, I said. He was suddenly very shy. 'Anything,' I said. 'You know that.' I liked him. I really did. More than anything, he was me-centred, if that's a phrase. I'd never had anybody this gone on me before. 'I'll do anything,' I told him. 'You name it, Walter, I will do anything. The answer is yes,' I said. I knew he felt guilty about the teeth thing.

He took his time in telling me. At first, I wondered if he'd read something new. We scanned all the books. But it was nothing new. When he came back, he said he just wanted to know that I'd be in bed waiting for him, that was all. 'Well, of course,' I said. Christ, what was that? 'A woman to come home to,' he said. Me. 'And would I?' 'Yes,' I said. 'Of course,' I said. 'It's a pleasure.' Didn't he know by now?

He gave his little half-sure smile, grinned at himself, then found his money and went out whistling down the stairs like a kid with the promise of a box of fireworks. It got me. There was something very touching about him always.

Anyway, I began to undress slowly, scattering my clothes about the room, thinking of him, his simplicity. A woman to come home to. All his talk of whores, his being around, his bits of black in Africa, the elderly dressmakers who'd raped him – it was all talk, or meaningless in some way. He just wanted me. There... Waiting for him.

Well, I got into bed and turned the sheets back. The girl who owned the flat had been given some perfume by her father who was in ICI and went abroad a lot. I didn't think she'd mind – it was for a social purpose – so I rubbed some on, soaked myself for once. Then, as he hadn't come back, I got out of bed and put the record player on, something from some show. I pulled the curtains and put the side light on, stretched myself, then took my hair down. I wore it long then, quite unsuitable but he liked the feel of it all over him, so I did everything I could. But he still didn't come. The record finished, I got up again, changed it. Then that finished and I found her album and looked through her records. What was the best tune to be done by? She had

116

this long-playing Shirley Bassey. Very old. Big Spender. 'The minute you walked in the joint I could see you was a man of distinction!' I knew he'd like that so I put it on, went back on the bed and waited.

What he could never understand was that I wanted it as much as he did. I don't know where he got his ideas about women from. He professed to be very knowledgeable about whores, but that was all. Perhaps he wanted me in a whore's get-up. I didn't mind if it would help him. So I waited and waited. The record was finished by the time he came back in. I stayed in the bedroom. I heard him put down the glasses, knew he must have seen my clothes strewn over the place leading to the bedroom, but he didn't come in. I heard him sit down in a chair and start to cry.

I couldn't understand it. I went in. He was hunched up in the chair with his hands over his face. He'd been gone an hour. Six large scotches on his own.

I wasn't annoyed, just curious.

'What happened to you then?'

He shook his head, looked away from me.

I looked at all the booze he'd bought, and the beer mugs, a little box of liqueur chocolates which he'd bought for me. Perhaps he'd been overspending? Perhaps he'd stolen something. The second-hand car trade was full of flies. I leaned over to him. Again, it was like dealing with a child.

'You haven't spent too much money?' I said.

He shook his head again, still not looking at me.

I felt so foolish, drenched in that perfume.

'Tell me?'

'I haven't got the guts,' he said.

'Oh, come on…'

'I can't.'

'But what is it, Walter?'

He looked at me then, through his fingers, the testing adolescent.

'I had a plan,' he said.

I thought he was referring to the weekend.

'Of course,' I said. I'd told them I was going home in College, and at home, I told them I was staying in College. The plan was mine too.

'I was trying to put you up the spout,' he said.

That wasn't news.

'And?'

'Get you to marry me.'

I knew all that.

'And?'

'You see, there's something I haven't told you.'

I had no idea what it could be. But with Walter, it could have been anything.

'I've been married before,' he said.

There was no central heating in the flat and I felt cold. I didn't know what to say. It was a surprise at first, a surprise more than a shock. But I was cold. I felt goose pimples up my spine so I went instinctively into the bedroom to get a wrapper. But when I went off, he started to howl. So I came back still shivering.

'So?' I said. 'You've been married?'

'Yes.'

'Well?' I said. His breath was coming in little choked

sobs and his eyes were red from crying. He must have been crying into his whisky, crying all the way up the stairs. It wasn't like him. I wanted to comfort him. So I was flip. 'Is that a reason to keep a lady waiting?' I said. I knew it was silly and trite, but I had to say something. And he grinned then, relieved, I suppose.

'No,' he said.

'Oh, come to bed,' I said.

He picked up the liqueurs. There were two boxes, not one, a very expensive Dutch kind.

'I brought these for you.'

'Bring them to bed. Bring everything to bed.'

I knew there was an electric blanket on the bed and I'd switched it on.

'Come and tell me,' I said.

I went into the bedroom and presently he came through holding a load of booze, the beer mugs, the chocolates and a bottle of wine. Then he dropped the lot on the floor.

'Oh, get in,' I said. 'Quickly.'

He took his clothes off sheepishly and folded them carefully.

'D'you want a drink?'

'I don't need it.'

'I do.'

'Well, have it. All you want.'

It took him almost five minutes to get himself into bed and in the mood to tell me. His story... He'd been sent away to this public school on the Herefordshire border, a cheap, tatty place exclusively for eleven-plus failures, the sons of would-be gentlefolk. He was utterly miserable, half

119

starved by the sound of it. He'd stuck it until he was seventeen then one day he'd got a grip of this maid. She was sixteen too. He was getting over tonsillitis in the infirmary, which was a tarted up dormitory on its own, and she'd come in to make the bed. There was nobody about so I suppose, for something to do, he put his hand up her, she didn't object, and for a month they were at it in the laundry cupboard. I don't know why he told me but he had to say she had a moustache and immensely hairy legs, a short, stumpy little thing with intense beady eyes. She was practically MD, he said, but when he got her pregnant her parents got on to the Headmaster, the Headmaster got on to his stepfather, and they all had a meeting in the Headmaster's study one November afternoon.

Other people's lives…

I could just imagine it, shouts from the playing fields echoing from outside the room, Walter in a grey suit with the school tie, spots all over his face and the girl dressed up with her bulge, his stepfather and her parents with the Headmaster in the chair.

'It's not as if it was a sudden temptation on the spur of the moment,' the Headmaster said. 'I understand there was a regular rendezvous right under Matron's nose.'

So, what were they going to do? Some kind of compensation, you'd suppose. But not a bit of it. Walter's stepfather told him he'd discussed it with his mother and he had to marry the girl.

'What?'

I couldn't believe it. I knew he didn't get on with his stepfather but I didn't want to know mine either.

He said his mother'd written him a letter. She couldn't come herself in a matter of this kind. Edgar, that was the stepfather, would know what to do for the best and she was sure he'd do the honourable thing.

It was like some Victorian melodrama.

'What did the Headmaster say?'

'He said I had to leave, of course, and I had the honour of the school to consider.'

'Jesus Christ...'

'They said, whatever happened afterwards, I had to give the child a name. They all agreed about that. Then I'd get a reference, they'd give the girl some money, and I'd be found a job. But I wasn't to see her again.'

'But if you couldn't see her, how could you marry her?'

'Oh, I married her. But they took me away after and she went home with her parents.'

'You didn't even...'

'No,' he said. 'They wouldn't even let me kiss her. They thought it was best. I was only seventeen. It was the week of some crisis. Perhaps they thought there was going to be a war.'

'It's incredible,' I said. I hardly believed it.

'Oh, it was just a formality. A marriage certificate for the girl.'

'But didn't you see her afterwards?'

'I tried to, but they put her brothers on to me. Very unpleasant. They'd all agreed we weren't to see each other, and later on, my stepfather fixed the divorce.'

'Without you ever...'

'Yes. It was an indiscretion that I'd have to get over.'

121

'And the child?'

'It was born but I never heard any more. They signed something and there was a lump sum given instead of any kind of payment by me. I wouldn't be surprised if they did very well out of it. Her old man was a rat-catcher on a farm.'

I didn't laugh. 'Your father-in-law,' I remember saying.

'Well, it worked out,' he said. 'They were happy. Then I went to work as a shirt salesman, a junior, and it was all over until now.'

'Why until now?'

We were talking in the dark, lying side by side under the blankets but he was lying on his back staring up at the ceiling. He was so alone.

'I don't know,' he said wearily. 'I kept telling myself I was too young to do anything, but I reckon I should have stopped it.'

'And not married her?'

'Oh, married her and tried to make a go of it.'

'Oh,' I said. I was sorry he said that.

'I mean, I'm supposed to have got over it. "Put it right out of your mind," they said. "You've got off scot-free and the rest." But I keep on thinking about it and the kid.'

'Naturally... and me?' I said after. 'Where does that leave me?'

'Don't you understand? Perhaps that's the only kid I'll ever have?'

'Oh, why?'

'Look at you?' he said. He looked at me. 'I've been banging myself sick.'

'Thanks,' I said. How alone can two people be?

'Oh, it isn't just that, I'm a bloody mess,' he said.

'D'you think I don't know?'

He looked away. I could see him wondering, going off into that scatty mind of his. Then I said a fatal thing: 'You can't go back,' I said. 'Only forward.'

He was so relieved you could feel the blood coursing in his veins.

'You don't mind then?'

'You didn't want to marry her, did you?'

'Doris? No, she was awful. And she married again.'

'Well, then... Oh, come here,' I said.

So that was that. We had our sex weekend, the first I've ever enjoyed. It snowed, I remember, a freak November fall, huge flakes that evaporated as soon as they landed on the window sills. We didn't go out and gave ourselves time, inventing new ways until in the end I was sore with having it, and there were red marks over my nipples and cuts under his buttocks where my fingernails had been. We had a shower together finally, like footballers in a visiting team. 'We've come good,' he said. He always thought he'd be an international at something. Perhaps this was his game. We were so close together then, it was impossible to think of being separate and the only minor irritation was when I had to explain my cystitis to the college medical officer. I looked him straight in the face and said I was struck playing lacrosse. Other people's nervousness is the best cure for your own.

Poor Walter. He thought me nervous. And had such hopes then.

We were driving through Marlborough before Ifor suggested dinner. The sausage country, I thought. That would have killed Walter, but I'd better mind my Ps and Qs now.

'I know a little place,' he said.

I smiled. Thinking about Walter when I first met him always made me feel sexy.

'Whatever you think best,' I said. The trouble was, you couldn't live on memories. I'd always have a certain tenderness for him.

'A rather trendy place.'

'Oh?' I said. How conventional can you get.

'Are you interested in food?'

'Very.'

'You look like a good cook.'

'And what do good cooks look like?'

'Well rounded.'

'I'm not sure that's a compliment?'

'It was intended as one.'

Oh butterfingers... It was like going out with Fred Astaire, I thought. There'd be a waltz in a minute. I had a moment's doubt on how to behave. Should I be intelligent or tarty? I wondered what it must be like having a slim, successful, urbane father with whom one did one's little bit of consulting and who forked out now and again. Better still, another non-sexual relationship, the kind I had with Bryn. Then I thought, should I tell him about Walter? No, you couldn't tell anybody about Walter. Why did I have to think of that weekend? I didn't know. The more I thought about the whole incident, the more I thought of his stepfather's point of view.

'The young ass has got a maid in trouble at school. I'd better go up and sort it out. Of course, it will cost. These things always do.'

Anybody else but Walter would have dismissed it after a few years. You can't keep on harping on what's happened to you. I didn't. But Walter had the capacity for giving a lingering attention to the things that hurt him. He licked old wounds and played with them. No doubt he saw the child as Paderewski or something. With him not getting the credit. He'd tell me the bit about the rat-catcher's daughter, but in his mind he'd cook up something wonderful that was marvellous for everybody except him. He did himself down even in his own mind. And yet, I thought, like a lot of these boys from the cheap public schools, the moment they got out and found they didn't fit in with the network and the middle class blah-blah, they had to suffer all the rapacious turns of fortune of the real world, the world below. Like the second-hand car trade. He didn't last long selling shirts and he was soon down to dirt level where only cash mattered. Perhaps that was partly sociology. He'd had to become fly. But the root of it was that nobody wanted him ever, parents, school, employers, no one... Not even me finally.

I sighed.

Ifor gave me a glance. It was dark now and he'd switched the lights on. The instruments on the dashboard gleamed like little clockwork faces and the engine ticked away. It was a long drive.

'You're tired?' he said.

'It's longer than you think,' I said.

125

'We'll have a drink before dinner.'

'Lots,' I said.

He grinned, concentrated on the driving. He used that car like a purchased penis.

But I was glad he left me alone. He must have sensed my aversion to chat. He seemed accommodating. I watched the road signs flash by, mused. Perhaps I'd have it off with him. Perhaps I wouldn't. Somehow, the urgency had gone. What was I going to do about Walter? He'd have to get better first. I'd have to get him out of hospital but that would take months. In a way though, it was convenient, I'd live my own life, look around. I didn't feel the slightest shame. In a sense, I'd always carry his ashes around with me. He'd been distributing these all his life.

Presently we drove off the main road to this roadhouse. I noticed straight away there were chalet bungalows behind it. He came round to open the door and practically lifted me out, keeping his hand on my elbow. He was squiring me, all that. He took a long time locking up the car. Walter'd always said of his cars – if anybody stole one, he'd be sorry for the thief. He checked and double-checked the boot, then we went into the cocktail bar.

'D'you want to spend a penny?' he said.

Perhaps he thought I'd pee myself with nervousness rather than ask. 'I'll tell you when,' I said.

He flushed. He wanted to go himself. I wasn't used to new people. That's what marriage does for you.

'Sorry,' I said. 'I'm a little out of practice. I'll go in the bar and wait.'

So he went off to shake it.

He'd said the place was trendy. I didn't see it. The cocktail bar was called The Bamboo Room, a thatched roof over the bar, cane stools, straw everywhere, a cheap phoney Jamaican decor, posters of titty girls, bongo on the tape. There was a drink-flushed military type with a worn-out blonde in the corner standing up. They were staring into the gin and quarrelling quietly.

'Ronald definitely said...'

'He didn't.'

'Ronald told me...'

'He said nothing of the kind.'

'He told me yesterday...'

'I think we'd better leave it, don't you, darling?'

I did. The woman looked at the barman and ordered another drink, putting a smile on. She was a brassy forty-five with that ginned-up, Home Counties, Sunday morning look, a loud horse-box voice, always last to leave the bar.

'Harold's very good to me,' she said of the barman when he filled her glass.

Pissed, I thought. I'd taught in Maidenhead for a year in an attempt to leave Walter and knew the type, big teeth and woollen knickers.

Ifor came back rubbing his hands. Somehow I knew he'd washed them carefully.

'What will you have?'

I wanted a bacardi and coke, but for some reason I said;
'A large gin.'

That would give him confidence.

'Splendid. Two large.'

The barman seemed to know him. 'Tonic?'

'Tonic, ice and lemon,' I said. We were being watched by the other two at the end of the bar.

I felt up to tricks. Their asinine faces and awful accents depressed me, both public school. Although I'm Welsh, I have a pretty anonymous voice, a small edge as I emphasise certain words, more bite than lilt. I winked at Ifor, gave him the nod.

He didn't understand.

I hid my face behind him, nodded again.

He made a face, still didn't understand.

'Cheers,' I said when the drinks came. 'Cheerio!'

'Cheers,' he said. He was still puzzled.

They were still watching, the woman pricing my clothes.

'Well, father,' I said in a loud voice. 'He may be Jewish but he's the father of my child.'

He nearly jumped through the thatched roof.

'What?'

'His family are creating stink,' I said poker-faced.

He didn't think it funny at all. Everyone in the bar was listening and pretending not to.

'Shall we sit over here?' Ifor said, pointing to the corner near the window.

So we moved over out of immediate earshot.

'What was all that about?'

'Those people,' I said. I lowered my voice. 'I don't like being priced.'

'Father?' he said thoughtfully.

'What?'

'You're a little embarrassed at being seen with someone of my age?' he said sheepishly.

Oh, dear... 'Not if you're up to it,' I said.

'Is that a joke?'

'Try me,' I said.

He didn't seem to realise what had hit him all of a sudden. My silence on the journey must have given him a certain impression. I'd dropped a reminder in now and again, but then if he was going to chat me up, it was going to be so slow and oldie worldie no doubt. And in the end, we'd have a bit by accident. But I didn't want it his way, I wanted it my way. But I'd better cool it, I thought.

'I'm sorry,' I said. 'I just couldn't help looking at those people. I thought I'd send them up but you didn't twig it.'

'Oh,' he said. He looked pleased that I'd included him.

'A little leg pull,' I said heavily.

'Yes,' he said. 'Thick of me.'

'Yes,' I said.

We were talking in lowered voices. I looked over his shoulder and gave the woman a bold stare. She looked away hastily. Then they started up their Ronald bit.

'The last time, Ronnie said...'

'Oh, dear,' I said. 'I've nearly put my foot in it, haven't I?'

'Warn me next time.'

'I like having fun, don't you, Ifor?'

'I've not had any for a long time.'

I didn't want to know why.

'Nor me,' I said. I took a good pull at the gin. I saw him watching. 'It's all right,' I said. 'I've got a stomach like leather.'

'You don't look the kind who'd pass out on me.'

'Have you had many of them?'

'One or two.'

'Unpleasant for you.'

'I'm not a ram,' he said in a small peeved voice.

'That's your age talking,' I said. 'We'll have to get over that, won't we?'

There was a moment then when he wanted to leave and not be bothered with me. I don't know why I laid it on the line for him so quickly. Perhaps because I was so recently free, I thought; well, released anyway. But we'd got off on the wrong foot and it was entirely my fault. He wanted to do his bit of flirting, I suppose. But I was coiled like a spring. And it was a come-on. Perhaps he wanted to be a dirty devil first? But knickers, I thought. It was either on my terms or nothing.

I said, 'We seem to have got off on the wrong foot, Ifor?'

'Yes,' he said.

'Sorry,' I said.

'Getting along with anybody is difficult,' he said.

'Wife?' I said.

'Yes,' he said.

I made a face. Nothing was new.

'Husband?' he said.

'A prince,' I said.

'Ah...'

'Recently deposed,' I said.

'You're too young for that,' he said.

'How old am I?'

'Twenty-seven and a Scorpio,' he said with a smile. 'I have all the details.'

I didn't like that smile. 'Tell me, did you select me? I've only got six years experience of actual teaching but have they got a file in the Ministry? This one does, this one might?'

'Oh, stop it,' he said.

'Sorry,' I said again. 'What are we going to talk about then?'

'You,' he said.

'I'm very uninteresting.'

'Your husband?'

'He's very interesting.'

'Ah...'

If he said Ah like that again, I'd spit. 'And private,' I said. 'See?'

'Good,' he said. 'Wife too then.'

'Splendid,' I said. 'That's a pact.'

So, we made a start. Then he said: 'Is your Aunt banned too?'

'I could see you fancied her?' I said, just jokey.

'More my age, you mean?'

There it was again, the peeved note.

'Oh, listen,' I said. 'I don't care.'

'I'll tell you something,' he said then. 'Something terrible.'

'Yes-yes?'

'I have a thing about being stared at in restaurants.'

'So?' I said. 'Let's always meet in the dark.'

'I'm glad you said always,' he said quickly.

Pitter-patter. We were still swimming a poor crawl.

'When the time comes,' I said. 'We'll meet under the table. Like dogs,' I said. 'And put the lights out.'

'What'll we eat then?'

'Dog food,' I said. 'It's quite edible but it makes you bark.' Oh, what did I mention that for? I felt sick suddenly.

'Something passed over you then,' he said.

'Wise old owl,' I said. 'If you take a good look, you'll see my glass is empty.'

Instant attention. He called the barman over, just a forefinger. Walter always had to shout or threaten to call the manager.

'Another tonic, Madam?' the barman said.

'Thank you, Harold,' I said. Quick, me. Harold smiled and went away.

I was warming up, but then he said; 'Do you like dirty jokes?'

'Oh Christ... No,' I said. 'I thought English was your subject?'

'The etymology of the dirty joke is rather fascinating actually.'

And his father was a miner! 'Ifor,' I said. 'Be yourself.'

He didn't say anything then. When the barman brought the drinks, he tipped him, but again didn't say anything, just looked hard at the drink, then picked it up and drank it all. He was having a struggle with himself, I could see. But I didn't care. I wanted someone to help me.

'You're really rather remarkable,' he said then.

'No, I'm not.'

'All your generation.'

'I never mix,' I said. 'I don't know about the others.'

It was all ruined. Ashes again. If anybody else came in,

132

I'd let them pick me up. I'd rather be done against a barn door than this.

'Have I said something?' he said.

'Dirty jokes,' I said. 'Sick, aren't they?'

'They're a lubrication.'

'For what?'

'Silence.'

'And male bonhomie,' I said.

'You don't like men?'

'I've had to behave like one.'

He nodded wisely. I wished he wouldn't do that.

'And you?' I said. I wanted to snarl suddenly. I saw his watch. 'If I asked you nicely, would you give me that watch?'

He looked startled, covered it with his hand.

'Certainly not.'

I grinned. 'Oh, so it's not love then?' I had him.

'D'you want another drink before we eat?'

'Why not?' I said. I needed something.

This time he went up and got them himself. A crowd came in, my own age, a beautiful-looking boy in the gear, white and tan shoes, maroon suit which showed his figure and a broad white belt above his hips. He had lovely hair flowing over his coat collar and deep intense eyes that looked right into me. But he was with someone.

Ifor came back.

'It's all gone wrong, I'm afraid. Isn't it funny how things can go wrong so quickly?'

'Balloons pricked,' I said.

'Yes,' he said.

It was all I could do not to move in my seat so that I could strip that boy.

'Well, cheers.'

'Cheers.'

It was awkward now, it would be awkward later, it would be awkward all day tomorrow. Awkward, awkward...

'Where are we staying?' I said. I didn't know.

'My secretary booked two rooms in a hotel not far from the Ministry.'

'Where's that?'

'It's in an annexe actually. In Belgravia.'

Why had everything gone wrong? I didn't know but I didn't have the heart to pick up the pieces. I wanted that boy but I couldn't have him. So I felt savage.

'Do you sleep with your wife?' I said suddenly, staring through him.

'No.'

'Sleep around?'

'Sometimes.'

'When you looked at me in school, what gave you the idea?'

'I didn't have any idea.' He was going white.

'None at all?'

'No.'

'But you thought, "Perhaps"?'

'I thought it would be nice.'

'Nice for who?'

'Both of us, I hoped.'

'When exactly?'

'I don't understand.'

134

'When exactly did you think you'd get it in?'

'I didn't, don't know,' he said. He was stammering.

'You're the sort who sends roses,' I said. I sipped my drink.

'Only after,' he said.

His bit of stuff, I thought. He shouldn't have said that.

'Yours is a contemptible generation,' I said.

'Yes,' he said.

He looked away. I'd been boring my eyes into him and snapping. Perhaps he saw my lips curled. He was playing with the bracelet of the Rolex. I saw that it was too big for his wrist and was about to say something about that too, but when he looked back at me, there were tears in his eyes.

'Oh, Christ,' I said. 'Tell me lies, feel me, get me pissed – anything. Don't do that.'

'You have a very savage tongue,' he said. He was hoarse.

'I have?'

'Yes. Why?' he said.

I didn't know. I shrugged my shoulders. I looked past him. The boy had gone.

'You're very young,' he said.

'I don't feel it.'

'You don't realise what effect you have, that's what being young is, being ignorant of other people.'

'Thanks,' I said.

'D'you want to go?'

'No,' I said. The boy might come back. I'd given him one look that said everything. You never knew.

'Well, you don't want to sit here torturing me, do you?'

'Oh, come off it,' I said.

'Why do what isn't pleasant?'

'Is this a schools broadcast?' I said.

'Please,' he said. 'You have a beautiful face.'

I looked at him again. He meant it. And I'd hurt him, I could see that by his eyes. He was still pale too. I sighed.

'All right,' I said. 'Let's start again.'

He finished his drink. I was eating him up. A lock of hair had come unstuck, spoiling his perfect grooming. It made him look older, greyer. I age people, I thought. I thought about it like a discovery.

'Connie,' he said. 'I don't want you to do what you don't want to do.'

Now I did feel old. Older than him. 'My life isn't like that,' I said. 'I don't know what I want to do.'

'Well, how about eating for a start?'

'Eat, I will,' I said.

'I must eat or I can't drive.'

The breathalyser. I thought of Walter again, carrying himself into the driving seat. 'Be okay if you keep an even speed of ninety!'

'Right!' I said hard. 'Feed the inner man, Ifor.' I couldn't help sending him up.

He called for the menu and sent for the headwaiter. Food chat now. I hardly listened.

'They do a very good pâté.'

'Pâté for me then.'

'I don't know if you like halibut, or there's duck?'

'Duck,' I said.

'Orange sauce, Madam?'

I didn't like the look the Headwaiter gave me. No reason, I just didn't like it.

'*No* orange sauce,' I said.

'But...'

'Have you gateaux? I hope there's a selection.'

'I don't know about wine,' Ifor said, studying the list.

'Let me chip in?' I said, nasty again.

'It's driving,' he said.

'I can drive if necessary.' I thought of Walter again, 'Had a great trip. Wrote off an E-type.'

'That won't be necessary.' So he ordered wine.

I was still giving him a time. So I said, 'If you want to, we can stay here. They have stables at the back.'

'We'll see,' he said.

'Good,' I said. 'As long as you attend to the food.'

The boy wasn't in the restaurant either so I ate myself silly. After the duck, they brought out a trolley loaded with gateaux, some of it fresh with rich cream and nuts. I had two helpings. I ate like a girl out of school, keeping him waiting after courses so that he began to tipple from the bottle, had to order another, and by the time we finished, he couldn't possibly drive.

'See about a chalet,' I said when the coffee came.

'Are you sure?'

'See about it, then I'll be sure.'

He nodded and got up from the table a little unsteadily. He'd stoked the drink away by now. There were other people in the restaurant so he drew himself up, very tall and distinguished, and stalked out. I didn't pay any

137

attention. I'd eaten so much I thought I'd explode. When he came back, he was very jolly, ordered brandy. There was a chalet vacant at the far end. He could drive the car up. He'd cancel the reservations in Belgravia.

'Wouldn't the Ministry get to know?'

'No, it just means claiming subsistence instead of presenting bills.'

'What about me?'

'I sign your expenses.'

He had it all worked out.

Presently, he paid the bill, tipped everybody, put away his little gold note case and we left. I could see the waiters looking at me but I didn't care somehow. He walked me to the chalet, opened it up, then went back for his car so that we could make a quick getaway in the morning. Unseen. I went in, switched the lights on. There were two single beds, several easy chairs with print covers and a little writing desk. For the commercials, I thought. Their order books. On the walls were flower portraits cut from women's magazines. It was the sort of place that Rachel would call reasonable considering. Considering what, I never knew, but it was a category.

I sat on the bed and thought of Walter as I undressed. I'd always had a feeling adultery was sad, furtive little lusts, inconvenient phone calls, deceit in envelopes – all the book stuff. But I just felt flat, more guilty that I'd upset him than anything. I didn't know I could hurt anyone that easily. I didn't want to hurt anybody. If I wanted anything, it was fun, I thought. Why couldn't sex be fun? The meal wasn't even fun, I just ate like a pig, didn't say much. I felt let down, depressed. I'd made him angry, a man of fifty-five. Him and his watch and car and chat. The etymology of the dirty joke. Shit.

I'd got down to my panties and bra when I heard the car purring up towards the chalet. I sat on the bed wearily. I remembered that shower with Walter in that flat. I felt like a footballer now, a pro who didn't want to go on – who'd rather be doing the garden. Was there something wrong with me? Perhaps I ought to try girls or something. I heard him shut the door and check all the locks of the car. That car... There must be something chronically wrong with a man like that and I didn't want to know what it was.

He came into the porch and knocked at the door. Knocked!

'Yes,' I said.

'Ready or not, I'm coming,' he called. He was born when? Nineteen-bloody-eleven, I worked it out.

He came in and eyed me.

'Oh, you've undressed?'

I unclipped the bra. See, I thought, my full ripe breasts.

'Why?' I said.

'Oh, there's a little stream down at the bottom of the garden. It's sweet.'

Sweet... 'And no doubt there's a moon,' I said.

'I just thought... Sorry.'

I took everything off and got into bed, leaving my clothes on the floor. I was as tidy as a squirrel in school, hoarded everything, tins, boxes, all labelled, but then I had monitors, slaves. At home, I'd got like Walter, always in a rush in the mornings. We put things away by leaving them where they dropped. It was quite unlike me, and yet I did it. I saw him looking at the mess. I wasn't doing my educational image any good.

I looked at him, just looked at him. He'd brought my grip but I didn't need anything.

He stood there, holding it disconsolately.

'You don't think I'm going to wash, do you?' I said.

I thought he'd say something like 'You young ladies!' but he didn't, just shrugged, put the grip down, opened his own suitcase and took out a pyjama case. A pyjama case! From the case, he took out this pair of fancy blue pyjamas with a red stripe down the trousers.

I stared at them.

'French,' he said.

He went sheepishly into the bathroom to undress.

Would I? Wouldn't I? I didn't know. I didn't care. I was tired by now, mildly boozed. The food made me feel heavy and sluggish. The one curiosity in my mind was what he was going to do with the watch.

He came in wearing this pyjama uniform, looked at me again.

'Well?' he said.

I looked at his trousers but he didn't even have a hard-on. Well, I thought, it's not so bad then.

'Good night,' I said. I turned over on my side and closed my eyes. It was so embarrassing, such perfect strangers.

I had to wait a full minute before he got into bed and then he wound the watch carefully, put it under his pillow and put the light out.

A dirty weekend, I thought. I'd be better off with milk bottles.

But in the night I woke up and saw him lying there smoking. He had his back to me and was lying on his elbow. He coughed once or twice, then ground the cigarette out. He sighed and turned restlessly, folded his hands behind his head and lay there staring at the ceiling. Perhaps he couldn't sleep because I was there. Perhaps he had indigestion, perhaps he felt guilty, perhaps he'd realised how boring he was, an old man who couldn't sleep.

I don't know why, but suddenly I threw the blankets off.

He didn't move, was unaware of me, or scared.

I got out of bed, my bare feet making wet footprints on the tiled floor, and stood looking at him.

He blinked, couldn't believe I was there.

I kept staring at him.

He didn't move.

Then I moved forward, took a handful of his blankets and pulled them off him slowly.

At first, he tried to stop me.

'No,' I said.

I untied the pyjama cord to give myself room and then sat on the bed and began to work him over gently.

'Not if you don't want to,' he said.

'I hurt you, didn't I?'

'Yes,' he said.

'I'm not like that,' I said. 'Not really.'

I kept my hand there, using each fingernail.

'But...'

'Sh...' I said.

So he just lay there until he could stand it no longer, and finally he caught me as I wanted to be caught, and with little choking sobs he got rid of his loneliness and for a minute, no more, we were together and I could feel his bony hips and the bristle on his chin and I held him tight-tight all the way along his body. I didn't feel anything special, no orgasm, but I didn't let him go for a long time. Then, drained, he moved off and kissed my breasts, a fey, romantic gesture. I saw only his bald patch. Pale dead skin.

'Give me a cigarette,' I said.

He lit one, looking about a hundred-and-fifty in the light of the flame. I closed my eyes.

'You wanted it as much as I did?'

Men always said that to me. But I didn't, as it happened.

'No,' I said. 'But it's all I can do with men. This and destroy them otherwise.' I knew the truth at last.

'Oh, rubbish.'

'Yes,' I said. 'Look at you last night.'

'What you said was true.'

'Was it?'

'Yes. And now?'

'I don't know, Ifor. I don't know anything.'

'Thank you for now anyway.'

'On the house,' I said.

I didn't think of Walter then, just me. We lay a long time like that in silence. He got the blankets back on the bed. I didn't want to move and wanted somebody beside me. But then he got worked up again, found an urge from somewhere, but it was no use. He wasn't ignorant and found the homing spots, but I'd done my good deed and pushed him away.

'Be a friend,' I said. 'That's all. Just be a friend.'

He lay there on his elbow looking at me.

'You're a funny girl,' he said. It was the nicest thing he'd ever said.

'Yes,' I said.

I went back to my own bed then, didn't say any more. If Walter knew, it would kill him, I thought. What was the matter with me? I couldn't think straight. My guilt came in patches, sometimes a flood, sometimes never. I tried to tell myself over and over that it was impossible to do anything about Walter any more. As it happened, I didn't crucify him with my tongue any more. I'd tried all that. What could I do that I hadn't done then? Nothing, I thought. Your own faults are so difficult to grasp. You think you understand what you're doing but there are blank areas, things left unsaid, actions left undone, the *persona* you present without realising it. One thing occurred to me that was new. In the whore's bed, as it were. And that was, that I was never wifely. I was never anybody's little woman, never sentimental, and perhaps he knew it too well. Perhaps the awful thing was that he needed to invent these little pastiches of his because he couldn't get close to me any more. That was sex again, I thought, the great chest. Remove the condom and what have you got left but ashes. I never needed him and perhaps he knew that I'd given up without admitting it to himself. If that was true, then I'd murdered something by creating the seeds of that self-dismay in him.

If it was true, I thought, I couldn't bear it.

So I didn't sleep all night. My dirty weekend.

Ifor woke up, whistled as he shaved, the new man.

I had a thumping headache.

'Is anything wrong?'

'Nothing.'

'Would you like an aspirin?'

'No, thank you.'

'Coffee or something?'

'No.'

'I've ordered breakfast.'

'I never eat breakfast.'

'D'you mind if I do?'

'Not a bit.'

When it came, he tucked in, bacon and eggs twice. I went into the bathroom when they brought it. He was all right, I thought. He'd had everything he wanted.

'Sorry?' he said gently when I came back in.

I shrugged my shoulders and began to dress.

'Guilt,' he said. 'We all feel that.'

'I'll be all right if you just don't talk about it.'

'There you go again,' he said cheerfully; 'the gentle savage.'

Oh, no... Fred Astaire again.

'D'you know why we do things?' I said. I didn't mind him eyeing me dressing.

'Because we want to,' he said.

'Even hurt people?'

'If we want to.'

'Why do we want to?'

'Because we are inadequate on our own,' he said.

'Why, on our own?'

'I don't know why,' he said. 'But I've never had any real happiness on my own.'

'And you're happy this morning?' I said.

'Yes.'

'Because you proved something?'

'No, you did that.'

'Oh, did I?'

'This is a little embarrassing,' he said.

'Oh, gee up,' I said.

'The fact is, I feel I'm more bearable.'

'Just a fuck?' I said, hard like that.

He flushed. 'You didn't leave me quite so alone, did you?'

'No, I suppose,' I said. I thought about that. Then I twigged something. Sex was important to him, it wasn't to Walter and me. Because we'd had so much of it. But it was all we did together, I thought again. Apart from that, not a single communication. I'd had these thoughts before, but never so clearly. My adultery was not on that bed but in the mind, the act of separating myself from him months ago. I was another one who fired him, but never actually gave him notice.

I clipped my bra.

'It's very easy to deal with you,' I said.

'Me?' Ifor said.

'Yes. You just want your little trumpet to blow.'

'There you go again,' he said. He was as jovial as a scoutmaster. He'd had it in and now he was Prince of

Wales. Whatever I did or said, he'd had it away once at least. Men... They made a currency out of it.

Well, we learn all the time, I thought.

He put on his watch after breakfast and everything was like it had been, except he had that quiet confidence because of his trespass. I got a duster and wiped the dew off the Jag and now he looked at me lovingly, the girl who always did the right thing.

I kept my tongue in check, we chattered away, but when we drove into London, he turned his thoughts to the working party like a good Inspector should.

'You'll find there'll be a lot of people talking,' he said. 'Personally, I find it better to say as little as possible until it gets to the committee stage.'

'Ah, but you would,' I said.

'What?'

'You haven't got any actual experience at all,' I said.

He grinned, looked at me as if I was very young which I suppose I was.

He wasn't a bad sort, Ifor, an old broiler who wanted his oats; not much more. Even on the floor, Walter'd make four of him.

CHAPTER FIVE

WALTER

I don't want to sound unreasonable but have you ever noticed something? Doctors are bastards! They go on holiday whether you get better or not. Absolute bastards. They don't lose any sleep. That New Zealand registrar... Silken git. No prognosis. Can't be definite. Can't say. Look here, I wanted to shout, if it's plugs, change the plugs. Trouble with the sump, spanner out! But they can't say. He can't say. Nobody can say. Chemotherapy, he said. That again. What is it? Drugs. Streptomycin. Every day. And bed rest. In bed all the time? All the time. And don't strain at stool. Stool – what the hell is stool? No, he can't have an enema, can't have a bronchoscope. Bronchoscope – I could stand a cinemascope. I'm BI, bloody immobilised. Everybody wants to look at the eye, Eale's disease, old Joey the floaters. Two days I'm here, they've brought a load of blackies up from downstairs, just to see the Eale. 'Habari,' I say; 'Bwana Mac'wber poxed up!' Not a flicker in response. Medical students, little bastards preparing to be bigger bastards. They've come up from Hearts downstairs, where the action is. That's where the oxygen apparatus rattles in the night, where they actually run. Not up here.

'No, Mr Lacey, is everything all right, Mr Lacey? The mobile library will be around on Wednesday but of course, you can't read. No, you must use the bed pan, I'm afraid there's no question of you going to the corridor toilets. It's the same for the other patients on your grade. No, Mr Lacey, I assure you the needle is new. The fact is you haven't very much flesh. No, Mr Lacey, the food is the same for everyone. Special diets are for special cases. No, you cannot be woken later, the night staff have to get ready for the day staff and they don't only have this ward to deal with. No, they cannot put the thermometer in your mouth while you're asleep. (If he's bitten the end off, give him bread, just a slice.) I'm sorry, Mr Lacey. Yes, they *are* sprouts. They're grown in the hospital grounds and that is not insecticide. You please yourself whether you eat them or not. No, Mr Lacey, stout is only given on the doctor's recommendation to post-operative patients. This is not a hotel, Mr Lacey. The staff are doing the best they can. You ought to feel lucky you haven't got cancer...'

The sister had a whining voice, left nothing unsaid. For two days, I lived for Wednesday, Consultant's rounds. His name is Hughes, Mr A. L. ap Hughes, it says on the card above the bed. The staff lower their voices when they talk about him. He's worked his way up from pigshit. Personally, I wouldn't be surprised if he does experiments without anaesthetic on stolen animals. It's not that he can't say, but that you can't hear him, the Count of Monte Cristo with the permanent sore throat. Rounds, tidy up, bed straight, locker frisked: I could gob on the floor. Then the procession, Glory Boy, the Registrar, Houseman, Sister, Staff Nurse, the probationer trailing behind carrying the heavies. They came at a rush round the beds. The probationer'd done my hair, slicked it back with a wet sponge. I wasn't to move. 'Just lie there, Walter. Any questions you want to ask, you ask. Wednesday's the day. Mr A. L. ap Hughes.' He could have been on skates, he moved so fast. Flames of death, I thought. He went round the ward like a gnat in a petrol ad! Jet-propelled, old Esso-face.

'This is Mr Lacey. Eale's Disease.'

'*Ah*...' from the back of the throat.

'Doctor,' I said.

'Just a minute, Mr Lacey,' the Sister said. 'Here's his chart. X-ray here. Temperature's up.'

'*Haw*...' said Tonsillitis. He was a North Walian with a moon face, agricultural colouring, wisps of hair sticking up at crazy angles, a flannel shirt behind his white coat, a crummy old blue tie so threadbare you'd think he'd tied it around the chicken coop. And big boots. Boots! And no voice.

'Ho,' said Tremolo.

'We're having a WR done,' the Registrar said with a smirk.

149

'*Hoo hoo.*'

'Haemoptysis,' the Sister said.

'*Ah, haarrgh.*'

The Sister offered him an ophthalmoscope, but he shook his head.

'Doctor,' I said again.

He nodded, smiled, patted the foot of the bed as he would a cabbage, and then he was off, bolting for the door like a startled poacher, his short body bent double by the length of his strides, and they were all gone, Wednesday rounds over. I hadn't got a question in.

Brilliant man, the legend said. He could tell just by looking at you.

One day, I'd ask if he was an astronomer as well.

'Walter,' Rachel said on the Saturday; 'The Sister says you're being difficult.'

'Where's Connie?'

'Patients can be discharged for their behaviour, you know.'

'Where's Connie?'

'She's in London.'

'London?' I felt scared. I was so conditioned by cheap films, she might have said Las Vegas.

'I expect there'll be a letter for you.'

'There's not been a word. Five days.'

'Did you get the dressing-gown and slippers?'

'Yes, but...'

'Did you write to reply?'

'No, but...'

'Two of a kind. Here, I've brought some grapes. Shall I

put them in the locker or on the locker? I'll bring you a fruit bowl next week.'

'Put them where you like. What's she doing in London?'

'I'm coming to that. This is the marvellous news. She's been appointed to a Schools Council Working Party on Compensatory Education.' She pronounced it with emphasis. For all I knew, it might have been the Dead Brides of Frankenstein.

'In London?'

'She has to go up to represent *all* Wales once a month. It's an Enquiry into the Backward and Deprived.'

The Backward and Deprived... Bull's Eye again.

'If she wants to go poncing around the country,' I began to say.

But she interrupted heavily: 'It's an honour, Walter.'

'Honour...' I lay back against the pillows. They'd drops in both eyes now, both pupils were dilated, but I saw her looming large beside the bed, teeth glistening as she made the pronouncements; then they came slowly together and clenched, as unnaturally white as piano keys. I remembered she used a peculiar bleach of her own to clean them.

She covered them when she smiled.

'I couldn't bring you anything to read so I brought you a jigsaw.'

'A jigsaw?'

'You can pass it on to the other patients when you're finished. It's Drake before the Armada. Navy, I thought you'd like that.'

Sailors don't care, I thought; it's something to do with the salt in their blood. Oh, where was she?

'Now then,' Rachel said; 'Tell me, how are you feeling in yourself?'

I just lay there. They'd increased, then reduced, the amount of streptomycin I was getting because I was resistant to it and had to be de-sensitised. Orders from Old Glory after he saw my temperature chart. But it meant I was going off into comas in the nights, waking in a sweat, then slipping into semi-consciousness for parts of the day. They were irregular bouts and followed no pattern. I was weak and getting weaker. They reckoned it would take six weeks to straighten me out and they weren't going to bother to X-ray me until I was getting the full dose. Nobody would say much more. It all depended on the strep', and my being able to take it.

Some of this I told her, then my mind passed to Connie's trip to London. I was at once suspicious. Jag-town, I thought. Personally I'd always thought it a place where very dim people came into their own. But who was I to shout? Modest Walter.

'I've left some eggs with the Sister,' Rachel said. 'She said there's no reason why you can't have them as you're refusing to eat.'

'I'm not refusing to eat.'

'They don't like people who are difficult, Walter.'

'I'm not being difficult!'

'That's not what she told me. Of course, she only hinted.'

'But you can read between them,' I said.

'Between what?'

'The lines,' I said hoarsely. She had this effect on me.

152

'Yes,' she smiled. 'But I've found out one thing.'

'What's that?'

'You can have sweets. Lucky, I brought some mintoes.'

Sweets, grapes, eggs, jigsaw, advice, homilies... Rachel. What could you do?

'You'd think she would have dropped a line?' I said.

'Yes, you would,' Rachel said.

I could see she disapproved. She began to eat my grapes. Testing, no doubt.

'She went on her own?'

'No, there's an Inspector of Schools for the area with her. A Mr Evans. He speaks beautiful Welsh. Must be near retiring,' Rachel said carefully.

Ah, I thought. So she's gone on a bat on her own.

'Iestyn couldn't come today because his wife isn't well and he's looking after the shop. I get the impression he feels he's done all he can.'

'Tell him not to bother,' I said.

'That isn't very kind, Walter.'

'No, I don't want him to have the bother of coming all the way here.'

'I came on the bus myself.'

I knew she'd gone to a lot of trouble, knew she disapproved of Connie not being here, although she wouldn't admit it.

'Has she rung up?' I said suddenly.

'No, but the lines may have been out of order.'

She's covering up, I thought. She doesn't know what or why, but she's covering up. Her face had taken on that impassive matriarchial look, as when she didn't want to give anything away. And she talked and talked, destroying the silence as if it was an evil compound in which fears would breed. She just sat there, scything away with platitudes.

'One thing you always learn in hospital, is how much better off you are than other people. I sat next to a cancer on the bus.'

'What?'

'The mother of a cancer patient.'

'Oh, yes.'

'They've burnt half his glands away.'

Oh Christ, Rachel...

'Deep heat treatment,' she said.

She'd inform herself every week, I knew.

'And there's one man whose wife's hair is falling out with the drugs,' she said. 'Side effects, they call it. She's on this Endoxana.'

'I'll see what I can do by next week,' I said.

'Why are you so flippant, Walter?'

'Why not,' I said. What was she doing in London, the very first weekend I was in? It was as if she couldn't wait.

'We haven't always got on,' Rachel said.

Oh no, confessions, re-examinations.

'...But there's no need for you to feel unwanted,' she said.

I suddenly had tears in my eyes. Those who use bludgeoning tools must always win if only because they strike the whole body. Out of hospital, I was a champion door-closer whenever she was around, the expert vanisher. Now she was unavoidable, my only visitor.

154

I blinked away my tears. 'It's the strep',' I said. 'I'm resistant to it.' As I said it, I knew she'd tell them on the bus.

'*Will* is very important with Tee Bee,' she said.

'Yes.'

'The *will* to fight it,' she said.

'Yes.'

'Without *will*, nothing succeeds.'

'Drugs,' I said.

'*Will* first,' she said.

In a minute, she was going to tell me to pull myself together and heave me forward into a new life when I came out. She was like that, a pusher for living, and she went at it two-fisted. I could never understand why she had never married but never liked to ask. You'd think she might have hi-jacked somebody at the bus-stop. She was capable of it. A thousand different attitudes separated us, nearly fifty years of life, my scrambling, her living. She gathered everything to her like a crab, digesting all, using all. Her strength was in her face and in her every expression, this difference between us. Perhaps we were saying different things to each other so often because neither comprehended the other's experience. The generations went about anyway like people lost in a maze. Now it was all sex and fun, but in her day the simple kick was bread and butter. And God, I thought; Houdini the first. But it was too complex for me to understand. I didn't want to think anyway. Except that she reminded me I was wanted. Very simple. Very cosy. Warm. Toasty. Nice to be nice.

But why had Connie stayed away?

I didn't ask her and stuffed a grape down as Rachel abstained and looked interestedly around the ward. There was a collier opposite me with a hundred per cent silicosis and TB, a full house, as he said. He was propped up on raised pillows because he couldn't lie down, a thatch of silver-white hair crowning a sunken-cheeked face that was nearly all chin and coal scars. His name was Dai Gash and you could see the shape of his skull. When he settled back for the night, his coughing was like a self-created Coal Board philharmonic, an orchestrated wheeze that could vary from a low staccato note to a high piping falsetto. He was fighting for his life and would not give in. For some reason, he had no visitors.

'A nice-looking man,' Rachel said. 'He has *no* visitors.'

'No,' I said. I knew she was underlining that, a moral tone.

'I'll pop over and have a chat.'

Myself, I was always glad to be left alone. She waddled over and sat beside him.

'My Aunt,' I called.

He grinned as if he knew about aunts.

You couldn't help admiring her. She couldn't pick up a match without involving herself. Dai had no visitors, she became his visitor. I knew she would be a regular on the visitors' bus, a mine of comfort and information. She could solve everybody's problem except ours.

When she came back, she found we had relatives in common. She would.

'Mr Gash is *riddled* with silicosis,' she said.

I knew that.

'His family has gone to his boy's graduation at the University.'

I didn't know that.

'A proud day for him.'

'Yes.'

'Worked all his life in dirt and water and now this – out of the pit.'

How Green Was My What, I thought. She thought about an everyday happening and before you could say Keir Hardie, it had become sociology, a symbol, a piece of flag-waving, the keynote of a sermon. You'd think we did it alone, that there wasn't an errand boy in Leicester who ever moved house. She was brimful of sagas, invented them, seized on them, doing her own jigsaws like a weaver of national dreams, all on offer to the tourists or whoever cared to listen, and all inapplicable to all the situations I ever encountered.

But perhaps she sensed the rottenness of our own myths. We couldn't live without any at all.

I said, 'Why didn't she come?'

She looked at me long and hard before she left, honest Rachel.

'I don't know,' she said. 'I just don't know.'

That night they had the telly at the end of the ward and they turned Dai Gash's bed so that he could see, just him, the fruiterer in the corner who'd been in before and was the TB expert, and the fourth man, a lag by the name of Mush, one of the docks boys from Tiger Bay. I hadn't spoken much since I came in, because of the strep' comas, and now I didn't want to join in. They had the Saturday film on and

157

I just lay there quietly by myself. When it was dark, the eye never bothered me. It was quiet except for the odd moan from the hearts downstairs and you couldn't hear much with the telly on. A moth fluttered in from the window and circled the little screen. Nobody could get out of bed, but the fruiterer wouldn't let anybody kill it anyway. Bad luck, he said. He had no ribs to speak of and had lost one lot in the old days when they did the operation under local anaesthetic, and you could hear the ribs falling one by one into the bucket under the table. Some memories, he had. But now they were all quiet, three men and a moth, and Gregory Peck.

I thought of her then, when it was dark and no one could see my face. The cow... Who did she think she was cheating?

But steady on, I told myself. I had my optimistic moments, usually when the boss was reaching for the cards unknown to me, or when I was brewing up or whistling cheerfully in the outer office. Perhaps it was what Rachel said, a promotion. I didn't understand these things. And perhaps she welcomed a trip away from Rachel. The moment she qualified, I remembered, she went to Maidstone. To get away from me, I thought at the time, but it worked out all right. It does no harm to get away from someone, I thought. I'd always been a great leaver before I was married. I ought to understand the same need in other people. I went on thinking like that, all the reasonable things. Even on your uppers, there's always a part of your mind that behaves as if it's still resident in the desirable semi-detached, as the estate agents say. And monkeys can dream in the zoo.

The moth was trying to kill itself as I lay there. It had come in with a dive-bombing whine but now it was charging wildly, making low-level runs at the centre of the screen, hitting the glass and sliding down to the corners, a tiny thud indicating its obsession. It was fascinated by the light and would not give in, but still nobody did anything. There was a cat-and-mouse search going on in the film, Gregory on his face, a jungle clip from a war story, crickets chirping in the silence. Of course, it was impossible that the moth knew anything about that. It saw only the light. I wondered what would happen if the set were switched off. Would the moth retreat, pick itself up off the floor and fly away? Or was the light the fatal attraction, once seen never forgotten? Did the intensity of the light drive it crazy and make every other light unacceptable?

People could be like that, I thought. As well as my being ineffective, she thought me romantic and childish, I knew. Things hadn't turned out as she expected, she said, the phrase of my life. But whatever happened, I couldn't change my view of her. I knew that as something final. Even in the gutter, men had some things which they clung to, I believed. It might only be a memory, a picture in the mind which remained constant on recall, and even if everything crumbled in my life, there remained the image of everything she had been. Perhaps you had to go through life like that, holding the perspective clear about the people close to you. But it was in the past tense, as if you started at a certain point and then slipped down from there, only remembering people as you passed them. Ever

159

after, they seemed distant because you were constantly moving away. So where did that leave me? To the view that nothing will be better tomorrow, I thought, back where I started, the lowest of low.

And I didn't believe that. I just couldn't. Even though everything in my life led me to that conclusion. Perhaps it was because I'd been surrounded by lies ever since I started work. And almost everyone I knew in the work situation operated by one confidence trick or another. Take selling. You didn't push a good car. You let it sell itself. You let the mug see himself in status-warming situations. Owning that car was like joining an expensive club, you let him feel. He was becoming a member through your cooperation. You were the proposer, the hire-purchaser was seconder, he was very lucky to be able to join. And it was the same with shirts. You never pushed the quality product directly. Let him fumble with the cheap stuff, then slip the winner in.

'Now, of course, sir, if you really want a shirt, not just something to wear...'

For the mug who wanted two collars, there was the utility stuff, but a real shirt, the shirt of shirts, that meant joining a fraternity. All the top sells went in this way. And naturally, you had a bogus technicality to throw in.

'It's a double-reverse process on the loom actually, that special ribbing. They have to re-set the machine to get the quality which, of course, explains the cost. Ultimately, there's no substitute for hand trimming and only a certain number can be made in this way. I'm not sure whether that's the last...'

160

I'd invented lies like this which were still in use in the trade. Even as a kid allowed to take over in the Christmas rush, I'd make a distinctive sale. I had the confidence not to push. But whereas the others got to believe in what they were doing, I'd got sick of it. Something had snapped, so from shirts, I went to cars, and finally to motor cycles and scooters, and then I knew I was at dirt level. Even in the crummiest car showroom, there's an obligation to get the product to the end of the street. The burk had to be able to drive it away, but with bikes, we mostly had kids on the receiving end, and it was the salesman's job to begin the instruction if they couldn't drive them away.

At first, I did it conscientiously, but once you made the sale, there was always pressure to get back to the shop. The fitters couldn't be spared to help you, so finally you just put the kid and the bike outside the door, and some days I used to wait for the crash, my ear cocked as they did their first revs and ground away at the gears. I used to tell them to bring a friend with them, mostly working-class kids on their way home from work on a Friday, embarrassed at signing forms, being in an office, all anxious to be away, jet-setting along the open road. We'd hammer them for the leathers, boots, mirrors, helmets so that sometimes they didn't even have the price of a gallon of petrol left. And when the fitters were busy, I'd have to go out with the van to bring in the wrecks, a job I did in a hurry about once a month.

Speed, I thought, speed and lies. In the motorcycle business, you learn fast. There the con is easiest because of the low-grade customer and they're hooked before you start. One death and I was out, and after that, I'd sell anything else, but not on wheels. Feed it to my canine friends, I am a white man after all.

So how did you learn? Only by learning about yourself. She used to say it didn't matter, my success. She wasn't hooked on it, she said. And she didn't want the things that went with it. You live a short life actually, she said. She didn't want things because she had a thing about things. We were never good customers. They didn't rush to us in shops. We had no air of that. So learn about yourself. If you had nothing to occupy you, perhaps it was a mistake to have a marriage the only thing in your life? I had nothing else and I sensed it was dangerous. A public school man can put his hand to anything, they said. Mix at all levels, captains of commerce, industry, kings. Shit... With me, it always ended with kind smiles.

'Walter, I'm very sorry but...'

'It's quite all right, sir.'

'We're having to expand in the workshop, cut down on sales.'

'Absolutely. Rationalisation, I quite understand.'

'And in the circumstances...'

'Do the same thing myself.'

'No hard feelings?'

'Never.'

When they put the telly away, they moved Dai's bed back into the file and we settled down for the night. He had to stay propped up on his pillows so I could always see him, his routine. First he took his wrist watch off and wound it, strapped it to the towel rail on his locker. Then he had a night cardigan which he put on over his day cardigan, blew his nose, did his hair, folded his hands in front of him and waited for sleep to come. After the night sister'd been, he'd have a smoke on the quiet if he couldn't sleep, slipping the ash into an envelope. When he thought nobody was watching, he'd do arm exercises, flexing his shoulder muscles, moving his fingers from side to side. He'd got soft, he told us later. Out of trim. He had to keep a bit of a grip, he said. Lungs like little hard bags because of the dust, see. It was a matter of fact as he said it. He didn't complain. He hadn't worked for five years. But he was trying to keep his grip. With TB, and one hundred per cent dust, his full house.

Lessons, I thought. You always had to find something to live by. Courage, I thought. What was it? I didn't believe in any of the conventional things. We all grow up with clichés that I never believed in anyway. I didn't think it was forgetting the self, acting without regard for his own safety, as the citations said. That was a different thing, a test to which you reacted instinctively, often with skills that demanded testing. It was something else, not so much leading with the chin as just going on. And on and on. There was no reason for it if you were looking for reasons, but it was the act of going on. It didn't depend on intelligence, it defeated intelligence. Neither did it depend on knowing anything. You didn't get it from a book or a sage, you found it in yourself. You stopped screaming and took whatever was coming. There was something silent about it. It was beyond words. If

163

anything, you said less and less, finally nothing unless it was a joke. You rode the punches, as they said. And if you couldn't stay on your feet, you stayed upright in your mind. You didn't squeal. Never be a squealer. If I could learn that, I could learn anything, I thought. That way, you had a chance of a private self.

Dai couldn't sleep that night. He must have seen me staring at the ceiling. I'd stopped coughing but the weakness was there, the paper-thinness of bones stretched out and muscles already growing slack and the strep' inducing this fever and weakness. It was taking me a long time to get used to it. But I had a new thought come in Gregory-Peck time, a whizz wrapping on the package. I looked at Dai as he lay there. Taking it all the way along the line, I thought. He saw that I was awake and nodded.

'Aye aye,' he said.

'Aye aye,' I said.

'Laying a bit thick tonight,' he said, referring to his sputum.

'Yes,' I said.

'I got a horse going for me on Monday,' he said. 'I think I'll have a dollar on him.'

'Over the sticks?'

'On the flat. Jasper's Fancy,' he said. 'I think I'll have it on the nose. You got to have something going for you, haven't you?'

'Yes,' I said. Something going for you, I thought.

'Your auntie,' he said.

'My wife's actually.'

'They're a type, they are.'

They were.

'They eat men,' he said with emphasis. 'There's one in every family around here.'

'What makes them tick?' I said.

'Appetite.'

I laughed. He laughed. Perhaps we were both thinking the same things.

He began to cough then, deep in his chest. He shouldn't have laughed perhaps. It was very unsettling at night.

Eventually, he cleared his throat and filled the sputum pot. Filled it. Six fluid ounces if you want the details.

'Helluva thing, isn't it?'

'Helluva thing, sure.'

Basics, I thought. When you come down to it, we are neither as separate nor so special as we think. And everything that separates us comes from outside us, the way we speak, the clothes we wear, the things we own. We have very little that doesn't leave us or can't be shed. And ultimately, we are alone. In the very last breath we address ourselves alone. And no one else.

So she didn't come. No doubt she had a reason. It was something I had to bear. Acceptance, I thought. Was that what I'd learned at last? Somebody once said I had a grasshopper mind. Well, grasshoppers had to eat grasshoppers, I thought. The huge joke in living was that we had to live with ourselves always. And our minds. Our luck... I got up on my elbow and peered at the floor where the telly had been. But I couldn't see the moth.

The moth is dead, long live the King, I thought, meaning me.

But why didn't she come? I'd get the details out of her even if I had to claw them out. The cow... I knew all right.

CHAPTER SIX

CONNIE

People have a capacity for making themselves suffer. Even people like us, Walter and me. It's because his life is trite, meaningless, of no consequence, unimportant. What he does with it, I mean. I'm different. What I do has social consequence and matters. I'm involved, worthwhile. I have skills, am capable.

So Ifor said. I told him everything. Everybody needs a confidant. Even me. Even if it was Ifor. Stay the weekend, he said. Talk it over. I knew he wanted another dabble, just that, but even knowing it, seeing through him – to the core, as Rachel would say – I stayed. The price was his interest in me. But even though I knew that he just wanted to get it in, his little piece of gristle, I also knew I'd stay. That was another need. Somebody else. You could see through someone and still want them. Transparencies were necessary too. Nobody gets seduced, brother. There's never been a seduction in the history of the human race.

The upper échelons of the education world were a total flop in my book. There's where we are, I thought, my lot in our little hut, and where they are, Belgravia.

The annexe was a whole house. Uniformed porters, notice boards with raised plastic letters like they have in hotels, *Birds Eye announce their presence in the Buckingham Room*. The compensators were on the top floor, a Professor in the chair, a man from the Ministry taking notes. He was so thin and scrubbed, black beetle dress, bowler and umbrella, a coconut voice, so precise and *nice*, I wanted to stroke him.

Ifor was most concerned we made separate entrances and we stopped the Jag a block away. Now, he's paying for it, I thought, his oats. 'This is the nosebag,' I said. 'You pay for everything.' I arranged to see him later. He suggested one or two places. 'Make it expensive,' I said. And we fixed on one. Nosebag or not, he didn't seem to mind.

I left my grip in the car and followed his directions. He was going to arrive later. It was a sunny day and there was a little park with a tennis court and seats in the centre of the square. Belgravia impressed me. London is impersonal and too big to comprehend. It always made me feel small. Nearly all my life I'd lived in tiny rooms, grey places. Architecture was something that happened in the county hall, nowhere else. I walked around the square looking at the huge houses. In the valleys, people hang their curtains plush side out so that people in the street can see what they've got. They live with the lining. Here, the lining was visible. A moral there, I thought. If Walter had been with me he would have said this was where *They* lived, the people who ruled our lives. I didn't feel that, just curious.

There were several nannies sitting beside prams in the park. Servants, I thought. I had never even been in a house where they had those. The other half remained the other half, who never worked. What did they do with themselves? Perhaps they just didn't get up. But they had to do something. Of course, there was tennis, the theatre and parties. Fun, I supposed. A woman of about thirty-five came out of a house, crossed the road and spoke to one of the nannies, who stood up deferentially. She'd on this aubergine couture piece with a mink collar and croc boots. They were so real you could smell the swamp.

'I shan't be back until after lunch, *Nannay*.'

'Bo-bo,' she said to the child in the pram. Then she went away. She didn't touch the child, I noticed. Walter said his mother never touched him. Why did people send their children away to school? So they could go off on the knock unhampered, Walter said. Scandalous. A rational man wouldn't say things like that. I didn't know. I watched the woman stride away across the park. Her face had seemed so calm. Perhaps the rich never lost any sleep over their children. They employed other people to do it for them. Perhaps their women were merely supportive, elegant decorations. To keep that cool look, they needed time. Bolshie thoughts, I said to myself, Walter-thoughts. I suddenly felt very Welsh, meaning inferior. I wanted to get over the feeling of being a little

Welsh schoolmistress using her fanny to get on in education. It was quite funny and I wished I could tell it to Walter. About someone else.

My dalliance by the gardens delayed me. When I got to the place, Ifor and I arrived at the same time. I looked straight through him.

'Good morning, Mrs Lacey,' he said. He was wearing a light grey trilby he'd hidden from me in the car.

The hall porter was in earshot, holding the door open.

'Good morning, sir,' I said without thinking.

'You'll find the conference room on the third floor.'

'I'm much obliged,' I said.

As soon as I got into the room, I was suddenly afraid for Ifor. They were all so old and stinking with educational experience. I thought they'd immediately suspect I was there because he was slipping me a length on the side. Such Walter-phrases tumbled over in my mind. The secretary had this wafer-thin nose, a waistcoated wraith with delicate skin.

'Mrs Lacey?'

'Yes,' I said.

'We're most grateful you could come at such short notice.'

'Oh,' I said. I couldn't think of anything to say.

He was staring at me and liking my youth, big tortoiseshell frames that fitted cruelly on that delicate nose.

'Have you come up today?'

I blushed. 'Last night.'

He didn't say any more because the Chairman came over

holding a sheaf of papers. He had come down from the North, was tweedy and soiled, like an unsuccessful bookie.

'This is Mrs Lacey, Chairman. She's fitted in at short notice.'

'D'you do?' he had a wet palm. 'Know Cardiff,' he said. 'Entrancing civic centre.'

'Yes,' I said. There was an ornamental goldfish pool in front of it and once, after Walter went on a fishing trip with one of his boozy employers, they caught a tope, stuck it in the back of the car and dumped it into the pool in the early hours. To greet the park keeper. They were as disappointed as children when it was never reported in the press. Even the press was against Walter.

The Chairman took this proprietorial interest, ushered me around, squeezing my elbow. Professor this, Doctor that, then we came to the women. Christ, I thought. Educational women were worse than the men. All so unlovely. Was I cruel? I hoped not. Because people couldn't do anything else, why did they have to go into education? It always seemed to be so sad for everybody. No doubt we all had a contribution to make, but why was there this terrifying gap in looks between the teachers and the taught once you passed a certain age? Were the spinsters people who could never commit themselves, victims who became aggressors and inflicted their own rules, standards and codes which were so manifestly unsuccessful in their own fulfilment? But I checked myself. Bitch! Fulfilment, I thought, I couldn't shout.

Ifor came up and ignored me, fingering his collar as he did it. I watched him speak to another HMI out of the

171

corner of my eye. Nobody seemed pleased to see him. Then we all sat down, there was an opening address, a paper read by the secretary. The tone of his voice bugged me, then the sociologist's phrases began to fall thick and fast, *the intangible reinforcement condition, psycholinguistic abilities, perceptual discriminations, a thorough grasp of the behavioural sciences.*

I soon realised I was out of my depth and angry with myself for being there. It seemed you could not get on in the educational world without the capacity for making other people seem dull. There was this special language in which the informed spoke to each other, but not to me. When the discussion opened, I made no contribution. I had nothing to say to them. I could see the secretary looking at me. One word and he would have applauded, bent his nose and grooved the table, I was sure, but I said nothing, looked blankly out of the window at the trees in the distance. When they served coffee, I felt I ought to offer to wash up. It had no interest for me, but it annoyed me. I did not see the relationship between this and the children I taught. No doubt they were well-meaning, but whatever they compiled, I knew at once that they could not speak to other people, only themselves. Whatever directives came from outside, nothing changed unless the teachers changed, meaning *their* attitudes, *their* skills, *their* energy, I came out with the impression I was leaving a private world which was pushing itself along, expanding its activities, puffing itself up as it listened to itself, its self-importance odious and its effectiveness doubtful. The panel would gain by the experience, few others. I knew in my bones that for the most part, they would produce a pamphlet that would stay unread on the shelves.

'I know,' Ifor said when I told him.

'Why then?'

'Separate worlds are self-perpetuating. They pass each other, seldom communicate.'

'What's communication then?'

'Caring,' he said.

'And what do they care about, these people?'

'The problem, one or two, then papers on the problem, status as a consequence of the problem. Being in on it, the illusion of power.'

'And the kids?' I said. I thought of my lot, Arthur so pleased to pour tea for the Headmaster, mine host. That meant something to him.

'Perhaps they care, but they couldn't face them for the rest of their lives.'

'You too,' I said.

'Yes,' he said. 'Now.'

'Why?' I said.

'Those who can, do.'

'And those who can't?'

'Manipulate.'

'And who do you manipulate?'

'I sometimes wonder,' he said. 'I write reports mostly.'

'And will you write a report on me?'

'I'll probably be asked to give an opinion,' he said with a smile. 'You know what it will be. I admire you.'

Fans, I thought. But our elders are so sad: our important elders sadder. But I did not want to dwell on them. I wanted to spend. I'd cashed a cheque before we left. Now I wanted to shop. It occurred to me, I'd never had a father to take me shopping, a little more of this, my dear, a little more of that. I wanted to indulge myself; be indulged. Fun things, I thought. That was what I wanted.

We'd met in this Spanish restaurant behind Swan and Edgar's. There was an indoor patio, a glass roof, elderly Spanish waiters and a taped guitar. Then portly sherry men, heads together in the corner, and little bits of things on sticks to nibble. I was the only woman there.

I said, 'I must shop.'

'Why not?' Ifor said.

'Would you like to get something for your wife?'

'Heavens no. She'd suspect something.'

So it had come to that. Suddenly, I felt sorry for all the lies in other people's lives. You'd think somebody else caused them.

'Have you got any children, Ifor?'

'A boy', he said. 'He's just finishing at Oxford.'

'Bright?'

'Yes.'

I could see he didn't want to talk, but I couldn't think of anything else left to say. We'd dealt with education.

'D'you think mistresses improve the character?' I suddenly wanted to be bright and brittle.

'Depends.'

'On what?'

'Of their nature, they are impermanent,' he said.

'Everything's impermanent,' I said. He sounded like he

was going to do a Blue Book on the subject. 'Are you tired, by the way?'

'Tired? No,' he sounded surprised.

'I just wondered. You didn't sleep much after?'

He gave that wandering look around the restaurant again. Some men like to talk about it, but he didn't, I could see. I was struggling for conversation now. Again, he was self-conscious of his age. It was getting tiresome.

'Well, I must shop,' I said. 'Imperative.'

He didn't know what to say.

'You ought to see me shopping,' I said. 'I whizz through things.'

'And always get what you want?'

'Alas, yes,' I said. 'Until today. Inconsequentials today.'

I had the yen to do things I never did. Be extravagant. Waste. Forget. Squander. Perhaps it was having it outside the shop after all these years, perhaps it was just an aversion to that awful jargon in Belgravia, the distance from Walter, Rachel, home, all that. But I had it on me, the genie.

'A hatchet to the boats,' I said, getting literary for me.

Of course, he didn't understand.

'I'm going to burn them,' I said.

He looked alarmed. Did he see consequences for himself? I didn't have the heart to make him realise how unimportant he was. In a minute, he was going to say something cautionary and wise, but I could do with a day off.

He called the waiter and ordered. I didn't know much about Spanish food so I let him squire me again. I was enjoying it after years of Walter's glaring and arguing. He wouldn't be told, would do things like refuse to taste the wine, or demand fresh horseradish, and once he'd counted the sauté potatoes. It was so boring.

We went into the restaurant, a handsome tip and we were at a window, slightly raised above the other tables. *Gambas* for starters, then little bits of squid and garlic. I like picking, eating with my fingers. He ordered a sole for himself, I had a steak with special garnish, then loads of wine, dry and white. Pigging it up again, I thought to myself. Six months of this and nobody'd look at me. I saw strawberries and cream, tiny mountain strawberries. Delight, I thought. They served immense quantities, then he couldn't finish his, so I did. The way to my crotch is via the *à la carte*, I thought. I felt hilarious, wanted a big floppy hat, earrings that chimed. I passed the strawberries one by one behind my teeth and squeezed, playing with my saliva. It was like something out of the *William* books. '*Crumbs*,' I should be saying. 'Oh *crumbs...*'

But he enjoyed my eating. Good, he's enjoying something, I thought. I felt benevolent. After the brandy, he had a cigar. On my suggestion. If only I could bring him out a little. I wanted to get rid of his guilt and not have anything hanging over him. I was tipsy too, I suppose.

I said, earning my keep; 'The cigar suits you.'

'Affluence,' he said.

'No, fun. Isn't it fun to be mellow?'

He grinned. Suddenly he looked like a collier living it up after Twickenham, cigars and all. His worry deserted him.

'That's the stuff,' I said. 'Come shopping? I'll have

176

parcels. You know what London is, you can't leave a shoe lying around.'

For some reason, that set him off, the first time he came to London, the year of the General Strike, all that. The Welsh can't forget. Sometimes I think they prefer remembering to living. The latter they can't abide. But it made him happy, jawing away.

I gave him big eyes, rapt attention. How to get on with men! Listen, nod, squeeze, open, close, above all, eat. Nearly every man I met wanted me to be sorry for him eventually. Underneath anyway. Perhaps it was the stars, a collision of the planets, magic? I was Scorpio's child, somebody told me once. People threw themselves on my mercy. Magical for them. Magic, I thought. I would like to believe in reason *and* magic. Magic for weekends. Anything but sociology.

He was talking about Arthur Cook, whoever he was. Some devastating reply to this heckler who kept on shouting, 'Figures can't lie.' To which this Cook replied, 'Ah, but liars can figure.'

Ho ho, I thought. Scintillating stuff. But I smiled. Or giggled rather. You can never show your face.

When the time came to pay the bill, I stood up and then hurried him away in case he dwelt on it. Always the provider, I was rather pleased with myself at my capacity for extravagance with other people.

'Quick,' I said outside. 'We'll get a cab.'

'But...'

'You can't park without a nervous breakdown,' I said. 'Cab!' I hailed one.

177

Chelsea first. I went at it in a rush, dragging him with me, out of the cab, along the street, down this flight of steps into a boutique I knew. I sat him down and began to try things on. Mongolian stuff with fringes, fun furs, warmth without cruelty. It sounded like us, his ambitions for us. But when I found a sleep suit, he began to gasp. It was like a French farce, me parading, giving myself the eye as I tried things on, asking for his opinion. For some reason, he'd brought the trilby and I could see his fingernails slashing into it. The sleepsuit was a brown snakeskin print in shiny satin, totally whorish. I traipsed around the shop to let him look. Nobody else paid any attention.

'Well?' I said.

You should have seen his face. I thought he'd had angina.

'Well?' I said again.

But he made a show.

'As long as you've got an electric blanket,' he said.

That was brave.

He said he'd pay for it and I let him. What I didn't say was how shocked I was with the dirtiness of London. In these women's changing rooms, they strip off with the pull of a cord. I didn't realise nobody wore underclothes any more, a few didn't wash either. I felt very provincial. So in the end, I stopped the damage he was doing to his hat and cut it short. I'd this avocado maxi with the lace-up bust, the fun fur and the sleep suit. The moment I got on the train, they'd date, I knew, but I didn't care. I was in that mood. Foolish is as foolish does – is that it?

When we got back to the car, I could see he was exhausted. Feet, I thought. London always does that to the feet. Then I thought we'd take a hotel room and he could lie down or something. Simply that. But I knew that if I said it, it would offend him. So we were halfway out of London before he said he'd wanted to stay the weekend.

'Why didn't we?' I said.

So then we turned around again.

'Where did I want to stay?'

'Somewhere I'll never be able to go again,' I said. 'Somewhere special. I'll leave it to you.'

It wasn't that I was on the make, but I didn't see the point of not having fun. Perhaps for the first time in my life, I had the same need for gaiety that Walter had.

'By the river,' he said.

'No, not the river.' It sounded like that full moon the night before.

'I thought of Henley,' he said.

'Full of types,' I said. I'd been there.

'The centre then? The trouble is Americans.'

'I like Americans,' I said.

'D'you mean a suite?' he said.

Jesus, what an impression of me. 'I'll leave it to you, 'I said.

He got out of the car to phone then. In a minute, it would get sad again, I thought. Unless he kept on drinking. Walter used to say sometimes it was dangerous to stop drinking and he was right. A mood was like a note of music. You struck a chord once and it reverberated if you kept on striking it, otherwise it passed into nothingness. You either kept striking the same note, or you changed the tune.

'Well?' I said when he came back.

He looked really tired now.

'I've booked two rooms.'

'Two?' I said. Did he think I wouldn't let him sleep?

He didn't answer. Perhaps he did.

It was huge, glossy and swish, a staff of under-managers, black-suited Swiss, and an immense doorman, much bemedalled, who looked so important, he might have been the Morality Officer. Then, a reception desk as big as an air terminal. People kept coming and going. Checking out, they said. Father and daughter again, we made our way to our two rooms with the porter. I felt ashamed of my shabby little grip. Walter used it for taking flagons to the off-licence. Ifor had this expression on his face as if he were putting up with me, my purchases. Nobody flickered an eyelid, the Carlton Tower service. We were soon imprisoned upstairs like two refugees the Ministry were paying for.

Before it got sour, I said, 'I'm going to have a sleep. I'll give you my key.'

He couldn't understand why I wanted to give him the key.

'So that you can come in when you want?' I raised my eyebrows.

He looked at me blankly. It was as if I'd asked for money.

Alone, I thought I'd bath. I left a mess again, clothes trailing all over the floor. There was a radio and I switched it on, clicking the knob and finding a Schools Broadcast with my unerring instinct. So I put the radio off, ran the bath.

The silence of big hotels. Oppressive. Unbelonging. I had a feeling of being in transit. What was I doing here? The porter said ring Room Service if I want anything. I picked up the phone, ordered champagne. Everything I was doing was obvious, cheap and nasty, I thought. I picked up the phone again and cancelled it. The bath was still running. I looked out of the window at cold, unfamiliar London. Then I rang Room Service again. I would like a pot of tea, I said. The voice was dutifully attentive. It would be done. Suddenly, I didn't want to be on my own. There was too much time to think. I turned the taps off, let the bath run out, didn't bathe. Then I saw the first package, slipped into the sleep suit. When I looked into the mirror, I noticed my fingernails were dirty. I couldn't see anything else, just my dirty fingernails.

I began to cry for no reason at all. Just sat on the bed and cried. Why the hell did he have to get two separate rooms? There was a knock on the door, an Italian-looking boy with the tea. I nodded at the dressing table. He did not look at me, went out again. I'd have a cuppa, I thought. I did, and lay on the bed staring at a Hogarth print on the wall. People didn't change. They fluttered their puny little wings and stayed in the same position. I felt I was in prison myself.

When Ifor came in, it must have been an hour later, I'd fallen asleep. He was in a blue silk dressing gown. He wore a collar-attached shirt but had taken the collar off. The neck band was open showing a red mark where the stud had pressed against his neck. He sat on the end of the bed, playing ruefully with my foot, not saying anything. The collar stud upset me. I stared back at him as I would a stranger. He stopped playing with my foot.

Then he said, 'It's Walter, isn't it?'

'Not particularly,' I said. It wasn't just then.

'Care to tell me?'

'No,' I said.

'I thought we might try a show later,' he said.

'Might as well,' I said.

'Why don't you have a sleep?'

'I've had one.'

'You're not very easy to be with now,' he said.

'Everything comes and goes,' I said.

I couldn't make the effort, that was all. I didn't want to be on my own. I didn't want to be with him.

'I like the evening attire,' he said. He was trying his best.

I made a face.

'Let me see the dress,' he said.

I didn't say anything for a minute, then I stood up, slipped off the sleep suit, opened the package and took this maxi out. I knew he was watching me and that was part of his pleasure, but so what? He was getting precious little else. When I put it on, I left it unlaced to the button, another whore's rig.

'You like wearing clothes like that?'

'They're just clothes,' I said. The fun had gone out of everything. So we sat down and had more tea, and then I told him about Walter and me, everything exactly contrary to what I intended. He did his nodding, the wise old sage bit, then all the things about how capable I was. Very boring. He had a shrew of a wife himself, gin-lost now, all coffee mornings and bridge leagues, and they hadn't really a thing to say to each other. That was boring too. I sat there saying to myself, any minute now, he's going to tell me that she didn't understand him when he said:

'She doesn't understand me.'

'He must have seen me stare. I couldn't get over the fact that whatever was wrong with me, he was worse, a feeling of superiority that was quite unjustified, and yet I had it. For something to do, I stood up and did my parade in the clothes again. I could see him working himself up, but I stalled him.

'You know what you'll be like if you get yourself worked up now,' I said. 'You'll go to sleep in the theatre.'

I felt I'd been married to him for twenty years. And he looked grateful.

'Where would you like to go?' he said.

I thought he'd made a mess of the hotel so I looked up the paper and chose a Restoration comedy, rich and frothy, all bosoms and chat. I wore the fun fur to the theatre, and the maxi, and felt like something out of the British Home Stores, the way everybody else was dressed. Everything I set out not to be, I became, I thought. But when he got back up there in the bedroom, he was doting on me. He'd bought half a bottle of scotch (why *half*?) and the gleam was back in his eye.

I sat in the little armchair and stared at him hard. Surely, he couldn't want it all that badly, a man his age? And if he did, we'd had it once out of charity which he must have known. What next!

But he wanted to go on seeing me, he said.

I looked at his face, the peculiar colour of his cheeks caused by the tiny ruptured blood vessels, his old eyes, rather fine white eyebrows and thin lips. He was distinguished and tall, wasn't disgusting. He didn't make me shudder, any of the things you're supposed to feel. But he didn't get through to me as a human being.

What did he want?

'A friend,' he said.

Didn't he have any friends?

'Acquaintances.'

'People like you less as you get older,' he said.

I didn't see that.

It was a difficult thing to explain, but he had reached the age when he saw through everything, people's motives, vanities, pretensions. He was tired of it all.

He made a little speech standing up all the time as if he was addressing some education committee.

'Ifor,' I said when he finished, 'You're a scream. But you don't click with me all that much.'

The way I said it made me vaguely ashamed. Click, I thought. He must have an excellent degree.

He said he wanted to know me better.

'But why?' I said.

Perhaps he could help me.

I knew that I'd always have to earn a living and didn't see the harm in that, except it fitted in with the bad image I had of myself, greasing in the time-honoured way.

I shrugged my shoulders, said something about looking a gift horse in the mouth, and no more. He kissed me goodnight finally, a father's kiss, and went off lugging his bottle of scotch to his own room.

Perhaps he knew what he was doing, because the moment I got into the sleep suit, I didn't feel like sleeping, didn't see why I shouldn't have a drink, went in, and that was that again. We seemed fated to single beds, his bony hips and knees, the pyjama trousers with the stripe down them. This time he kept the watch on – I'd taken him by surprise – and I felt it cold against my skin. We'd finished then, and when I mentioned it, he took it off and held the face up for me to see.

'It's luminous,' he said proudly.

What can you do? Men are children.

He laid the bracelet across my chest and looked at the two of us as if we were all he had in the world.

I went to my room, half hoping I'd run into something menacing in the corridor, but no such luck. I'd helped myself to the scotch and slept easily, but in the morning, obvious of obvious, he'd strained a muscle in his back and couldn't even pick up his suitcase. He looked even greyer.

'Is it a disc?' I said.

But it was under his shoulder blade. I couldn't remember whether I'd thrown him about, and didn't like to ask. But I had to nurse him all the way home. We stopped for liniment at some chemist's and I rubbed it in his shoulder, laughing all the time.

'You'll have to get a roomier car,' I said. 'With infrared.'

But now he was grumpy and didn't say much.

Everything was slipping into the past. Disenchantment, I thought; I had it.

We didn't speak for miles and miles and I slept again. He woke me up when we passed the roadhouse where we'd been on the way up.

'You never saw the bridge and the little stream,' he said.

'No,' I said. I knew he'd think about it for weeks. Except for his pulled muscle, the entire weekend was like something out of the *Desert Song* for him, I was sure. He stopped outside the house and couldn't resist a romantic squeeze.

'Don't worry. I'll keep my mouth shut,' I said.

That pained him. Then we shook hands. He held his hand out and I couldn't ignore it.

'Thanks,' he said.

'Oh, Ifor...'

He was going to say something else, but I cut him short, picked up my grip and the parcels, and hurried away. I couldn't get in fast enough, and when I did, Rachel wouldn't speak to me. I'd missed a visiting day, the first. And it was a wife's place, all that. I didn't say anything but when I got to the hospital, the Sister asked me to come into her office, closed the door behind her.

He's dead, I thought. Dying. What a relief! Then I was nearly sick for thinking that. Walter always made a positive attack even when he wasn't there.

She said, 'I'm sure you won't be unduly alarmed. Your husband is having a little difficulty with the drugs.'

'Chemotherapy,' I said. I remembered.

'He's having to be de-sensitised to the streptomycin. The doctor thinks it will take a little time. There's no reason to be alarmed.'

'I'm not,' I said. 'Have the ophthalmic people seen his eye?'

'We're not expecting any improvement until he's had at least three months chemotherapy. If you would like to see the doctor?'

'It won't be necessary,' I said. 'I'm sure you'll do everything.'

A hard unconcerned bitch, I thought. She must be thinking that of me.

'Can I see him?'

'Certainly.'

'I won't disturb him?' I was hoping she'd say I would.

'He might be a little light-headed.'

I didn't say anything. Normal, I thought.

And he was asleep, lying there, his mouth open, dribbling. I hadn't brought him anything because I came out of the house in a temper with Rachel and myself, so I sat down beside the bed and looked at him. No privacy, the relatives of other patients glancing over. Without quite knowing why, I straightened the counterpane. My husband, I thought. I knew I wouldn't tell him. It would be like kicking a child in the face.

He didn't wake for twenty minutes. I opened his locker, tidied it, closed it again, ate a grape. Then I went over to the window, looked out. There were other patients strolling around the grounds with their relatives. There's always an atmosphere of hope in hospital. Little people hoping.

187

Forced smiles, jollity, gifts, hand-holding, embarrassed kisses. Everything in public. It depressed me.

When he awoke, he stared at me angrily. I sat down by the bed in time to prevent him shouting.

'Where've you been?'

I don't know how or why, but my confession came out like a child's blurted statement under threat.

'On the knock,' I said. 'Where d'you think?'

'You haven't...'

'The minute I got you in here,' I said. 'An Inspector of Schools. He's fifty-five, pulled a muscle in his shoulder, as a matter of fact. He was so embarrassed at the hotel, he had to say I was his daughter.'

He stared at me. 'Which hotel?'

'The Carlton Tower,' I said. 'D'you know it?'

'Nothing but the best,' he said. Then, he grinned. His hair was curly and untidy, as endearing as a wink. I always wanted to stroke it and did so now. I could see he didn't believe me. What can you do but involve yourself more deeply? Things get worse, not better.

'The Wasserman Test was negative,' the Sister said when I left. Hoping I wouldn't understand and would have to ask, no doubt.

'Charming,' I said. 'Utterly charming.'

I sounded just like Walter. Hope is made of tinsel, hangs on Christmas trees.

CHAPTER SEVEN

IFOR

Of that period in her life, she later said she was in a state of drifting aimlessly. She did not see the point of things, she said. When I came along, she did not see the point of me either, or of herself saying yes, or no. I was someone who came into her life. Rather ridiculously. As Walter had temporarily gone out of it. Of course, she thought about him. As she did of me. But both of us should understand that we were not the be-all and end-all of her existence. There was no be-all and end-all of her existence. She did not tell him but I had to understand that.

She really was remarkable, I thought, after that weekend. She hurt, provoked, demanded. Her language was wounding. I did not remember meeting any one person who could hurt me so much in so short a space of time. And often in the language of the gutter. There was something fierce about her unhappiness, and like a fractious child she communicated it at will. Although part of her seemed to be saying, 'Leave me alone,' another part forced its attention on me. This part said, 'Here I am, take notice.' It was she who broke the age barrier between us by speaking to me as if I was her undesirable inferior. Perhaps that was sex. Whatever it was, I knew that I could not leave her alone. The only attractive thing about my world is the young, and their reaction to us I find to be wholly commendable. I was a traitor to my age group because I did not admire us, and was quite content to play second fiddle to her. There comes a time in your life when you are quite happy to 'string along', in their phrase. In the weeks that followed, I thought I would adopt this role.

The fact was, I thought her beautiful. If she saw me as seedy, I saw the reverse when I looked at her. The conception of romantic love is quite out of fashion, and if I had mentioned it, she would have laughed in my face. She did that enough as it was, but whenever I saw her, she aroused feelings in me that I had not known for years. Words are inadequate things, and since I often wrote as many as five thousand in a day ('You think in bloody paragraphs,' she once said,) I was always at a loss in knowing how to describe her to myself when I was not with her. Her plumpness was intoxicating. She was tall enough to carry it off, I said. (She laughed as if I were a gossip columnist.) Her eyes were frank and inviting, I said. ('Enclose a stamped addressed envelope for a confidential reply,' she told me.) She had wonderful peach colouring, a ripeness about her that belied her childlessness, and a way of looking open-mouthed, her sensual lips wet and rueful when they were not twisted with scorn. She moved quickly when she wanted to, with absolute confidence, and had the habit of looking people up and down as if summing them up instantly, and always herself giving the impression of being a physical girl who knew what she wanted.

I was sorry for my inadequacies. I had a vain hope I would learn, but more than that, I wanted to be with her, an overpowering urge just to see her that was quite ridiculous in a man my age, but within a few weeks I knew that it was probably the last such urge I would ever have in my life. I never told her that, but at the root of my behaviour was the consciousness of last things which the young never understand. A man has to learn to age and I did not want to yet. In front of the path to the grave, what is selfishness and foolishness? I lacked so much and the most joyous thing in my life was my feeling for her. It was not inflamed then, as it would be, but I hid my consciousness of her away in my mind like an old man will treasure a precious stone. I asked nobody to sympathise, nobody to understand. If I was sly, it was because I had to be. In any kind of love affair, no matter how eccentric or how distasteful to outsiders, what one is doing is escaping from oneself, casting off old skins and starting again, oblivious to the debris of other selves.

But first things first. I remember I did not write to Gordon on the Sunday following, as I said I would. Nor the following week. Hilda noted my dilatoriness, stored the omission away in that part of her mind which she still reserved for me. Later, it became one of those recalled incidents which, as she said, should have told her. As if it was the first bruise in the matrimonial apple. I did not see Constance for some weeks afterwards, but when I did, she was pleased to see me. I began to take her to see Walter on visiting days, and sometimes we went on down the coast to a hotel for tea. I did not forget that she had twice come to me uninvited. I treasured that memory. For a month, we had no sexual connection and felt free as a consequence. But after a month, I wanted to see her more often. There had already been warnings of an envious world simmering outside us, but I'd ignored them. One day I mentioned her capabilities in the Office. She'd resigned from the Panel and somebody'd asked why. I said her husband was ill. There was an opportunity to discuss her and I seized on it.

'She radiates warmth,' I said. 'She is tolerant and accepting and immensely practical. If the occasion arises, I shall have no hesitation in recommending her for a more responsible appointment.'

Geraint Rees (Science) raised an eyebrow when I was talking. He is a colleague of my own age and equal seniority. Perhaps I enthused too much. I did it so rarely. Later, I overheard him talking to a junior. I hardly think 'shitting on your own doorstep' is a phrase to commend itself to a Ministry official. But I knew he was sounding a warning note. Which I ignored.

When I told her, she laughed. We had become very affectionate. There were times when we could laugh together at other people.

'They think I'm your bit of stuff,' she said.

'I'm afraid so.'

'And they're jealous.'

'Indubitably,' I said. It was the sort of word which she expected to come from me and I used it deliberately.

She laughed again. She was eating sardines on toast in a seaside hotel which stayed open for the winter. She retained her prodigious appetite.

'And what will you do?' she said. We had been walking by the sea and she had a high colour. Walter was improving and being prepared for surgery. He was putting on weight and getting excited about it, she'd reported. It put us all in a good mood.

'I shall do nothing I don't want to do.'

'Well done, Ifor,' she said. 'Do Inspectors get hauled over the coals, then?'

'Sometimes.'

'Then you'll have to give me up.'

'I couldn't do that.'

'I don't think I could now,' she said. 'You've become a habit.'

'And transport,' I said. 'There's always that.'

At first, my waiting outside the hospital when she visited Walter increased her guilt. There was something seedy about it, she said. But when our meetings became innocuous, she was reassured. I was useful to her. She liked my company. She had a need to get out of the house. I fulfilled that need. We did not touch each other. It was as if the physical happenings of that weekend were regretted, connections that we had made in spite of ourselves. We did not speak to each other in that wounding way. We had come together too quickly, had recoiled, and now were getting to know each other again.

Now we were civilised, she said, and the relationship was adult.

But for my part, I soon knew that I was doing what she wanted in order to go on seeing her. I doubt whether a man can say at what point his obsession started, any more than a man can look at his life in retrospect and pinpoint the moment in time when his future was settled. We become what we are, in a sense, and all the accidents of fate have as much effect upon us as our conscious decisions. Because of my age, she wanted to believe I was wise. I knew I was not. Age may enable you to select the things which people most want to hear. It frees you from the heat of the moment. It enables you to hold back, to wait with more patience, but in my case, the way I spoke and the things I said, were the mask of wisdom, not the substance. I wanted her as fiercely and passionately as I had ever wanted any woman. Where she was concerned, I did not believe in folly. Every moment I spent with her, convinced me of the futility of my life. I looked back at it, and it disgusted me. I had done so many conventional things. I had no lasting satisfactions. I was the guilty party in my own marriage, but my guilt had worn thin. However badly you behave you get used to yourself. More than anything, I had lacked the power of decision, the courage to free myself from what had become distasteful. I had told myself that I did not want to hurt people for so long that my passivity had become totally hurtful. All my compromises led to the diminution of myself and those close to me. If she taught me anything, it was to see the dishonesties of so much of my life, and the cowardice of the rest. A man can become a cipher, a piece of flotsam, almost without his knowing. And he has only himself to blame.

Telling her about myself was like shedding a great load. There are some who talk about themselves easily. Talk is cheap in Wales. We have a gift for it, the speciality of all impoverished peoples, but I was the exception, perhaps because I had done so much in my life to disguise my origins, and cloak my real feelings. If there is one thing that Englishmen of my generation hate, it is feeling, the expression of any unacceptable emotion by their standards. Learning to live with them, attempting to become acceptable to them, had cost me dearly when I was a young man, but now without quite realising it, she made me see that the seeds of my inadequacies were rooted in my lack of courage years ago. Everything has a beginning, even dismay. It was my good luck that meeting her was the beginning of a new awareness of myself. Her directness startled me at first, then took on the role of the surgeon's knife. She was no respecter of persons, and free of that awful Welsh trait of ingratiation which I encountered daily. In a curious way, it was as if I had come the full circle to re-encounter in her the directness of the *werin*, that valley sharpness, the same truculence and insolence of the colliers I remembered as a boy. She affected to despise sociology and professed a total indifference to things Welsh. She could not understand that I was the pip squeezed from the orange, the product of both, victim and assassin.

One day we were talking about families. Soon after her father died, her mother married a Polish newsagent, an immigrant who had prospered and by whom she had other children. The family was scandalised. From being doted upon as a small child, Connie found she had to make readjustments. Then the shock of her mother's pregnancy, and of being handled by this foreign stranger, coincided with the failure of the business. Her mother had made a dreadful mistake. So she abandoned her mother.

Speaking of it, she told me that no matter how the situation was described, the feeling of standing unwanted in a state of trauma while her mother's world appeared to be collapsing around the hearth was a unique feeling from which she had never fully recovered. All the descriptions in the world, no matter in what scientific terms they were couched, did not alter the intensity of the feeling and its effect upon her. If she could think of any comparison, it was like being burnt, slowly and deliberately exposed to fire, and ever after she had a nose for such situations, a sense of them, which was one of the reasons she could detect this feeling of hurt in children. She never verbalised about them, she said. She wouldn't dare to intrude, but having sensed their hurt, she made allowances. It was as if there was some parallel scent of charred flesh which victims of parental disharmony carried with them and which she could recognise because she had had an experience of similar intensity.

There was no substitute for it, she repeated, and all the difference in the world between the idea of it, and the reality. It was one of the things which drew her to Walter and she called it a mark of living, the bruise of the world's unhappiness.

I said it was a romantic conception; it explained her compassion and capability, but limited it. Then she got angry.

'You're so smooth, aren't you?' she said.

'No,' I said. 'But you're only talking about one layer of experience.'

'Mine,' she said. 'Mine and Walter's.'

'It's one area of experience,' I said clumsily.

'That's what I mean, you're like all the rest of them, a describer.'

'I have to describe,' I said.

'Not to me, you don't.'

We were talking in a bar again, tucked away in the corner of a pub I knew where there was a coal fire and where we were left alone. The heat in the room flushed her cheeks. She wore her hair long and it hung loosely about her shoulders. Her chin was stuck forward aggressively and her eyes were narrowed. Everything had been so cosy, now she was suddenly hating me because I had contradicted her. I did not say anything for a moment. I wanted to tell her so much and did not know how to begin. She was excluding me from any possibility of experience and it was ridiculous. People dismiss you because of what they see and what they imagine, not what they know. One carries a certain image. The world takes it for one's real self, and in most cases, does one an injustice.

'One...' I began to say.

She swore again, turned her head away impatiently.

197

'What's the matter?'

'One!' she said contemptuously. 'There you go again. One!'

I didn't understand.

'I'm talking about me,' she said. 'Me! Me! Me! Not one...'

'I...' I began to say.

'That's better, What makes you bleed, Ifor?'

'That's what I'm trying to explain,' I said. 'It's not any one thing, or even two things. Everybody doesn't have one traumatic experience.'

'Traumatic,' she said contemptuously. 'You can't get off your horse, can you? I said, what makes you *bleed*?'

I didn't answer for a minute. I was nervous of saying the wrong thing. She was so impatient and contemptuous. She looked as if she might leave at any moment. The landlord came in behind the bar to see if we needed anything and I shook my head nervously. When he went away, I still didn't say anything. It was as if my whole life was being put on trial.

I couldn't be detached or amused, or pass her off with a witticism. She couldn't stand a trite answer. She liked acting frivolously on occasions, but she seldom spoke frivolously. I had to remember that every time I saw her, she came to me from a direct contact with Walter's suffering. It made me conscious of being a bystander in her life and I already knew that my feeling for her was much more than that, even if it was not reciprocated. Feelings seldom are, I have found, and while in one sense I despised my carefulness, in another I knew that I had to calculate. People think of the lecherous, bald-headed seducer, not the man who has to ration glimpses of himself in order to fulfil his need. The one is cunning, the other careful. I was learning all this and behaving accordingly, but at the same time, experiencing a wild sea of feelings such as I could not remember encountering for years. And now she was taunting me because of my guard, my care. When she spoke about herself standing forlorn in the face of her mother's difficulties, it was natural that I should take the mother's part. Whatever the child felt, the mother had an obligation to herself. What about her traumas? That things hadn't worked out, that her Aunt had removed the child from the situation, may have solved Connie's difficulties, but it was naive and selfish to suppose that it did not create others. Nothing is simple, and in a family, no one action is ever isolated or free of consequences for all its members. But I knew that everything I would have to say on the subject was a commonplace and would offend her.

I said eventually, 'Cowardice makes me bleed. My own.'

I think she was startled.

'My naivety,' I said. 'The innocence of me, my lack of the things you have, your directness, honesty, your reaction to pain. In short, the dreadful amoeba-like quality of me, that's my disgrace.'

When one speaks the truth, a truth that has been forced out of one, there must be an extra edge to the voice, a tautening of vocal chords long trained in the presentation of platitudes that communicates a new image at once.

'Christ,' she said. 'That must have cost you something.'

'I don't think I'm altogether beyond redemption,' I began to say.

'Oh, don't get bland,' she interrupted. 'Tell me.'

'Tell you what?'

'How you've discovered you're so oily.'

My reaction was to smile. She was having her effect on me daily. The next time I had to give a lecture to some dragooned schoolmasters, I would probably begin, 'Frankness is a relief.' And in my mind, see a picture of her sitting as she was now, her mini skirt and net stockings, a familiar reminder of her youth, all deliciously increasing my discomfort. No doubt the picture of her would vanish the moment I consulted my notes, or some Ministry brochure, but I was a different man through knowing her even so. When I began to answer, an answer that must have taken weeks in the telling, I knew that I was fighting for a handhold on her life, that was how serious it was to me.

'It's a process,' I said. 'And it needs a trigger. You're the trigger.'

She saw me looking at her and smiled.

'Well?'

'Where do I start?'

'At the beginning. Sex,' she said. 'How about that?'

Like all her generation, she was frankly curious about sex and quite uninhibited. It was very difficult to explain my inhibitions, and even more difficult to convince her of its lack of importance by comparison with all the other events and attitudes that carry one forward to where one is at any precise time.

I said, 'That's Chapter Two.'

She grinned, 'But he gets it in the end?'

'Now you're being smart,' I said. 'And trite.'

'You tell me,' she said coolly.

She didn't think she was being anything other than normal and somewhat wry. I tried to explain that in one's life, there is not necessarily any one single happening which stands out as a watershed, but rather a process, a multiplicity of happenings, the simple fact of geography and the circumstances of one's birth. She had no conception of what it was like to be a scholarship boy, or even to stand out amongst one's fellows at an early age because one had won some small approval from adults outside the home.

'You've got to see me in a sailor suit,' I said. 'Standing in a Board School hall and being praised for my handwriting.'

'Your handwriting?' she was incredulous.

'It's still immaculate,' I said. 'A Sunday School teacher taught me an exact copperplate. To this day, I am asked to inscribe presentation cards to colleagues.'

She began to laugh. 'Copying,' she said.

'Yes,' I said ruefully. She had hit the nail on the head.

If only the young knew what absurdities we had come through. We tended to dwell on the economic hardships, measurable statistics of deprivation, numbers of unemployed and duration of unemployment. We had calories on the brain. What was never realised were the attitudes we had to reject, the pressures of long-dead opinions and mores which survived and hurt long after they had ceased to be expressed. I had escaped the jingoism of the first war, but the dead hand of Welsh nonconformity lasted much longer and shaped my boyhood.

'You should see me in a blue suit,' I said, 'the trousers serge and shiny, my face scrubbed and beaming as I signed the pledge, a little gold medal with the face of Thomas Charles of Bala resplendent on the lapel, and the conviction stamped in my mind that I had only to be respectful to my betters to get on in the world.'

She laughed again. I doubted if anyone could see me like that, but like that I had been.

'And in school, I sat next to a poor boy who wore his sister's shoes and whose only ambition was never to be late, never to be absent, even if he had to put garlic in his socks to stop him whooping when he had whooping cough. He had an overriding ambition. After four years of this meritorious behaviour, he might, if he had not missed a day, nor been late or insolent or surly or unobliging, win the most coveted prize, a pair of working boots with hob nails and steel tips, the envy of his school mates.'

She looked bored. But I couldn't escape this memory. That's what separates us, I thought: memory. I dwelt on it.

'I carried a blotter with me to school, my own,' I said. 'And a pen wiper, my own store of nibs. If I was sent on a message, I ran all the way. When I passed a scholarship to the County School, I was stood up in the pulpit in chapel as an example to others. There was even a pious hope I might go into the Ministry.'

'And then?' she said.

'I had a blazer and a cap and a schoolbag in which I carried my books which were wrapped in thick brown paper so as to be able to hand them over at the end of the year in the condition in which I received them.'

'Oh Ifor,' she said. 'You're hopeless.'

'Exactly,' I said.

'You were a swot.'

'The prince of swots. To this day, my mind is full of useless information. "Chicago is the second city of the United States in commerce and manufacture and has a population of roughly two million, seven hundred thousand, and is a meat-packing town," I said breathlessly.

She did not laugh.

'When did you begin to think?'

'Yesterday,' I said. 'Perhaps today, I hope tomorrow. Since I met you anyway.'

'You're a bloody fool,' she said.

'I have to be careful in what I say,' I said.

'You can't alter what you are.'

'Can any of us?'

'Perhaps,' she said. 'You don't answer questions, do you? All this Welsh whimsy.'

I thought about that, felt it to be unfair. Then I didn't. I began to be obsessed with the idea of explaining my life, and presenting it in such a way that she would understand what I meant by processes, the congealing of attitudes, until really, the idea that there are courses of action which you can choose is erroneous. The young do not understand about poverty, nor respectability, they have little idea of possessions being a part of you. They keep up with peculiar Joneses if at all; they have no conception of what it is like to worm one's way up a ladder like I had to, and not knowing that, they have equally no conception of the self-disgust that comes upon those for whom this course of action has become repugnant. They do not understand regret. They are only immediately sorry for themselves. I tried to think of ways which I could explain but it defeated me.

Then I went back on the past, trying to recall incidents which at this distance, I could say were meaningful. It was curious how so much of what had happened to me was entirely an educational matter, a depressing context.

'You're a walking stick of chalk,' she once said to me. 'You stink of it, Ifor. For Christ's sake, I'd rather the watch.'

She pulled my leg about that watch. I became so self-conscious I did not wear it when I met her. It had been Hilda's father's bequest to me.

At another time, I was trying to explain Oxford, the fact that my father's branch of the NUM, his lodge, had given me a suit of clothes and an overcoat. I was by then the local boy made good. I could assimilate information, I saw relationships between things, and I could regurgitate, later argue for and against this case or that. But as soon as I got to Oxford, I found that I had a third-class mind. And I had neither the appetite nor funds to socialise, preferring to keep myself to myself, or remain in the exclusive company of one or two others like me who never really fitted in. If there was one thing which I had to do, it was to come away with a good degree, and I did not do that, although fortunately there were few who understood the niceties at home. When I took teacher's training in another university, it was with the sinking feeling that perhaps all my efforts would have been cheaper for my family if I had gone to a provincial university. They were pleased enough that I was out of the pit, would always have a white collar job and a pension, and in those days, to be free of wages and receive a salary was a golden accomplishment. Do that, and you had done well.

'Ifor, it's so boring,' she said when I attempted to tell her.

'I know,' I said. 'And it was five years of my life.'

'Well, didn't you get a bit then? You know? Up the backs? Is it the backs? On the river or whatever it is. In a punt, is it? May Ball,' she said. 'I've heard of those.'

'No,' I said. 'I never socialised. I couldn't really afford it, and I didn't want to.'

'What? – Live it up?'

'No. I didn't have a penny to spare.'

'But you must have had a fingerful of some woman?'

'No,' I said. 'I was a virgin when I was married.'

'Oh, Christ!'

Now she looked at me as an object of genuine compassion.

'Poor Ifor.'

'Yes,' I said.

'But didn't you feel girls, you know? Nearly get it in?'

'In the Army,' I began to say.

'But didn't you... in the Army?'

'No,' I said. 'They showed us a VD film. It frightened the life out of me.'

'But you were an officer?'

'I was dressed as an officer but underneath I was still me.'

'Poor you then,' she said, disapprovingly.

'Are you any better off?'

'I don't suppose,' she said, 'but I was never as thick as that.'

'It's very hard when two worlds collide,' I said.

'Collide?' she said scornfully. 'Who's colliding?'

I was silent, fearful of saying anything for a moment.

Then she said. 'How d'you get on in the Inspectorate then?'

'The Civil Service is the same as the Army,' I said. 'The most acceptable Welshman is still the most presentable imitation of his English counterpart.'

'By keeping your mouth shut?' she said.

'By being relatively harmless, yes. We are all of us tea cosies.'

'Pooh,' she screwed up her face. 'There's not a man in my life that's a compliment to me.'

'You must attract us.'

'You can say that again.'

'Still,' I said. 'Such as we are, here we are.'

'Yes,' she said. Her unhappiness was immense. 'Oh, us.'

I had never any conception of what she was thinking. Men inflate themselves to impress women, I had thought, but her experience was quite contrary. They fell on her mercy, she said, one hand extended for comfort, the other reaching for the trouser fly. It was a fact of her life which depressed her. She said she yearned to be chatted up. I said I would do my best.

'Don't bother,' she said. She groaned, but then sensing my discomfiture, held my hand, a simple spontaneous gesture that delighted me. We had neither of us mentioned my son and I was grateful for her silence on that score. A man does not fail in one direction but many.

We had other immediate worries. Her Aunt had taken a dislike to me, objected to my calling at the house.

'She says people will talk,' Connie said.

'They are already talking,' I said. I remembered Geraint Rees (Science). We had been lucky so far in not being seen, but our luck could not hold out.

'It's not that I care about people, but I don't want her getting into a state,' Connie said.

'Do you think she suspects anything?'

'What is there to suspect?' Connie said. 'She just doesn't like you coming to the house.'

I was used to people disliking me.

'You must have the eye,' Connie said wickedly. 'And she says she's surprised at you. A man like you must have a position to keep up.'

I laughed. 'I suppose I have.' That I had recently returned from a journey of nearly two hundred miles to count the number of infants' toilets in a remote North Wales primary school in response to some question in the House did not inflate my ego. Whatever I was called, I did a clerk's job.

But I quite liked her Aunt.

'I don't suppose she has any idea of why I like being with you?' I said foolishly.

'Oh, yes she has,' Connie said. And she made a face. 'Ychafi.'

I think that solitary word of disgust depressed me more than any other she had spoken. I swallowed hard. It was as if it had come back down the years, an expression of disapproval such as my mother might have used, but for others, not myself. It caused quite disproportionate feelings of resentment in me. But it was how others would always see us, I thought. There would always be something grubby in their minds when they looked at us. Perhaps it was her youth and my age, the years between us, and our marriages. No doubt her Aunt would have her stand by Walter's bed like one of those praying women in the Sunday School bible class engravings of my youth. For some people, nothing ever happened in the world. They were bound by the conventions as certainly as I had been. And such wretched conventions too! They certainly wouldn't understand how she freed me of them, and made me look at myself again. If I had any chance it was with her, I thought, and I could be sure everything and everybody would get in the way unless I was indifferent to them. And ruthless too. Of course, at this time she had no idea of the intensity of my feeling. I kept it hidden. But the idea of not being able to call at the house was repugnant to me and I said so.

'Well, you can hardly blame her,' Connie said. She sounded abstracted as if my confessions had driven her off into a separate part of her mind where I did not exist. If you bored people, they escaped somehow or other.

'Why not?'

'Well, it is unusual.'

'To have friends?'

'An elderly friend,' she said with a smile. 'You know what people are like. It's your little bit of gristle they're thinking about.'

I flushed. She hadn't spoken like this for weeks.

'And Walter,' she said before I could say anything.

'I know that, but surely your Aunt has no idea?'

'People who've never had it, never want other people to have it.'

I did not want to pursue the matter. 'Am I going to meet you on the road in future?'

She shrugged her shoulders; 'If you like.' She lit a cigarette, inhaled and blew the smoke down her nostrils, studying me coolly.

I wanted to hurt her for that. But I had to say, 'I'm sure you don't care tuppence whether you ever see me again.'

She looked in her purse insolently.

'I haven't got any change at the moment.'

I looked away. 'Don't,' I said, wounded.

'What?'

'Be like that.'

'Like what?'

'Cheap and unfeeling.'

'Oh Ifor, you're a strain.'

'Don't see me again then – ever.'

'I didn't say anything,' she pouted. 'Why get annoyed?'

'You know,' I said. Every love affair has in it the elements of a reversion to the adolescence in which we learned to feel and took our tiny steps in caring for someone else. Most of us don't progress much, I thought.

'If you want to know, I was thinking of Walter,' she said.

'It occurred to me that if you ever met him, you'd get on like a house on fire.'

'You don't really know what I'm like.'

'Oh, yes, I do. You'd have to buy a car off him or something first, but once you broke the ice, you'd be a right pair.

'A pair?'

'Of grousers,' she smiled tartly.

'Thanks,' I said. I saw myself in the sailor suit and scrubbed collar again, scorned by the collier lads. I had a browning photograph of me like that somewhere. The seeds of what I was at that moment were contained in the photograph of that eager little boy.

She leant forward and put her hand on my knee. 'Don't you see?' she said. 'I think it's funny, the resemblance. Women are supposed to be seduced by hearty types in blazers, or footballers, or drummers or something. But not me, and that's what I can't get over. With me, it's always necessary to have a bin to pick up the pieces.'

'You imagine it,' I said.

'You have a short memory,' she said cuttingly.

'Well, it's because you want to then,' I said. 'People do what they want ultimately.'

'Is that so?'

'Yes, it is,' I said, irritated.

'You're not going to get all profound on me again, are you?' she said. Now she sat well away. This night she wore a black leather coat. I think it was called the wet look. The lapels parted revealing her breasts, so firm and youthful. I wanted to hold them both in my hands and shake her. And she knew it. She crossed her legs defiantly. Everything you desire, you dislike at some time or another. Now was the time for dislike. She tossed the cigarette into the firegrate.

'I'll tell you what then,' she said flatly. 'Why don't you invite me back to meet your wife?'

'No,' I said at once.

'Has she had a breakdown or something?'

'She wouldn't want to be disturbed.'

'Because she doesn't understand you?'

'That's a cliché.'

'You said it first, Ifor.'

'It would be quite improper,' I said without thinking.

From insolence, her expression changed to scorn: 'You sound about two hundred and fifty!'

I began a series of awful jokes, anything to cover my embarrassment and dismay.

'Methuselah never let his wives mix,' I said.

'Wives?'

'Women,' I said.

She moved her hand to reach her purse again but I caught it and held it, squeezing her.

'Don't,' I pleaded. 'Please... How did we start on this?'

She withdrew her hand and as she did so I saw the skin white where I had gripped her.

'Gristle again, is it?'

'And nothing else?' I said desperately. 'Nothing at all?'

'You're getting intense, Ifor.'

'Yes,' I said. She hadn't answered, I noted. It was as if all I had said was in vain. Sexuality and nothing else mattered.

'Well, don't,' she warned me. 'Just don't.'

I did not say anything for a moment but when I finished my drink and took her to the car, there was the same distance between us. She walked a little away from me, taking care that no part of our bodies should touch. I wanted her now but was too angry to say anything and I couldn't touch her. She sat apart from me, crossed her legs tightly, the threads of her tights making the tiniest sound as her flesh ground the nylon together. Then she did up her coat, buttoning it deliberately and pulled her coat collar up. I wanted to tear the buttons loose, but I did not. I did nothing, put the key in the ignition and reversed the car, scraping the wing in the process. She looked around alarmed but I did not stop, drove straight out on to the main road. I had been drinking scotch and had taken more than the legally prescribed amount, something I rarely did, but now I did not care. It was intolerable that my feelings should induce such humiliations. I sensed her body taut under her clothes, saw her eyes staring ahead from the corner of my own eye. I wanted her, tart or not.

Then I calmed for a moment and concentrated on the driving. It occurred to me that I had once accused Hilda of never being able to play the whore, an essential in every woman's marital armoury. Poor Hilda. But it was more than that. At one level, part of me wanted a deeper, fuller, richer understanding with a warm and vibrant human being; at another, my desire was sudden and violent, ultimately destructive. But I would never have such a desire again, I thought. Never! And then I smiled, attempting the calmness which I thought she expected. But she soon destroyed that.

'I know what it is,' she said as we drove.

'What?'

'You're getting the itch again.'

'I refuse to discuss my feeling in these terms,' I said at once.

'Platonic friendship,' she said scornfully. 'I wouldn't be surprised if you had a hard-on.'

'I will not come down to that level.'

I could see her examining me curiously. Then she smiled. 'My Aunt's quite right,' she said in a different tone. Now she was teasing. 'You look so fit, that's the trouble.'

'I play squash,' I said stiffly.

Then we did not say anything for a mile or two. Had I ever met a man who did not respond to compliments, I wondered? So I purposefully said nothing.

'You're not sulking, are you?'

'No.'

'Oh, good.'

'Why?' I said.

'I was wondering something. D'you know anything about the Revival?'

'The what?'

'The Welsh Revival.'

'Of course,' I said testily as if it were a question suddenly put to me by the Welsh Joint Education Board. 'Certainly.'

'My Aunt reckons the Ministers would work these girls

213

up with their conviction of sin – all that, then the local lads would lie in wait for them on the way home.'

'Nonsense.'

'Yes, they'd have their drawers down quick as you like. Just imagine all that thick rough flannel against your skin.'

Bitch, I thought. 'I don't believe it,' I said.

'It would be nice to think so.'

'Your Aunt has a vivid imagination and if you think you're teasing me, you're not.'

'Aren't I?'

'No.'

Silence again. Again, I did not break it.

Then she said, 'It's not easy for me either.'

I put my foot on the brake and stopped the car. She looked at me startled as if I were going to turn her out. Then I said it all.

'The curious thing is that everything about us is stunted and warped. Our failures are accretions which cling to us physically, but we have to shrug them off. We have to find what feeling there is between us and declare it bluntly. And we have to act on the strength of our feeling. We have to be eloquent and bold and never mind being thought ridiculous. We have to throw caution to the winds and marvel that any one human being can affect us so and pursue it to the end, this feeling. How else can I reveal what an abject failure I am without knowing that in the very act of telling you, I'm dismissing it? For myself anyway. D'you think I tell you so that you can pick at it and sneer like a dog a bone? Well, do you?'

She stared at me and did not say anything for a long

time. Her eyes were small and bright in the darkness. She did not take them from mine. A car hooted as it went past, then another long silence.

Finally she spoke despairingly; 'You can't *will* things to happen, Ifor.'

'I don't have to.'

Again, she was silent.

'Perhaps it's better if you say nothing,' I said dismally, but she caught my hand, held it. 'It's not as if I don't know why you're silent.'

She looked away but still kept hold of my hand. The silence was oppressive, more than it had ever been, as wretched as my fumbling overtures and her destruction of me in that motel. I always blundered, I thought, always. When should you declare yourself? How much should you expose? If she said anything risqué now, I would hit her. But she did not. She said nothing.

'Excuse me,' I said, and withdrew my hand. I started the car again and drove her home, stopping on the hill below the house. As a matter of habit, I got out of the car first and went round to open the door for her. She got out slowly, awkwardly, then hesitated, looking at me gravely, and suddenly came close to my face, put her arms around my neck and kissed me sloppily, her face wet with tears.

'Connie.' I said.

'Saturday,' she replied.

I held her roughly, conscious even then of the incongruity of me kissing a girl on the street and how it would look to other people. But I held her just the same. A month ago I would have dropped my arms and looked shiftily around. I said, 'I can't talk to you in public places.'

She examined my face carefully: 'All right.'

Then she turned and hurried up the hill. She looked suddenly smaller than she really was, small, ungainly and common, I thought. But mine.

Joyous clichés came flooding through my mind as I drove home. There's no fool like an old fool, I said to myself. And in my mind, I recalled an admonitory phrase of my school days, grave words spoken to crop-headed transgressors isolated on the platform of the assembly hall. 'You are heading for serious trouble.'

If Geraint Rees (Science) ever said anything again in my hearing in the Office, I would tell him very quietly and calmly to fuck off, a phrase I had never publicly used in fifty-five years of life.

'Saturday,' I repeated over and over again. 'And Saturday is just the beginning.'

CHAPTER EIGHT

RACHEL

I watched her get out of the car, what she did in the street, heard the door click downstairs; a nice picture, I must say. I thought for a moment before I went downstairs as I knew I had to. One or two observations...

They think we know nothing, people my age. We are dismissed as so much chaff. Mostly, they lower their voices or raise them when they talk to us, or put on false smiles as if they are talking to the mentally deficient, the *twp* as we say in Welsh. Three halfpence short of a shilling, you'd think, not all square. Either that, or we are too old to understand. Indeed, I do not understand the pace of things, all this rush, but the ungodliness of people is no surprise to me, or their nastiness. But to hear them go on, you'd think they'd invented folly. The problem is, how to get through to people, as they say. The most important things in this life are giving and caring, and those who are denied the opportunity have my sympathy more than any others. But to get it across? You can only try and even as you try, memories haunt you.

But try, I did.

She was in bed by the time I got down. I have always had access to their flat, a mistake perhaps.

'I want to talk to you,' I said. In this room, she had brought Walter first when it was my downstairs sitting room. Then he came again and again, a different car every month, making remarks that were quite impertinent in the hearing of a woman my age.

'I'd rather you didn't say anything,' she said now.

'But I'm going to just the same,' I said.

I sat down uninvited. There was a light still on by the bed. It showed the strain on her face. There was strain there that day too, the day Walter came. Walter Thingammebob, I used to say, the Rodney. He was like the wind, spent every whipstitch as if money burned in his pocket. But one thing I noticed, he was straight with money even if he didn't have it long, always leaving coppers if he used the phone, unlike some she'd brought previously who'd ring London long distance without so much as by your leave. And he had a nice way with him too, gentle. He thought me a dragon but I put a face on for him. If he had quite a wrong impression of me, it was me holding back. The truth was I didn't mind his nonsense, like trying to marry me off to some publican in Tintern Abbey where he took us to have a salmon tea in one of his cars, the draughts going down my neck like billyho. Very nice, but tinned, it turned out, because of the pollution in the water. The point was, he was *giving*, not *taking*, that day.

I thought of his face now as I looked at her avoiding my eyes. No great catch, I thought when I first saw him, but then I'd thought that myself of another, long ago. There was all the difference between Walter's face and the one she'd just left, this Inspector. I knew what was going on in his mind the moment I saw him, that twist about his mouth, the sideways flicker of his lazy eyelids. Despite his Welsh chat, they told me more about him than if I had read a book about him written by himself. Only one thing he wanted, and that to steal for his body in glorification of himself. It is the oldest story in the world, the older man and the younger woman, the one seeking what he has lost, the other finding out what is in front of her, any port in a storm. Soft, I call it, like all wishful thinking. They snatch at each other's bodies in the dark and think it is important.

Only, of course, I had to put it in my own way.

'Listen to me, please. A man of his age is only looking for a bouquet. A new bit of red for the old cockerel to disguise his strut.'

'Very funny,' she said.

'Not for me.'

'It's none of your business.'

'If you're living here, it's my business,' I said. Another mistake. Never remind people of their obligation to you. They can't forgive you. 'I suppose his wife has no objections? As half-soaked as the rest of them?'

'We haven't met,' she said.

'What about Walter?'

'Oh, Walter,' she said in the way she had begun to speak of him ever since he went to hospital. She picked up a magazine as if I were a stranger, or some old crone she'd met in the hairdresser's.

I felt my heart beating as I watched her. Ordinary people can do the most extraordinary harm to themselves and others. Had I done her harm? What if her real mother was here now? No wonder I could hear my heart beating. The consequences of your actions linger in your mind all through your life, lapping like waves through your consciousness. But steady now, I thought. I had to hold myself together.

She turned over the page of the magazine and went on reading.

I didn't want to speak, suddenly. I saw Walter's face again, his hands. When they held hands in the beginning, it used to turn me over inside. If they but knew, I was not seeing them, but myself, not in the same position but as near to it as I would ever get, standing waiting against the barrier in Cardiff Queen Street station when the boys went to France, the first time. Just them holding hands reminded me of the time my hands held another's in that way. It was years since I had thought about it, but seeing them brought it back, another wave going through time, and returning to me now.

The grandfather clock struck the hour upstairs. That Education man must be home now, lying to his wife. Then my thoughts went all of a jumble. Once, I felt another hand in mine, I wanted to say, and then I knew with that intuition you have, that there's only one chance for some,

220

only one. I knew that, because once I had felt another's hand in mine. His name was Dafydd Rowlands, known ever after as Fusilier Dafydd Rowlands, and three other words, *died of wounds*. My secret, that hand of his. No more than the hand, of course. Shrapnel could rip his insides out in France but he was Mutt and Jeff put together when it came to moving his lips one foot towards mine. He never kissed me, alas, and the hand he gave to me was because he was no great catch either. (If that was what she was thinking about behind that magazine.) No great catch as I was no great catch, or Walter. But it was my hand he held, pressing it over the barricades at the station. Of all the crowd in khaki, he was the only one not smelling of drink, the only one who didn't smoke. And he had a farm too, and silly as it sounds, a way with sheep. He sat across from me in chapel, much too slight to be a farmer, too delicate he looked altogether, a slight stammer if the truth be known – no great catch. 'Give them a chance to get a word in, gel,' my father said many times, but it was my stare or my talking, or just the plain fact that I wasn't all the rage and never would be which did me in in that direction. I'm not entirely sure, and like my father said again, 'Face things you have to, gel.' And I have always faced them four square.

Except now. Another page turned. She was going to wear me out with her silence in that bed.

'You will learn to bleed for a hand that has touched yours,' I wanted to say. 'Yes, you will.' If the touch is right, fingers to fingers, the pressure of a wrist, the coarseness of that rough old khaki, wrist tendons straining

221

as you pull away. At the time, I was hoping that he wouldn't cry in front of the others, that they wouldn't put on him because he was so delicate. I had grown up with him in the same chapel, on the farm next to his farm, and up until the last war, there were hedges I could visit which he had trimmed with a bill-hook, branches that he had touched, his wrists making up for his size with their skills. He was local, a part of our past, our people. *Dafydd Rowlands, died of wounds, France.* Only the Shonis called him Dai. To me, he was full name always, and the other three words that they put on the memorial which I never visited, just the hedges until they pulled those down to make a council estate. My shy fusilier... The world was no better for his dying, nor people wiser.

They tell me I wander. I do not. I see too many things at the same time. And I had to say my piece.

'If you tell me I do not understand, you insult me,' I said. 'But you're not carrying on like that from this house.' My voice was frail when I meant it to be strong.

She put down the magazine.

'Don't upset yourself. There's nothing you can do.'

'I can shut the door.'

'It wouldn't make any difference.'

'But what d'you see in a man like that?'

'He needs me. It isn't as sordid as you think.'

'Ask his wife.'

'His wife isn't interested in him.'

'But Walter?'

'Sooner or later, Walter must stand on his own feet.'

'You mean, leave him? You will leave him, your husband?'

'Well, I'm not much good to him, am I?'

'You haven't looked after him.'

'He can't even look after himself. Oh, please, I don't want to talk about it. Some things have to be private,' she said. 'They have to be.'

'It's not having children,' I said. As if I didn't know, as if I hadn't wandered about like a broody hen upstairs ever since they had been living with me. 'That's the root of it, isn't it?' I put my finger on things.

'Not having any privacy is intolerable,' she said. Evading.

'Face it,' I said. 'Perhaps when he's better you might have something to show.'

'It's me,' she said. 'Can't you understand? Me...'

'You?' I stared at her. Her face was wrinkled and childish like a child's again, a dumpling complaining because she was fat years ago. 'I don't know what's the matter with the boys these days,' I said to comfort her then. 'In my day, they liked a good armful!' But, of course, I didn't know. Then as now. We can only do our best to understand.

I said, 'How can you know a thing like that without the doctors...'

'Doctors!' she said. 'I just know it.'

'Nonsense,' I said. 'Well, if it's true, then you must have second best. There are other people's children. Adopt.'

'I don't want second best.'

'Face things you have to,' I said. I seemed to have been saying that all my life.

'No,' she said. 'I don't want to.'

223

'Well, I've had to,' I said. 'And you're lucky. There's still Walter.'

'He's hopeless. Even he knows it,' she said.

'Well, you married him for hopeless. I should have thought a woman's place was to put him right. Before somebody else does.'

'I only wish they would.'

'For shame on you,' I said.

'Yes,' she said. 'And now will you please leave me alone.'

'No,' I said. 'I'm not the sort.'

'Look, I don't want to quarrel with everybody.'

'Did I ever tell you about my one hope?' I began to say.

'I couldn't stand any of your folk tales tonight,' she said.

'Because of what you've been doing, I've no doubt? You go on like this and you'll destroy yourself, and your marriage,' I said. 'This man...'

But she turned over to hide her face. A wasted journey.

'Do you want anything then?' I said. 'Shall I get you a glass of hot milk or something?'

She did not reply. Perhaps I had done too much of that, fetching and carrying.

'Well, I'll tell you flat once more,' I said. 'You leave home for that man again, and it's the last time. I'll live alone rather than put up with that.' I said my piece, cards on the table, me.

But that night, I did not sleep at all. It was a long night for me, I can tell you. I began to think of myself. Perhaps the root of the trouble was me, my need for her all those years ago. On the day I went to collect her, I knew in my heart that I was doing what I wanted to do. But was it the right thing? You can steal children from their parents, entice them away by your indulgence. Nothing could be easier, given the will and the means, and I had both to be sure. My niece, Betty, did not know what to do. Since she lost her husband, she was a changed person. The new one was no improvement, there was another child on the way and Constance stood there, a little *dwt*, clutching my apron. I was familiar, her new home was not. Nor her new father and she blamed her mother for him, his foreign voice and temper. Oh, it was a moment, I can tell you. We Welsh people are very emotional. The cleverest hide it, we have a mask for every occasion. Sometimes we do not even know why we do things ourselves. But now I asked myself, did I play on Connie's emotions and wean her to me so that I could indulge myself? Who was helping who? No wonder I did not sleep all night.

I went downstairs in the morning. I caught her just before she left for school.

'Perhaps I should have encouraged you to see your mother more often?' I said.

'Oh, that,' she said.

'You've got sisters you've never seen.'

'I hope they're not like me,' she said. She was eating cornflakes, as composed as you like.

'I know you think me an interfering old busybody,' I said. She smiled. That was all.

'But I've faced a few things,' I said. 'Being on the shelf for one. And my face,' I said.

225

'Your face?'

'Everybody puts a face on for the world, and mine is the hardest in the family, harder than my mother's because she didn't have my experience in the business. She was on the farm.'

'You told me,' she said.

'You see, I went all through the twenties and the thirties in my little shop, keeping the bad debts down with the expression on my face.'

'Yes,' she said. She lit an after-breakfast cigarette, as she called it.

'If it was colliers I was refusing, it was myself I was serving. I had the warehouses to visit every Thursday and my own debts, the margin to be calculated every minute of the day.'

'Pressures,' she said.

'Exactly,' I said. 'If I have any epitaph, it was what one of the colliers called me.'

She did not ask me what it was.

'Maid of foul weathers,' I said. 'Mind, he was from our chapel, and I strapped him all through the '29 strike because he was the one I could trust.'

She stubbed out her cigarette.

'No doubt he had his eye on five Woods on the book,' I said. 'The collier's delight before the war. I kept a large Players on the shelf for so long you'd think it was a box of Havanas.'

She laughed. Did she understand? Do any of them?

'Let me tell you one thing,' I said. 'All we can hope for in this life is that we live by example, that some part of us rubs off on our time, on the people we meet, that this action or that has noted itself in somebody's consciousness, and although it is a seed that might lay fallow for ever and a day, every good action you do has my hope with it like a prayer.'

But as I was talking, she left. Did I get the words out? I can't remember.

An old fool was suddenly addressing the wall.

'I have to go,' she called from the hall. Perhaps I had been too direct the night before. My father always said, 'Give them a chance, gel.' But I was always direct. Was that why I was on the shelf? Of course, I had offers from the colliers when the shop was empty and the shelves were full, but I had too much of a way with colliers, one hand always on the till. And it was too late then. That was another thing I'd failed to get across to her. Sometimes you get only one chance, only one man for keeps, and when that is gone, none at all. *Was that the most important thing my eighty years of life had taught me?* If so, I failed to get it out.

When the front door slammed, I remembered it was weekday visiting for Walter. I got some Welsh cakes from the cold slab in the larder. (I kept them there, otherwise the flavour went). Then I put caster sugar in a separate packet. It took me a morning to get ready and as I wondered what else to take, it put me in mind of what she said about not having children. The root of the matter... Well, the food they ate wouldn't keep a thrush in the pink, I thought as I

227

laid out some eggs. There'd been nothing but biscuits, snacks, everything out of tins, ever since they were married. They hadn't seen my father feeding up a stallion he'd bought cheap on the market. I remembered that all the morning, cod liver oil down the horse's throat by a dropper, the best of oats, a charcoal brazier in the barn, a blanket from my father's own bed – everything you could think of until the moment was ripe. He'd even blow in the horse's ear if it was a Johnny-Hang-Back! You can give nature a shove from time to time. I remember him delivering a foal, the red muck up to his elbows, but a smile on his face. But I daren't tell them that. They only want to taste the cake, not bite it.

In the end, I took Walter the Welsh cakes, a dozen eggs, some mintoes and myself, and on the bus to the hospital, I thought of what I was going to say to Walter. About last night, nothing. No decks. I tried to think of something chirpy. There was a girl got on the bus practically naked. Everything on offer like a joint of meat at the butcher's. And the boy with her, indistinguishable. These days they stroke each other in public. In ten years, I thought, I wouldn't be surprised if there were signs forbidding them from going the whole hog on the top of buses. And ten pounds for a second offence! But I'd better not mention that.

I held the eggs in a basket on my lap. Walter was very sarcastic about my eggs in the beginning, but not any more.

'There's nothing you can tell me about the Tee Bee,' I said to the woman next to me. We had a nodding acquaintance.

'I expect,' she said. She turned away from me slightly. Youngish people do.

'Not when I've seen the sheen they get on their faces in the last months, the final blush of a false spring, and the weakness, the light going from the eyes and the body wasting, sometimes a pound a day going without a movement in the bed. When they stopped weighing them, you knew the jig was as good as up.' (Did I say all that? I meant to.)

'Everything has changed these days,' she said.

Some things had, thank goodness. She did not seem to want to talk to me, a grey old soul. Myself, I did not mind talking about these things since I had seen so much of them. Indeed, I had seen a look coming on people's faces, sometimes coming on the face of a man of forty or fifty, coming there suddenly in a week or two, a greyness that lingers there almost as if a grey cat had perched on his shoulder and the sheen of its fur cast a shadow against his skin. It was an unnatural look, I remembered, lines fixing on a man's face like scales. Their eyes began to stare too, looking through you and beyond you. Indeed, I got to know that look when I saw it, and was unable to help the look I gave in return. But you cannot say these things, only think them.

The woman next to me said her husband was a terminal case. Cancer of the lung, with what is called secondaries of the brain.

I hoped he had lived a good life, poor dab. These things go on all the time in everybody's life, but somehow we remain ignorant of them.

In that hospital, I had an arrangement with the Sister which allowed me to go up in the lift, something they do not normally allow. It takes me an age to go anywhere, but go I do.

'Well?' I said to Walter when I got there at last and put my parcels on his locker. 'How are you feeling *in yourself*? I always began with that. It seemed to me to be the most important question. If anybody asked me, I should always have the same answer. 'Fighting fit and I shall go on until I drop.' It would never occur to me to say otherwise.

Walter had news.

'They're going to operate,' he said. He'd got much fatter on my eggs and milk.

'Well then... Progress.'

'They're going to remove a segment of the lung.'

'Marvellous,' I said. 'And your eye?'

'They're hoping that if they remove the allergy, the eye condition will clear up.'

'Common sense,' I said. 'When?'

'Next week.'

'Excellent,' I said. 'You'll soon be up and about.'

I sat beside the locker, took the Welsh cakes from the bag and put them on a plate, then sprinkled the caster sugar sparingly. He hadn't said anything about her occasional absences and gave no indication if he knew what was going on. Now he looked at me with a grin.

'You're a turn, you are,' he said.

'What d'you mean, "turn"?' I said. 'Am I something from the music hall then?'

'You're getting very well known in this hospital.'

'I've always been well known,' I said. 'Not small fry like you two.'

He laughed.

'Well, it's true,' I said. 'Wherever I have been, I have made myself well known. On the farm, in the shop, and since I moved. I make myself plain wherever I am. Why not? I've nothing to hide.'

He laughed again. We never said anything about her at all. If he didn't say anything, I just went on talking.

'Only five in chapel, Sunday,' I said. 'And the blasted heating conked out again. It's getting like Rorke's Drift.'

'Where?'

'South Africa,' I said. 'South Wales Borderers and the Blackies. Don't you know anything? History, boy. "Imagine Welshmen fighting Blackies," my father said. "To fill whose pockets?"'

'I bet he was a case as well,' Walter said.

I gave him a Welsh cake, took one myself. Why not? They were wafer thin, even if I say so myself. The wet stone did it. Don't talk to me about fridges.

'Don't you call my father a case,' I said. 'Eat that.'

Visiting hours drag on unless you can think of something to say.

An MP had been round the wards the day before, he said. Sir Somebody or other.

'Their knighthoods stick in their smiles like toothpaste,' I said.

'Why?' Walter said. (They were all listening to me in the ward.)

'The frog in my disrespectful throat is the people they've

trodden on and deserted,' I said. 'Take my word for it, a Welshman who has got on in London has only done so at a price. He has served others not his own.'

'I didn't know you were a bolshie?' Walter said.

'Once they get to London, it's knives and forks with them. To fill their own bellies. And reason for ours. They should remember they are representing an unreasonable people and not be over-awed by traditions which have nothing to do with us. I'm not saying it's not very nice for them, very human, but the places they leave behind remain the same always.'

'You should have been here to tell him,' Walter said.

'You don't doubt that, do you?' I said.

'No,' he said.

'I've known a few of them,' I said. 'When I did my bit with the library and visiting hospitals during the war. When the wounded were in blue. But when I met an officer, I always summed him up by asking what he would have been like to Dafydd Rowlands.'

'Who?'

There... It was out. I had never said a word about him to anybody. So now I did. It was funny how close we had come together in these few months; Walter and me. When I finished, I dared him to make one of his remarks, but he did not.

'So you see,' I said, 'I could have had my fling too, perhaps?'

He smiled.

'I can see him,' he said.

'Wales is people like him still,' I said, 'not politicians

jugging up on the Pullman, nor sneak-and-run school-masters rubbing out road signs with green paint.'

'Oh, that,' he said. There had been a case in the paper that morning, an agitator rubbing out English words because they were not in Welsh!

'The university lot making a noise like cornflakes in a bowl,' I said. 'Snap, crackle and pop!'

He laughed so much, I thought he would hurt himself.

'Welsh is one thing,' I said. 'But I have always believed that it is what you say and do that matters, not the language in which you say it, Welsh or English. And to those language bombasts who talk about Jesus as if he was from Machynlleth, I say, have a care. If it's all in Welsh up there, pity help the old Arabs.'

I had to stop then, in case he should choke. As usual, he had found undesirable company. There was a burglar in the next bed to him with tattoos up to his elbows, a fan dancer and a palm tree. Not much sense a burglar having himself marked like that, I thought. I mean, he'd be so easily recognised! But I said nothing, just nodded. The collier that I saw there before was dead and buried. People pass out of our lives like bits of paper floating down a stream.

Walter said they'd told him the operation would be painless. Fool, I thought. I knew they would have to cut through the chest muscles. What did he think it was, a picnic?

The time came for me to go. I gathered my bits and pieces. I never kissed him, or anybody, in public, but for some reason he held my hand, gave it a squeeze.

'Mind to feed yourself up,' I said. 'You won't feel like eating after the operation.'

'You've never had an operation in your life,' he said.

'I've never been to Australia either, but I know it's there.'

He kept hold of my hand.

'Thanks Rach',' he said.

The impertinence. I have never allowed familiarity. It has always been Miss Morgan, or Auntie Rachel in full. I nodded and took my leave.

The Sister was waiting for me by the lift.

'We have every hope that his eye will clear,' she said. 'But of course, we can't know for certain.'

'He has come on splendidly here,' I said. What I did not say was that there had been a great improvement in his character. He had stopped squealing, as the colliers used to say. There were men for you. I wish I could write a book about my great loves. All in the head, but loves nevertheless.

It was another day before I spoke to Constance. She had brought some walking shoes back from the cobbler's. She said she wanted them for the weekend.

'The weekend?' I said. This was Thursday.

She nodded calmly. She was not going to take part in any more scenes, she said. It was hard on everyone but she had her own life to live.

That I should be witness of this, I thought.

'So you're seeing him again?' I said.

She did not reply. When you are old, one day is much the same as any other but I felt that this was a day when, if a bird had sung, it would have been a blasphemy. Weak people cheapen themselves. Weakness is self-perpetuating. The seeds of disaster where the self is concerned are inside us, not without. Unless we are careful, we carry the seeds of our own destruction around with us, and like seeds, we can scatter our own dismay on fertile ground. Everything multiplies, good and bad. We deceive ourselves if we say we are responsible only for ourselves. I thought of that poor woman's husband, a terminal case. We need more reminders of what awaits us, I thought. It did not frighten me, but then I had grown up with real things, not this froth that surrounds them now. I tried to think of a way to put it but there was nobody to listen. 'Surround yourself with cellophane, you can still break your heart,' I wanted to say. 'The easiest thing in the world is to find yourself at thirty, coming home to an empty house.' But I did not. And yet I knew in my bones which way she was heading. Oh, yes, people have always wanted to end their lives and there is a beginning to that, like everything else.

One good thing. Walter's smile was like a sweetheart's.

I could feel that weekend coming like a coaltip beginning to slide. The first lie is always the worst, a trickle to what follows. I knew what awaited her. I felt it coming. What pleasure is there for anybody in saying, 'I told you so?'

235

CHAPTER NINE

CONNIE

Rachel's voice reminded me of clothes flapping on a line. She nagged insistently, her conviction of my wrong-doing making her into a perpetual broadcasting station, the light of morality glistening in her eyes, transistorised, never-ending, needing no re-charging of the batteries. She thought she maintained periods of disapproving silence but she deceived herself. She never stopped, and her convictions never wavered. Sin, I thought, she traded in it like self-raising flour. I wondered if she had ever done a deliberately harmful act in her life. I doubted it. I didn't attempt to get through to her. It was impossible. I wanted to get away. Anywhere, provided it was out of the house.

Did people ever really believe in the wages of sin, things like that? What did they see in their mind's eye when they thought about it? Perhaps there were angels' wings

237

flapping? And the Devil? I wondered how he'd look nowadays? Probably wear a dinner-jacket, manage an amusement arcade; be exposed on commercial television if he did not interfere with the profits. An investigation in depth, the BBC having declined to touch him.

Everything she said was nonsense, I thought. Folklore. Platitudes. Memories twisted to a purpose, my harassment. Walter was getting better although his eye hadn't improved. They were fattening him up in preparation for surgery, which they rarely did these days but were going to in his case because of his eye, and some resistance to the chemotherapy. He had become addicted to the eggs in milk, watched his weight very carefully. He said he had made friends in the ward, a collier and a safe-breaker, one of the Cardiff lags with a face like a disgruntled monkey's who had done time for blowing the night safe of the Beachley ferry. I nodded to the two of them in the ward. Two conspicuously working-class types, one with a nervous tic, pale heads against the pillows watching me, ill at ease in my presence. Perhaps they knew I was having it off while Walter didn't. I didn't know, didn't care.

Rachel said I was inhuman. I said I was tired. Ifor said he loved me. What was that, I asked. He said it so often, it was better than silence. If people are persistent, they succeed. In anything. Even if they wear themselves out and you with it. I didn't *know* anything, that was the important thing. What does anybody actually *know*? About anything?

Walter liked his thief. He was called Mush, appeared to have no other name, gave Walter new excitements at secondhand. Going on a job, deserted streets in the early

238

morning, casing a joint, blowing a gaff, the police feeling your collar, being done for 'sus', creeping down the stairs in a house you thought was empty and then, a cuckoo clock goes off like a cannon behind you. Paralysis... Did no one ever think of the pressures on the burglar, his nervous system? Walter found a new world, scooped it out for himself from the men in the adjoining beds. He was always interested in other people's lingo. I knew the slang would become part of his vocabulary. He was happy in hospital and had settled in. He wouldn't scarper. I was glad he had found something. He was as pleased with it as a child with a new comic.

But Rachel nagged on, then was finally silent. Said absolutely nothing, stared, clucked, ignored me. I said I'd go. She didn't answer. It was absurd that I had lived with her so long, I thought. She was so convenient. Her helping didn't help though. Perhaps she realised that; perhaps her own realisation wound her up like a spring? She was talking endlessly, then, when she stopped, perhaps she found that she had nothing to say once the habit was broken? Communication, I thought, the problem of the age. But it was a problem only if you had something to say, and I had not.

She said that if I saw Ifor again, she would turn me out of the house. I thought of those ancient flicker-movies, a blank screen with the caption, WHO WILL CARE FOR HER NOW?

Ifor would. We do such predictable things, climb to the next step because it is the nearest.

Two days' silence in the house. I'd stopped washing

dishes. So did Rachel. I saw her face watching me from the bedroom upstairs when I left. It was like the past watching you. I thought of faces, their eyes closed, looking upwards at coffin lids, faces in queues staring at nothing, people in a tube, the sex adverts blurring behind them, 'our tights stretch tighter'. People looked at nothing like I did.

But not Rachel. She looked at me and Walter behind me, clicking his sputum pot, mates with the colliers and the lag. She would like that, sympathise. I expected no one to sympathise with me, confided in no one, my aloneness building up tensions like a steel band coiling. The hell with it, I was thoroughly dislikeable. There was nothing to be said for me, but I didn't care. I did not care.

Ifor began to talk about his life endlessly, the well-meaning scholarship boy in a sailor's suit, the twit at Oxford, the worm in the officer's mess, the messenger in the Inspectorate, the filler of forms, the creator of forms, the report maker, the collier's son who had done well and done nothing. It had taken him fifty-five years of life to realise that and now he wanted me.

Where did he want me? I kept on wondering. Why? How? He just kept reiterating it. He wanted me. Would we set up house in a small, smart, flat then? Perhaps I should also have a wrist watch, ritzy furniture, Scandinavian chi-chi, swish things? If only I wanted them, I thought. But I didn't.

He moaned on. His wife, Hilda. One of the Groesfan Williamses, whatever that was supposed to mean. A shell, he said, an empty shell. Played bridge, had a brother, a barrister, had declined a magistracy, was snobbish about his colleagues, disgusted his son who, in turn, was disgusted with them. Life cannot be as awful as that, I thought. It cannot be. For anyone. Walter said the people he liked were full of guts, he had found that out. He kept on having these conversations in whispers during visiting hours. It was all I could do to listen. Ifor said that perhaps Walter was right, perhaps guts was the thing? It was time we showed it in our own interests, Ifor said. Leave him, he said. And come to me.

It began to prey on me, his insistence. I gave him no sex for months. Why should I? I didn't want it myself. I didn't, then I did. Sex was a great cheat, I thought. He didn't, but I did. I didn't know who was mixed up, him or me. I stopped thinking about it.

Then his wife, Hilda. I began to take the view that if a husband strays, it's his wife's fault. Hard, I know. No comfort for the little women sitting at home under the drying napkins. But a view, mine. I was sure Ifor had always had his little girls. I didn't ask him in case he should bore me with the details. But I was sure. So why didn't his wife get something going for herself? She was not interested, he said. In the physical side, he said. The way people talk... What sort of woman was she then? It was difficult to explain but she was a lady. He could search for other words, but that was what she was. A lady. Dignified, aloof, cool, preserved, kept her distance, disliked scenes, even in her cups presented a front to the world. One did this, one did not do that. In the year she was President of the Ladies County Club, she cut down on her drinking like a social athlete getting back into form.

241

She organised only one charity for the League of Pity. (That was some league, I thought.) And she played her bridge, loved her garden, pruned the roses herself, cultivated a vine for the roots of which he'd once had to get her a sheep's head since this gave the crop a bloom, according to her. Her father had been an expert on vines. The bloom on the vine, I thought.

Yes, but what made her tick, I asked him once. He didn't know any more. Whatever was at the bottom of the bottle, he thought. She drank regularly now but with dignity. There had only once been an accident when she fell through the forcing frames in the greenhouse and the gardener had to get her to bed. Appalled that the gardener should dare to touch her, she stabbed at him with an ugly sliver of glass, cutting herself further in the process. They dismissed the gardener a few months later. He was a good gardener, but it was felt appropriate that he should leave.

I said, there must have been something alive in her mind?

'Did she know about me?' I said, 'or the others?'

'If she did, she said nothing.'

'She hates you then?' I said.

'She has passed even beyond that.'

Perhaps I was frightened then myself. It is no comfort to stumble across the emptiness of other people's lives. Their blight infects your own. We all of us have things in common and sometimes they are insidious. Everywhere you look, there is pretence and cosiness, but beneath the surface, everything is cracking really. I was sure of that.

Facades, I thought about. Pretence. The illusion of well-being. Things... Anything to kill silence. We must be the least silent age in history, needing noise to cover the blankness of our minds. When they looked back on us, what would they say? Only the machines were interesting, the people were not.

Then I was suddenly confronted with the Welsh thing, Rachel on about the past, Ifor on the English, blaming them for his own destruction of his roots. I'd never thought about it before. Somehow I always associated Welshness with quarrelling committees, with things going wrong, little political men with vested interests and families of unemployable nephews screwing money and jobs out of the State for their own special, personal causes. And the Language that nobody spoke much in the towns, unless it was to get on in the BBC or Education. Of course, I remembered the more emotive things, hymns at football matches, those great spasms of emotion that swept across the terraces of the football grounds, waves of feeling and piping tenor voices, patterns of song as intricate as a folk weave, but meaningless in terms of my present. Welshness was like a cottonwool fuzz at the back of the mind because Wales was always round the corner where I lived. Men remembered it beerily when the pubs were closed, or at specially contrived festivals – somebody's pocket and kudos again. We had come to be the St. David's Day Welsh and nothing changed in our lives ever. Rachel spoke of men like Bevan who had passed on, leaving a name for greatness, but in the bleak towns they left behind them, nothing was substantially changed there any more than it was anywhere else. Rachel harped on it like a Jewish matriarch. We were powerless, corrupting ourselves daily. The people had lost their will to be and only existed to be used by profiteers of one kind or another.

But it had nothing to do with me and when she stopped speaking at all, I thought about my dependence on her as a little girl. The warmth of being closely cosseted, her reading stories to me, examining my nails to check their cleanliness, my trips to chapel, more to keep her company than anything else, the little band of deacons growing smaller and smaller, and the sense of an old world passing as the congregation dwindled every year. It never affected me, I thought, except that it was cosy, a contained little world like a club for the elderly that was soon to vanish. And the moment I got away, I left it behind me soon enough. They say the past never leaves you, but it did me.

So I stopped thinking about it, and London, and Rachel. I stopped thinking altogether. There is always a time in your life when you can do nothing, just drift. Ifor was pleasant enough. No, he was *there*, and attentive. If people thought us a minor scandal, they were fools, I thought. Half of gossip is envy. I had a deaf ear.

Then Ifor got serious. At first, I was scornful. Love, I thought. I was unmerciful. There was no need ever to chat me up for his gristle. It depended on how I felt, that was all. But then I saw I was hurting him. He said I was cheap, thoughtless, diminished the quality of feeling by my cynicism. If you asked me what that was, I couldn't define it. I just saw through things, that was all. If I had anything to say to the world, it was, *'Don't tell me any lies!'* But looking at another human being who keeps on saying he wants you, cares for you, goes on and on saying it like a drill, what can you do but believe it eventually? You have to believe something, I thought. A mistake.

I never thought of myself as the cat's whiskers, all that. He wanted me to, because he did, he said. And that night in the car when I knew he wanted me, was like being eighteen again. I tasted the power of that again, the power of sex. Men's lines, I thought, their chat. Walter had all these special angles, but ultimately he got what he wanted from girls by throwing himself on their mercy. '*Hold me! I am a shambles!*' With others, it was knee in, and stop your breath, their hands like grabs, fingers for the clitoris like navvies searching for the magic button. But Ifor had an aesthetic, his own trail of woe, and a desperation that was rare in someone his age. I *could* not escape the conviction that men declaring their love were somehow ridiculous. It wasn't something you declared. There was no need for posture. But he was so dated in everything, I supposed there had to be speeches, and when he said, '*Saturday – Saturday!*' breathless like that, it was somehow touching.

Who wants to be a bitch? Who wants to be a bitch to two men at the same time? So I said yes, one nice thing I did. I thought I wasn't pleasing myself at all in anything, maybe I'd please him once more. As for the aesthetic of me, his feeling, that was something that went on in his own mind.

So I said yes to Saturday but Rachel created. When he rang up, she put the phone down but I found out and rang him at home, only he wasn't there and his wife answered.

'Yes?'

245

'Oh Ifor... Mrs Evans?'

'*Who is that?*'

I didn't know what to say for a second. 'Who is that?' in that Harrod's voice. Now what had I got myself into? I didn't feel guilty then, just wanted to avoid embarrassment, hers as much as mine.

I said. 'It's to do with some research he's doing. A project on compensatory education. My name is Lacey, Mrs Lacey.'

But I felt it stick in my throat, the moment I said it. You can listen to your own voice so blandly lying and even though that's the thing you hate most in other people, another part of you is standing back admiring your own coolness when you do exactly the same thing.

'Why don't you ring the office?' she said after a pause. Her voice was distant and forbidding.

'Of course. I'm frightfully sorry for disturbing you.'

Cool as cool. But I was excited, that I couldn't get over. Perhaps I felt then what Ifor felt, the elation that precedes your own destruction. I thought of Walter's burglar and that cuckoo clock. I could imagine every step down the stairs and then a sound behind you in the darkness, freezing your blood, stopping short so abruptly that you could count your own heart beats. You don't think of the old lady you might terrorise at the top of the stairs or the squeamishness of women who look at drawers which have been ransacked – you think only of yourself at the precise time.

I put the phone down, rang his office. I just got him before he went out.

'Make it Friday,' I said.

'But...'

'Don't you want to see me?'

'Yes...' he sounded hesitant.

'Then make it Friday,' my own voice was tense. I couldn't explain about Rachel over the phone. 'I'll get time off.'

'Has anything happened?'

'Nothing that'll spoil anything.'

I could hear the sigh of relief, then a note of excitement in his voice.

'You sound eager?'

'You ought to know me by now,' I said.

He told me later that when he heard that, he nearly came around straight away. That set the blood moving all right.

'Fine,' I said. 'The usual place.'

We usually met in a car park in the centre of Cardiff. I would catch the bus down from where I taught, he'd leave the door of the car open. I just got in and we were away. I liked the raciness of it, if that's the word. It was fun to make a getaway like that.

He said he'd make arrangements. Had I anywhere special in mind?

'Anywhere,' I said. Now it was my need that was communicating itself.

Was I sure that nothing had come up?

'Sure,' I said.

'You sound as if it's urgent?'

'If you mean what you say?' I said.

He meant it.

I put the phone down. Rachel's eyes were on me as she went down the hall. I didn't say goodbye, just walked out of the house. I had come home for lunch from school and now as I walked down the road, I noticed a cinema poster with a couple necking, her with a cleavage like so much sausage meat and him, ringlets in his hair, getting buried. This is what the public want, I said to myself. I felt elated, wild and bright.

But Rachel didn't speak to me again when I got home and by the Friday, her silence was poisonous, infecting me with her own foreboding that came across from her in waves although she still didn't say anything. It was Wagnerian, crashing chords of disapproval. Sin-sin-sin! The sun would never rise again, all that. Rachel approved of wife-beating in certain circumstances, I knew, but if she'd said anything I'd have made some smart crack about selecting the whips, which would have scandalised her all the more. I got out of the house fast, taking a grip without a nightdress, another cheap gesture.

But when I got to school, there was Bryn and I changed again. Guilt... I tried to tell myself, it was just a lingering thing from childhood. Nothing could be as sordid as the way I now felt. And what would happen? Another bit on the side, some comfort to Ifor in his snail's trail to the grave, and nothing much else. I still didn't think of Walter. But then I had the sense of something awful coming in a way that was frightening, as if my puny little life was destined for some grave attention. It was absurd but it was present. I shared a room with a girl once who had a horror of birds flying inside a room. It wasn't just the superstition that a bird brought bad luck, but she had a physical revulsion to being clawed by it, her eyes pecked out, the webbed feet sticking in her hair. When a thrush flew in through the window, I had to sit up with her all night. Later she heard voices, someone calling, and I kept saying, 'There's nobody there'. But my voice made no difference, nor my presence. She went off the rails after that, got herself pregnant by a railway porter, and the last I heard, she'd had a breakdown and gone inside for shock treatment. In a way, the arrival of the thrush was the beginning, something she'd feared. It was illogical, primitive and stupid. Having witnessed it, I discounted it until now when for no reason that you could explain, some part of the feeling came to me.

There was something awful waiting for me too.

I tried to be objective about it, Rachel threatening to shut the door (we paid a nominal rent), the possibility of divorce, Ifor getting posted to Bangor or some remote place by a disapproving superior, a prick posting as someone once told me they used to do in the Colonial Service if one of the chaps got a thing about a native. But it was none of these things, all of which were on the cards anyway and I knew it. It was something more intangible, some sense of catastrophe that was going to happen inside my mind and was altogether personal. That girl used to fear the bird getting inside her, and although it was nonsense, the fear of it and the sense of it was real. So much for logic when you create your own fears without external help.

But I didn't know anything definite like that, could foresee no actual things happening in any concrete sense.

It was just the feeling at the back of my mind, etched there with thick pencil, a shading without tangible shape, a darkening at the edges of reason. If that is reasonable.

On the Friday morning, Bryn was busy when I went into his room to ask him for time off.

'Of course,' he said. 'Walter, is it?'

'As a matter of fact, no,' I said.

'Well, you don't have to tell me,' he said. 'Anything else you want?'

But as he said it, I realised it was the end of the week and he was busy with his attendance returns and one of those complicated requests for information requiring the names of children born between certain monthly dates. His desk was a mess of papers and registers. He'd barely looked up when I entered. If he'd had a moment, I might have told him the whole story. I knew what he'd have said. Something coarse, which he sometimes did because he trusted me. Something like, 'You want your arse kicked', and I would have said something like suggesting he did it, and he'd probably have had me home for tea. He had these terrific 'teenage daughters', and recounted their daily conversation in scandalised terms. He'd once objected to an article in one of their magazines, TOP TIPS FOR PETTING POINTS and a nude illustration with lines leading to the spots. 'I bet nothing gets you at the base of the spine,' his daughter told him. Who created this age?

When he looked at me, I said, 'There is something. Have you ever had the feeling there's something awful waiting for you?'

He looked at me as if I were complaining about boys

looking up my skirt, filth in the junior toilets, the caretaker's fingernails – as if I were empty and frivolous, cheese-paring – a female. My image cracked with the one sentence.

'For goodness sake,' he said. 'Get your chest X-rayed.'

'It's not that,' I wanted to say, but I did not. And I knew how I sounded. I could see his irritation. He looked away as if to disguise the extent to which his mind was moving out of sympathy with mine.

I could have time off, of course. Nothing else. He might have responded, I thought, but why should he? Because I thought well of him? But Walter thought well of me once. It made no difference.

You get what you deserve.

As I left to meet Ifor, I thought again of Bryn's daughters. The twins would have made a beautiful pair of rugby centres, he said once, were actually red hot at basketball, but now it was dancing. When they wanted money to go to some rave-up on the Isle of White, he'd said no, but they went just the same, fending off lorry drivers with the same expertise as they did the French when they went camping. I liked Bryn's house, his poise with the children. He complained all the time, complained that he couldn't get in the bathroom, and when he did, their toilet preparations made him sick. As did The Hair, which was how he referred to the boys that appeared the moment he set out for his weekend's rugby orgy. He and his family kept each other at arm's length, but he was as proud as paint of them.

Something I never would be, I thought, but then, despite

what I'd said to Rachel, I wasn't sure. It was just a feeling I had, one of her kind. In the bones, as she said. I was twenty-seven, and nothing had ever happened whenever I wanted a child. But was it the root of anything? I'd never taken any serious advice, just drifted. It was hard to explain even to myself that I didn't need any justification for what I did. I couldn't believe there was any one cause for this or that series of events. That was too pat. You can just get tired of things and I had too many grey thoughts on too many grey days.

After I left school, I rang her again, his wife. I wanted to be sure he had left.

'Mrs Evans? I'm awfully sorry to disturb you again. I was wondering if Ifor – I mean, Mr Evans...'

That correction. The most obvious thing in the world. Only the obvious slips matter.

The bluntest weapons hurt the most.

CHAPTER TEN

HILDA

The morning.

I answer the telephone in the mornings.

'Miss *who*?'

But I need not have asked. A person of no consequence. Her voice was rather metallic and common. She said, 'Ifor', then corrected herself.

'My husband does not like being telephoned at home,' I said. 'He is not here. I suggest you try his office. Please do not ring again unless especially asked.'

I can manage in the mornings.

'That was tart,' my friend, Sue Parry-Jones, said. She had called and overheard.

'I don't like that word,' I said.

'Snuffs to you,' Sue said. She retains these juvenile expressions, despite the fact that she is my age. She has preserved better, however, like Ifor.

'Who was it?' she was frankly curious.

'Some school teacher with a paper for Ifor.'

'Oh?'

'He is collecting material for some project.'

She did not say anything.

'I dislike telephones,' I said. 'In the afternoons, I seldom answer them.'

'But what d'you do when the maid isn't here?'

'I look at them.'

'*Look at them?*'

'And will them to stop. Ifor discourages callers too.'

'Ifor would,' she said.

'I think we might try a sherry,' I said. Sue had called about a bridge weekend which she said was next weekend. I distinctly remember that. In fact, I was sure of it. She definitely said next weekend.

For some reason, the telephone conversation interested her intensely.

'Does he have many calling him at home?'

'Many?'

'School teachers.'

'From time to time. I prefer them not to. His colleagues are bad enough.'

'The Inspectorate?'

'Yes. I do not know one who is not banal.'

'*Banal?*' she said. 'What an odd word!'

'For educated men, they are a joke.'

'*Why?*'

'They put on such airs, yet are so servile,' I said. 'I have always discouraged them from calling. Why ever do you ask?'

'Arthur says he prefers the politicians to the civil servants. They may be crooked, but they dearly love their two-and-sixpence worth.'

I did not say anything. We seldom talk about Ifor.

But Sue persisted. 'Does Ifor go away much these days?'

I could not understand her sudden interest.

'From time to time.'

'Conferences and things?'

'Yes,' I said.

'Men and their conferences.'

'Yes,' I said.

She was studying my face. I poured another sherry. Why was she studying my face? Did she think I did not know about Ifor? What wife does not know her husband? I would not have mentioned it, but she changed the subject.

'How is Gordon.'

'He seems to be totally involved in a world of his own.'

'At Oxford?'

'Yes. He seldom comes home.'

She sipped her sherry. 'You ought to find something to do. Arthur says you have a good brain. Why don't you get your brother to speak to his cronies at the bar? They can't find anybody to be magistrates without political connections. I'm sure if you agreed, something could be arranged?'

'I could not sit in judgement on others,' I said.

'Oh, Hilly... You don't do a thing these days? Not even church.'

'I don't know why the church is repugnant to me. Perhaps because anybody can join it.'

'Hilly!'

I poured another sherry. 'Father was a magistrate.'

'I know he was. Why don't you mention it to your brother? It would give you something to do, darling?'

'No, I couldn't get up in the mornings.'

'Well, you can't expect them to hold the courts in the afternoons.'

'Father used to keep them waiting.'

'Times have changed.'

'You are trying to do good to me, Sue,' I said. 'Stop it. You know I have the gardens.'

I could see them through the windows. The herbaceous borders I planted myself, but we inherited the copper beech trees that fronted the drive. Although the house was comparatively modern, the copper beech trees were like Victorian sentinels standing augustly amongst so much modernity. In Groesfan, my father's house, we had three gardeners and a boy. Father used to inspect what they had done every day, and in the autumn, he used to be unreasonable about the clearing of falling leaves. They might work all day, if he found a leaf on the lawn when he came home, he would stare at it as if it were an intruder. We discouraged callers and intruders.

There were so few people with whom one could mix.

'Well, I must be going,' Sue said in a loud voice. 'Ifor away this weekend?'

'Oh, yes,' I remembered. 'A conference somewhere.'

'Why don't you come to the Club?'

'The days seem to pass without me getting out.'

'You'll have to snap out of it.'

'Will you have another sherry?'

'Heavens, no. I must go,' but she screwed up her face and peered at me again. 'D'you eat when the maid isn't here?'

'Of course I eat.'

'I only thought I'd ask.'

'I can't think why you called?'

'*Bridge*' she emphasised. 'We'll drive up in my car.'

I preferred not to drive.

'Well, I must go,' she said for the third time. 'There's no need for you to come to the door.' But then she paused and looked closely at me again. 'Hilly, I wish you'd look after yourself. Couldn't you get Gordon to come home more often?'

'He is embarrassed when he does.'

'Well, your brother then? He doesn't live more than a mile away.'

'He comes on Christmas Day.'

'For Christ's sake, Hilly...'

She was looking at me with alarm. I wish she wouldn't. She affects the mannerisms of the young and they ill become her.

'Couldn't you go to Champneys or somewhere? Tone up?'

'Ifor's been there,' I said.

'Champneys?'

'Sitz baths,' I said. He had spoken about those and a phrase stuck in my mind. 'They increase the tone of the muscles and organs lying in the abdominal and pelvic cavities.'

'*He said that?*'

'They have enemas,' I said. 'Quite out of the question.'

'Darling, you pays your money and you takes your choice. You don't have to have everything.'

'I am perfectly all right,' I said. 'I can manage in the mornings.'

She said she would ring to confirm. Her hats are rather a hoot. Even Ifor smiles at them. Creations, he calls them. Fluffy. She gave me one of her searching looks and left. She disguises her miseries by concentrating on mine.

The afternoon.

In the afternoons, I find it difficult to concentrate.

I feel guilty about my son.

I cannot think what people did before vodka.

I know far more than people realise. I still have a good brain.

Perhaps Ifor is a pervert.

I love my garden but I am beginning to find the weeding tiring. My back muscles must be affected by my liver.

I loved my father because he was so gentlemanly and fair. He went to especial trouble to buy individual Christmas presents for the staff.

Whenever vodka is mixed with tonic, it is perfectly innocuous.

My brother, Philip, was my mother's favourite. I was so ungainly it offended her. She said in my hearing that I loped like a horse. I never ran when she watched me again. When I was conscious of my ugliness, I used to crouch beside my father's chair and help him to take his slippers off, then buried my face in his feet. I would do anything to make him love me, but I had no need. He did love me. I cried for two days when he died and shut myself up in my room, did not appear for the funeral.

When I met Ifor, he was in uniform. He said yes to everything I suggested. When he was unsure of himself, he had a way of pursing his lips thoughtfully and making a little humming noise that sounded knowledgeable, as if he were debating everything. 'Mmmmm...' It meant, 'I will do anything to marry you,' so perhaps it was a feeling of a kind, if only for the acquisition of a wealthy wife.

He asked me to marry him in the courtyard of Castell Coch, a Victorian imitation castle built by one of the younger Butes who later gave it to the City of Cardiff because they found it impossible to heat, and, of course, death duties. In the autumn, the leaves come down from the forest like spray and sometimes seagulls fly up the river towards the valleys. What on earth are seagulls doing up there?

I have never had an orgasm. Ifor used to be premature.

He always closed his eyes but I opened mine and looked at him. On his face, the fevered, yelping expression of a copulating dog.

Gordon said, 'You smell, Mummy,' and made a face. I never tucked him up.

Vodka does not smell.

Sue Parry-Jones rang. I answered the phone, thinking it might be her. The convention is in Builth Wells. It is to be held at a hotel. Match boards. The man from the *Daily Telegraph* will be there. We might improve our game.

No Ifor.

My brother once suggested I should go to see a psychiatrist privately. 'If it's private, you can go to the house. It would be nothing more than an extended social occasion. Some of them are quite presentable.' I declined. Then he suggested the Roman Church, and I declined that also. I said, 'What I do, I do by choice, knowing it for what it is.' He said, 'I don't like to see you like this, old girl.' So do we communicate.

Sue Parry-Jones claims she met one of the Culbertsons in Cannes. It does not excuse her replying to a tentative One Club without a picture in her hand. But she had her difficulties too. When she went to the Investiture, her husband picked up a half-caste tart and actually brought her to their house and their bed. He was very drunk at the time and could not go himself to the Investiture because a firm with which he had connections was being hammered at the time. So she went with their daughter because they had previously ordered the ornamental chairs and paid for them. Apparently, Arthur Parry-Jones was in the cocktail bar of the Queens where he met a crowd who were celebrating. Their new Prince presumably. Later, they went to a club in the docks where Arthur met this tart. She suggested he took her home and the next thing he remembered was waking up in bed the following morning. The first thing he saw was the tart going through Sue's jewellery box and putting things in her handbag. Arthur expostulated and the tart said in a dreadful Cardiff voice which Sue imitates very well: 'You wasn't speakin' to me like that last night!'

Arthur emptied out her handbag, gave her ten pounds and persuaded her to lie down under a blanket in the back of the car. The garage communicated directly with the kitchen so there was no danger of her being seen leaving the house. But he had been drunk the night before, and when drunk, he was extremely careful in routine things. He opened the garage door and drove down the drive at breakneck pace – straight into the gates which he'd closed and locked the night before. He knocked one gate twenty feet into the middle of the road, so the girl ran screaming from the car which was how the neighbours got to know. Sue said she got it all out of him when she got back from Caernarvon, and now, whatever she feels, she tells it very amusingly.

I said, I could not forgive Ifor for bringing anyone to the house. At least your home is something you have tried to make between yourselves.

A fatuous commonplace.

Do all men need to prove themselves again?

Sue says that if Arthur went bankrupt, she would drop him flat. I don't know what I would do. I wish I could be amusing about such things.

Sue rang again. Again, I answered. She was in a state. The Bridge weekend is *this* weekend. I made the mistake.
Would I still go tonight? I said I'd ask Ifor and ring her back. It is not my mistake.

Was that today or yesterday? Sometimes when she has called, I cannot remember her calling, but I am positive she definitely said next weekend. But was that yesterday?

I had a little sleep. Cat-napping, my father called it. He had a lovely smile. It started below his eyes, drawing the corners of his mouth upwards until his whole face was wrinkled with affection. He smiled for me only.

I rang Ifor. He was at the office. He had to be away anyway. Had I forgotten? I had. I said it would mean me leaving on the Friday night, that is tonight. Was there a cheerful note in his voice?

'I'm sure you'll enjoy yourselves immensely,' he said.

'Yes,' I said. Was that for the benefit of the office?

'How are you going up?'

'Sue Parry-Jones will take me by car.'

'About when?'

'Seven o'clock. We plan to stay halfway.'

'Are you sure you can get into places?'

'Sue's checked.'

'Be absolutely sure.'

'Of course,' I said. 'Are you sure you don't mind being in the house on your own?'

He was purring into the phone, I could sense it.

'Not a bit if I know you're enjoying yourself.'

Sue will. 'Bye,' I said.

'Bye,' he said. 'I shall have to rush.'

Why should he have to rush?

The evening.

Madeira is nut-brown in colour like old mahogany. It is heavy, a ruminative wine. We do not have a maid on Fridays or Saturdays. The trouble with servants is that you have to get up to let them in. They enforce conventions.

No Ifor.

I wonder what he tells his little girls. His endearments must be dated. What do they say when they see his wrinkled skin close to theirs? How can they bear him to touch them? I should be ashamed to see a boy's skin next to mine. They have such clear eyes, the young. Their ignorance is manifold. The way they dress makes you want to scratch. However unhappy we are, we do not look dirty.

No Ifor.

He called me Chickee before we were married. I can remember it was the first endearment anybody ever used to me, except my father and brother. Chickee... I thought it absurd. On our wedding night, he said, 'We don't want to rush things, do we?' I smiled. I knew.

I wish I had a way of helping him, of not being inert. Sooner or later, he will be reprimanded by someone at the Ministry. Then he will be humiliated. He can pursue no course of action which will lead to any kind of lasting satisfaction now. Neither can I.

At fifty, a woman is dying, will only live again if she is wanted by someone. No one wants me. If Ifor were ill, I would nurse him. He is never ill.

The only person I have ever loved in my life is my father. Girls at school did not keep up relationships. I was not encouraged to make friends in the neighbourhood. My father said, all he ever met were ambitious grocers and Freemasons. My brother read law. While he 'ate his dinners,' father was dying. Father used to ask me to be a friend to my brother because he was wayward. He said he always knew I'd be as steady as a rock.

'Steady as a rock, old girl.'

'Good old Hilly,' he used to say. Away from the embrace of his protective love, I have continued to decline as a human being. I should have not got married at all. I cannot feel anything *deep* for Gordon. He is so self-possessed. He runs away. He welcomes conventions. He will not sit at the table when I am drinking. I never tucked him up.

Madeira is a nut-brown wine.

'Steady as a rock, old girl.'

One keeps one's money in several banks. The clerks and people do not earn enough to proscribe their tongues. The people they recruit these days do not give one confidence. Of course, they sign a confidentiality clause. But then so do people sign marriage certificates.

Father always had two banks, and at his funeral, my brother said the respective managers raised their bowlers to one another. It was not unamusing if it were not Father's death which had occasioned it. He would have had a dry smile for that.

I wish I could be funny, even dry.

Sue Parry-Jones is my friend because we suit each other.

She asks my advice on clothes and furniture. I have a little man from Splott who does things for me. He is very good on woodworm. I can leave him alone in the house. Once when I returned unexpectedly, he was hard at work. He gave me a huge cheerful grin. 'I don't spend my time stealing your apples, Missus,' he said. I rather like him.

Someone should tell the people there is no hope in their lives unless they can carve out islands of warmth for themselves. It seems to me, decent people have a place to hide, the rest are exposed by ambition or pretence. The scum comes to the surface, suns itself, slips into oblivion. Those who are happiest are never seen, have fewest possessions.

No Ifor.

Sue Parry-Jones at the door.

'Darling, you're not even dressed?'

'Mmmmm...' his sound from long ago.

'Hilly, you promised me? I rang again.'

'Oh Hilly, you confirmed it? Did you ring Ifor?'

'Darling, can't you say anything?'

'Oh, Christ, and you're not even fit to leave alone. I'll

ring Ifor. Look, I *must* go, I promised. I'll have to get Elsie. Oh, nobody'll come at this notice. And I thought you were a brick.'

'Hilly, speak to me!'

'Look, why don't you go to bed? Just get your head down. Look, I *must* go, I simply *must*. Here... Come on, let me take your arm? Hilly... *Christ, how much have you had*?'

'Well, don't just stand there? Oh, I shall have to ring Arthur.'

'Arthur? Arthur? It's Mrs Parry-Jones. Oh, all right. No, it doesn't matter. No, tell him I've gone on as planned.'

'You'll be all right provided you just sit down. I'll ring you from an AA box or something. Oh, Ifor'll soon be home.'

People's voices... their faces... nothing else tells you so much. But my own is so unfeeling, flat, almost monotonous. I belong nowhere. I'm so ungainly and unlovely. There is a French pastel on the wall, the décolletage so finely etched, a young girl's face with a curl over her forehead that she must have laboured over. It is exquisite and tender. She is so hopeful.

I cannot remember when I ceased to be hopeful. To be unloved is not so hard as to pass the point of caring. Never me... Never...

Even if people watch you, see you, listen to you, they do not understand. What does one have to do to communicate? My father used to say; ultimately, character is the most important thing.

'Daddy...' the small lost voice inside me was never expressed. Madeira is a nut-brown wine. There is more in the study.

I move very carefully in the evenings. Normally, I have things left out so that I do not have to exert myself. I dislike stretching in the dark. Maids understand me, I have found.

When a bottle breaks, it is an ugly sound. The feel of broken glass is so coarse until you find an edge. The edge is the precipitating thing. The edge is fine and easily distinguishable.

I will sit in here in the darkness. Nobody wants me. It would be better if I were not here.

I cannot bear my life and yet it has no high or low notes. I live without crisis. I have no illusions.

Perhaps one could dribble away quietly without any fuss like a bottle emptying. If only one could make a painless incision, but one cannot with glass.

Unless I turn my neck sideways...

I hate my neck. It is wrinkled, patched and scrawny like a chicken's.

That person's voice on the telephone was completely without generosity. Finally, I think that is the most devastating thing you can say about a human being.

CHAPTER ELEVEN

CONNIE

She cut me off when I telephoned her.

'Please do not ring again unless especially asked.'

I hadn't thought about her much. Married men and their bits on the side, I thought about, but wives not much. Nasty me. Her voice sounded far-back, that edge to it that made other people get on their toes, but not me. If she was potty, she was potty, I thought as I came out of the phone box. I don't have conceptions like cheating. If Ifor was straying, it was up to her to do something about it, their business, not mine. How can you get involved with people you don't know? Rachel believed in absolutes, not me.

'My husband does not like being telephoned at home...' It affected me, that voice, its air of putting down the locals, the kind of woman that automatically pushed past you in shops, third-generation money, solicitors on first-name terms, consultants to the house, all that. If he left her, she wouldn't miss him all that much, it was only the scandal of the thing, appearances. If he wanted out, who could blame him really? You can go just so far with the messes you get yourself into.

I was a tight little knot of bitter energy by the time I got down to the bus-stop, half-crying, half-laughing. People who spoke to you like that insulted you. She had no idea who I was, but she had to be beastly. Of course, it was irrational, but it worked me up.

They were digging the road up near the bus-stop. A navvy was waiting by a hole for somebody further along to come and inspect it. He gave me the look, young and curly-haired, a broad smile. I looked away, tried to think of something else. I could see the lumpy valley mountains in the distance, the industrial estate before them, a dark, grey landscape. Since I was a little girl, we always tended to go the other way towards Cardiff and away from the hinterland. We were nominally part of a town, but Cardiff was so near, eight or ten miles. When Rachel retired, she completed the move, seldom went back to where she had the shop. We were at a point in transit, belonging to neither extreme now.

The bus did not come.

The navvy kept up his stare. The ganger or whoever it was, was inspecting another hole further down the road.

The navvy began to croon obscenely.

> *Little Miss Muffet,*
> *Sat on her tuffet,*
> *Airing her curds and whey...*

There was an edge to his voice, a confidential note that meant he must have known he was going to get away with it. Did I look like that, I wondered. As easy as that. Did it stand out on me? I could have burst into tears. I was suddenly like a jelly for no reason. If he'd finished work and tried to pick me up, I might have gone with him.

But the bus came, went down to the coast, Upper Boat, Taffs Well, all grey places at the river's edge. I'd been to dances here, parties there, might have taught in one place, left hockey sticks in another, passed through them now without a thought. It's easy to belong nowhere, just an attitude of mind.

But when I got to the car park, Ifor wasn't there. I felt a blind rage. What did he mean by it? I looked everywhere for the car. He couldn't have written it off, he thought more of it than anything. I walked around finally. I hadn't had any lunch, thought we might start with a binge. It was as good a way of beginning a weekend as anything. Then I hadn't brought much money with me, and despite everything, the totality of me, my attitudes, I didn't like going into pubs on my own. It was so obvious. And I didn't want to leave the car park. He liked to move off at once and not hang about. The more I thought about it, the more seedy it looked. But no car. A traveller parked his shooting brake nearby. It was full of samples, dresses hanging up in cellophane bags. Rachel used to romanticise the sounds she had heard in the early morning, the tread of colliers' boots on the road. Where had I stayed where I heard the sound of travellers putting their samples into their cars?

I couldn't remember. Real men on the one hand and the praying mantis on the other. That was the difference between our experience.

The traveller gave me the eye then, paunchy in immaculate tweeds, a town-and-country check, full little red lips, a bland enquiring glance. Or was it me? Was I imagining things? But then he came over and asked if I'd lost the way, standing too close to do it. I smelt the gin on his lips and froze. It wasn't kindness, brother. I wasn't imagining it.

'Get lost!' I said with a minor little explosion of breath. I sounded like the kids I taught.

He went away pained, no doubt conning himself with the idea that he really meant to be of assistance. Men... cities... But I could never have lived in a village, the Welsh way of life, all that. There you lived two lives, your own and other people's business. I walked around moodily. I knew something about the city. After dark, it was no different from any other, only in public it liked to pretend it was. Most of the money made had passed out of it years ago. The rich quit, leaving the councillors to squabble over the rates. Walter'd met a Geordie whore once who'd had a real taste of things local. Taken out on the moors, she'd stripped off in some estate agent's car, got herself all ready, when the client asked her to get out while he put the seat down. She did, only he reversed the car and then beat it, leaving her naked and screaming after the vanishing car. She wandered back to the road, found a lorry driver but he had to have his pound of flesh and wasn't going all the way back anyway. By the time he passed her on to his mate and covered her in sacks, she'd had three jumps and not a penny to show for a night's work. She was not impressed.

Why did I think of things like that? Why did I find them ruefully funny? Walter had a knack of reaching the underside of life, and then passed it on to me. In a way, he was an educator, I thought. His subject was dismay which he taught with a grin on his face.

Finally, Ifor came, puffing and blowing.

'Where the hell have you been?'

I'd my back to where he'd parked and had to get in the car before he'd explain.

'Something's come up.'

'Oh no...'

'It's all right. I booked for tomorrow night, a little place near Hereford.'

'Apples,' I said.

'But they can't put us up tonight.'

'Well, there are other places.'

'I always like to book.'

'*And?*'

'I tried to get hold of you in school, but you'd left.'

'So?' I said. 'What made you late?'

'No special reason. I thought I'd give you a lift.'

'By coming to school?'

'It's all right. Your Headmaster was so busy, he hardly raised his head.'

'Timetables,' I said. I didn't say I'd rung his wife.

'But here I am anyway.'

He grinned. There was something very reassuring about

his consistency. And his worries, like booking somewhere for the night. He wanted it settled. My fears left me.

'Where shall we go?' he said. 'We don't have to be in Hereford until tomorrow night.'

'Oh, I don't know. Let's just drive.'

'You want to be back home in time to see Walter on Sunday?'

'Yes,' I said. I hadn't thought about it. Rachel would tell him something. But Ifor was thinking about it *for* me. He was convenient, took care of my fading conscience, everything.

'Then where shall we go?' he said again.

'West,' I said. For no reason at all. 'Let's go west.'

We went out through the grubby back streets of the city, hitting the A48 which joined the motorway, heading west, making for anywhere as if we were a pair of footloose adolescents. It was a relief to be moving, he was happy with his car, and I stopped thinking. This way or that way, it was time out of mind, as the song said, and the sooner we had a drink, the better. Perhaps Ifor always had that effect on his women.

But he worried about where we would stay and wanted things fixed. It nagged him. He didn't mind arriving anywhere, provided we had a reservation. He couldn't bear to arrive on the hop. It was a tiny thing praying on his mind like a maggot; and irritating. He said his wife was away playing bridge. There was nothing to worry about on that score.

So I said, 'If the worst comes to the worst, we can always go to your place?'

I said it mischievously, testing, out of the top of my head.

He said, 'You wouldn't?' all small-boyish like that.

The important thing was, would he?

Perhaps it was the hell of it, why I said it. Perhaps it was the novelty of sex in his own house. Perhaps it was schoolgirl daring, or just thoughtlessness. One of those things you say that strikes a spark, that is agreed without thinking.

'Right,' he said. He said it like he'd made a decision.

'Fine,' I said. I liked decisions, and not having to make them myself.

'Will you have any trouble smuggling me in?' I said. I was enjoying the risqué side of it now. Whatever people had thought before, it was anything except sex. It was innocent and grey, his weekly confessions, my listening, somewhere to go, someone to listen, each to the other, although I never said much. But now there was crackle.

He said he might have to put me under a blanket in the morning.

'A blanket?'

Then he told me some story about some solicitor who picked up a bird, found her at his wife's jewellery, then drove out and knocked the front gates into the middle of the road. He couldn't get rid of her fast enough.

I got touchy.

'Is that how you think of me?'

'You know it isn't,' he said.

And I believed him. But a blanket was too much, I told him. I said, no smuggling. I wanted it open. I didn't think of anything else, neighbours, or his wife. I should have thought this, thought that, but I didn't. The plain fact: I didn't. I did not, and I had time to think, oceans of it.

We got on to the motorway and drove past a huge steelworks as the lights came on, myriads of lights like stars, sprouting at angles, a giant construction of lights stretching as far as you could see, then left them, and the smoke haze and the withered stunted trees, and turned on to the coast road, another port, another town, and on past that to a peninsula where he knew a pub that served fresh cockles and mussels, more little things on sticks. Perhaps sea food gave him ginger. He knew all the good pubs, Ifor, and after that, we went walking on a storm beach miles away from anywhere and the breakers rolled in, their phosphorescence remaining so that it seemed there were just the two of us alone on that vast beach, me, holding his arm and the tide on the make and flooding, the expanse of it looking more like the Atlantic than the Bristol Channel. Whenever you get near the sea, it cleanses you, I thought. It makes you feel smaller in one sense and bigger in another, more wholesome than when you are hemmed in by the squalor and sameness of urban streets.

'We should have come here more often,' I said. I had to shout to make myself heard. He didn't hear, patted my arm, and we put our heads down against the wind.

There were just the two of us on the beach. First, we had to climb over sand dunes, past a caravan encampment. But now it was winter, the caravans were empty and a long promontory like the body of a worm stretched out into the channel, the furthermost tip being struck by the waves and the spray went flying up almost to the cliff top as the water surged beyond it. There was an easterly wind blowing and a full moon. We faced west, sheltered from the worst of it, but round the point we could see white splurges of foam on the water because the sea was boiling out there. It was a wild night suddenly, but I felt wild. The caravans looked inviting. I would have liked to have woken up in one, slept with the sea in my ears. I hadn't done that ever in my life. There were so many things I hadn't done, I thought, so many things I hadn't seen. Ever since I'd known Walter, I'd lived an indoor life. Pubs played a large part in Walter's life and I followed him. We never went away much, seldom to the country even, never to the sea. In a way, we hadn't given ourselves much of a chance, I thought. But we were town people. We'd never lived with trees, were ignorant of the soil. With us, it was work, bed, buses or train journeys to other pubs, other beds. Grey, I thought, our life was grey. At least, for one night, I was taking a step away from that.

We walked again along the beach, saw a light in the distance, a fisherman in oilskins carrying a storm lantern and a pack. He came towards us eventually, his waders making him slow and ungainly. He was puffing and blowing, head bent again against the wind in a sou-wester.

Ifor said, 'Good evening.'

He nodded, stopped to squint at us. His face was wind-reddened and his cheeks were chapped, a broad-shouldered, cheery little man, stumpy under the flapping oilskin. He opened his coat to get a match, showing a seaman's jersey with RNLI on it in red letters. You could smell fish on him. Bait, Ifor said after. He lit a cigarette using the oilskin and Ifor as a shield.

'It's a dead noser on the point,' he said.

'Getting up,' Ifor said.

'Very cheeky backsides,' he said.

We had a little country chat. He told us he was after the last of the bass. But there was nothing doing once the wind went round. He had a hope of a big loner, a specimen fish to dream about, I gathered. He'd come off the point at the other side of the beach and was going home empty-handed. Bass were a hard fish to catch after October. Sometimes there was a run of them when the wind and sea were right; surf, but not too much of it, wind in the west, and the water not too clear. They went for squid, soft crab, sometimes anything, sometimes nothing.

He gave us a little lecture while he finished his cigarette, then nodded and went on. He hardly looked at me. We were just two people on a beach, an excuse to pass the time. When he went, taking his smell of fish with him, we followed his light with our eyes along the beach and up the sandhills until it disappeared.

'That's the way to live,' Ifor said.

'How?'

'Doing what you want to do, when you want to do it.'

I didn't know. He looked the sort of man who props up bars in seaside places. We'd caught him out of doors. But it was nice that he hadn't looked at me in that way, just had his chat with the two of us. I held Ifor's arm tightly and he squeezed it into his side with his elbow. Very married, it was. Innocent and nice, I thought. I wished I'd had children, all scrubbed and waiting for me in one of the caravans. 'Mummy's on the beach.' Some chance...

But I liked the darkness by the sea and wanted to linger there, only it was getting cold and Ifor shivered.

'Once more along the beach,' I said.

So we did another turn about. I liked it in the dark, just walking with another human, my feet firm on the crisp sand, listening to a shell crunch sometimes, or finding seaweed to pop. We were having small things between us now, I thought, little tiny physical things, somehow free of the sex and guilt that bugged us elsewhere. Of course, it was a prelude, I knew, but it reminded me of what little else I thought about. There were logs which had been washed up by the sea to the foot of the sandhills, baulks of dunnage that were too big to lift. I had the reckless, girlish idea of making a fire but Ifor being so old, I didn't like to suggest it. I could have sat there through a blaze, watching the flames and toasting myself. But he might have caught cold and there was no certainty we could have got the wood to catch alight. It made me think of difficulties there must be when you were so different in age. I didn't mention them, but they were there in my mind. Perhaps, part of the strain on him, was that he thought he had to behave like a miniature gymnast all the time. As well as his guilt if he had any. And already I was conscious of keeping him out so long in the cold wind. Even on a dirty weekend, you had human thoughts.

'Come on,' I said. We'd sat down in silence on one of the logs. He was still shivering and although I couldn't see the colour of his face I could sense his coldness.

So we went back at a brisk pace. He enjoyed that because he was a good walker, perhaps liked to show off, and he strode out as we went up the sand hills which tired me. When we got there, I looked again at the caravans. If it had been Walter, we'd have broken in, just slipped a lock somewhere, or perhaps hired one if anybody could be found. But I didn't think it fair to suggest it, although the idea of sleeping with the sound of the wind and the sea in my ears remained attractive. A little thing, less than the presence of children, but another thing, a wistful thought blowing away in the wind like a leaf.

'Well,' Ifor said. 'That was nice.'

'Bracing.'

'Very agreeable.'

Agreeable... The moment we spoke about a thing, we spoiled it.

We drove up to a pub then, but I'd picked up a shell and examined it by the dashboard light. It had contained a razor fish and was shaped like a long cigar case, hinged on one side and open on the other. The colour was exquisite, fawn moving into white with grey whorls forming a pattern on each side of the hinge like two slender elephant's tusks moving into a point. It looked tropical and smelt of the sea, but you couldn't put it against your ear because it was almost flat. The markings were so subtle, colours fading into each other, that I wanted to keep it. It was beautiful on its own and I admired it.

'Would you like me to have it made into something?' Ifor said.

'I can't think of anything I want,' I said, otherwise the

way he was looking at me, it would be in some jeweller's and ruined within the week. It belonged where it was really, but I just wanted to study the colours.

He gave me a paper tissue from the glove compartment so that I could wrap it safely in my handbag.

It was clean near the sea.

But when we went into this pub, there was a crowd of surfers down for the weekend there, and Ifor felt his age at once. I'd forgotten about that, but the surfing lot were even younger than me and it affected him badly. I'd completely forgotten my apprehension earlier and was feeling better than I ever had with him, but now he had it on him, the age genie, and I felt his itch to escape. We had one drink and finished it. How did that girl manage with Charlie Chaplin, I wondered. Or the other one with Frank Sinatra? I felt that frivolous, but I didn't say anything again.

I could see he wanted to go so I suggested leaving, just to make it easy for him, and outside, he held my hand as we went to the car, and for the first time, for the moment, it seemed natural and right. As right as it could be, the way things were.

We ate finally in a three-star place on the way back, a large, svelte dining room. Italian waiters a little off, a place the steel company executives monopolised in the day and left bare in the night. People seldom live where they make their money. My appetite always amused him and again there was the benign aftermath of good nosh, a little too much wine for me as usual, and him flashing his cufflinks and producing an actual cigar cutter during the brandy. He had all the things, equipment for every occasion, representing an eternity of Christmas presents. I sometimes felt that if I had a filling loose, he would have produced some piece of gold equipment and snapped it in again.

But it remained nice, free of strain, until the moment came to go home. He paid, under-tipped which set the waiter back. Then we left a little uncertainly because it looked as if the waiter might say something. He left him a ten shilling piece which didn't seem bad to me, but Ifor thought they'd taken too long getting the bill, which they had. I didn't like the way he said, 'I don't think we shall come again', which was a bit much, I thought, but something had annoyed him and when we got out into the car park, we didn't hold hands and went separately into the car.

'If you like,' I began to say when we got in. I was going to say we could have stayed there, but I didn't get the chance to.

'Relax,' he said, very swinging. 'It's all right'.

'Listen...'

'No,' he said. 'I've thought it all out.'

So I didn't say anything else. If it hadn't been for the waiter, perhaps I'd have gone back myself. It was a night when you'd think twice about winding a watch, little things going wrong, then not being spoken of from the start. Except for the beach.

The drive back was tedious, threading our way back along the road we'd come. But he put the radio on, took it easy, and we didn't say much. When he was telling me about this solicitor and his bird, I gathered the houses had adjoining garages so at least we wouldn't have any trouble getting in at night. I tried to relax again. After a meal, it wasn't so difficult. I supposed we'd go in, have a drink first. Perhaps he had some records. He was the type who kept up with last year's scene. For himself, I supposed he'd have Flanagan and Allen, I didn't know. Would I sleep in the guest room in case of accidents, I wondered. It was very complicated, a jigsaw of anticipation. Whatever is happening to you, your curiosity remains. I was anxious to see into his house. Would it be all gold, like his jewellery? In what way would it express him? All in all, I expected something shifted carte blanche from a shop window, a designer's taste, mats you could curl up in, those dreadful furnishing shop paintings, the anonymity of affluence. I didn't know, but was interested. When we got up into the neighbourhood amongst the detached houses of the rich, he was tense again.

And again, I tried to draw back. 'Listen, Ifor...'

For an answer, he squeezed my knee and kept his hand there.

So I didn't say anything and we shot into the drive quite unexpectedly, changing down at the same time as he purred the car up round his courtyard into the garage which he'd left open. There was a workbench with a vice and tools hanging up in a neat row at the end, then the interconnecting door. There were no lights on in the house.

'Handyman,' I said lightly, but he didn't say anything, switched the car lights out and it was dark. We got out in silence. I heard him touch the car as he passed the bonnet and then the handle of the vice chinked as he touched that as well, as if to reassure himself that familiar things were present. Then he came round to my door to open it. There wasn't much room and as I got out, he grabbed me and bent me back against the bonnet of the car. He was rough now, and attacking. I wanted to be kissed on the hearth, but he didn't kiss me. Now he was greedy.

'Sh... boy,' I said. He always seemed to spoil it, never to pick the right moment. Perhaps he was elated, excited that he'd done it when he must have had some doubts about bringing me there. I couldn't stand straight.

I took his elbow.

'Inside,' I said.

He still didn't put the light on, still kept hold of my hand. I had the idea he was going to lead me straight up to the bedroom, but presently he found his keys, opened the door and led me through the kitchen where I could smell food, and through the hall outside until finally we were in a carpeted room where he found a light switch. It was what Rachel would call The Front Room, long and spacious with a large Adam fireplace and the rugs I expected, but the whole, neither vulgar nor shop-window, a pleasant unostentatious room that looked lived in. There was a hi-fi in the corner, the leads of the extension speaker trailing under the mat that reminded me of Walter at once. The only flaw in the décor...

'Will you have a scotch?'

'I'll stick to brandy.'

It was warm in the room, sidelights under paintings, a fragile pastel of a girl's face, the centrepiece. She looked sickly but chummy and ringleted, and I suppose, was easy to live with, her and her lost innocence, and a pout on her lips as if no one had signed her dance card for hours, a hundred years ago. I saw a shelf of condensed *Reader's Digest* books against the wall. I might have guessed, I thought snobbishly, but I felt quite at home. It wasn't as bad as I thought. There were cigarette boxes on either side of the fireplace. I helped myself to a Turkish, felt wanton.

'Well, well, well,' I said. 'So here we are.'

He brought the brandy out of a cabinet, poured a drink, stood close to me as he handed it over.

I looked over his shoulder at the thick purple drapes over the windows. I was sure no one could see the lights outside. Not a chink.

'Here's to us then,' I said. My feet had got wet walking, then dried out, but were still cold. 'Can I take off my shoes?'

'Your feet,' he said, almost compassionately. 'I'll get you a bowl of water. You can bathe them if you like?'

He said it eagerly.

'If you just put the fire on,' I said. There was an electric fire in the middle of this huge fireplace.

He said they only lit the fire on Christmas Day. Christmas Day was about the only thing in their married life, I thought.

'Of course,' he said, then knelt down and switched the fire on.

I sat down and took off my shoes. Fortunately, they had dumpy, square toes so I wasn't too wet, just uncomfortable. He sat back and watched me, quite friendly. I thought about my earlier apprehension and dismissed it again. It was so much more relaxing to be in somebody's home.

He put my shoes near the fire to dry. I inhaled the cigarette and swallowed my drink. He looked at me shyly like a boy.

'It's great to see you here,' he said. He'd picked that phrase up from me and I'd got it from Walter, 'Great to see you'. But I didn't mind being with him. I'd have thought he'd have been ashamed. Whatever had hit him in the garage had disappeared as quickly as it came. I just smiled, didn't say anything.

'I think there's some old brandy,' he said.

'Open it up,' I said. He liked doing things for me. It gave him something to do, changed that benign stare. They kept the brandy in the other room and when he went in there to get the bottle, a clock chimed in the corner, an ancient grandfather clock. I did not feel like the burglar.

He was gone perhaps two minutes and when he came back, he'd taken his jacket off. Hello, I thought. Perhaps he'd dreamed up something orgiastic like rolling around with the pouffe, but he'd said his wife always objected to him taking off his jacket in the house when he was first married. It was the sort of thing tradesmen did.

I felt sorry for him suddenly. Nearly everybody's life is a mess. Nobody gets what they want. Everybody settles and he seemed to have more regrets than most.

I finished the brandy he'd given me first, then took a pull at the vintage in the new glass. It was like syrup. I made a face.

'No good?'

'I'm awful,' I said. 'Tinned salmon, tinned pineapple, the coarsest brandy. I don't know about many things,' I grinned.

It didn't matter. He'd get me another.

He was so obliging, I felt grateful. The first bottle was nearly empty but he said there was more next door and he went in to get it again. I stood up and wandered about the room. It wasn't full of nick-nacks but there were one or two things he'd brought home from the Army, sandalwood boxes, some kind of African ju-ju, and then I found a touched-up picture of what must have been his wife on horseback. She couldn't have been more than twenty when it was taken, hair in a bun, aquiline nose, pudding face, a vinegary expression even then. The print had been coloured and the colours didn't add up to much. It looked like an old Japanese print. She looked dated, bored, wasn't smiling, the sort of snap only a father would keep. I wondered why they'd kept it. Perhaps the horse had played the role of wristwatch years ago. The horse looked fine.

I put it down before he came back into the room. He must have been at the drink reserves again. Nice to have reserves. He was smiling freely now, a little too freely.

'Here we are,' he said. He'd brought the bottle. I was glad he wasn't declaring his affections again. He looked like a butler in his shirtsleeves and actually wore gold arm bands to keep his shirtsleeves up. I felt fond of him. I was glad we'd come there. The strain seemed to have gone from him too.

But the drink he'd poured was a stiff one.

'I don't really need it, you know?'

'Don't you?'

'No.'

'That's probably the nicest thing you've ever said to me.'

'If it is, I'm sorry,' I said. 'I don't say enough, never enough.'

'You're here, that's enough,' he said.

I put the drink on the mantelpiece and smiled at him. Now it was too hot in the room and I could feel my face burning. I didn't want to be too forward or too pushing, but I didn't want to hang about thinking of things to say. I went towards him and kissed him suddenly, keeping my eyes open and putting my arms around his neck so that he would be in no doubt.

'Well,' he said, holding me. He seemed to have a new confidence.

I wanted him to have that. I didn't mind him.

'Shall we finish our drinks first?'

'Oh no,' I thought. Every time it had been me who had gone to him eventually, and it looked the same way now. He would never learn.

'Here,' I said. I turned around for him to unzip me and felt his fingers tremble.

'Surely you know now, Ifor?'

He didn't say anything for a minute. I slipped out of my clothes without self-consciousness and although he was startled again, I wanted him to have a ball for once. He'd made no attempt to undress.

'What was that in the garage then?'

He looked sheepish, didn't say anything.

I thought, perhaps the familiarity of the room might be putting him off. I quite understood.

'Show me where?' I said politely.

He looked at my dress on the floor. Probably it was the only dress that had lain there in years.

He finished his drink quickly, then took my hand and – finally something got to him because with his other hand he switched the light off and then he was taking his clothes off in the dark.

'There's no rush, boy,' I said.

He kept holding me with one hand. It was trembling.

'I'm not going to go,' I said.

But he was wild suddenly and there we were again in the dark and I could feel him shivering, his desperation, the fever of it, the yearning and lack of skill that was tragic in a man his age. Nobody had ever taught him anything, I thought. I tried to talk to him.

'Darling,' I said. 'Darling, please...' but it was as if sex had become something on the commercials, no good when you got behind the gloss on the package. Everything you read was lies, and finally your own lies hit you in the face.

Was it my fault, I asked after. Entirely, I thought. I had brought him to a point where he had no right to be. Everybody outside would say he was the villain but everybody outside was a fool. Whatever had happened to him, he had never grown up. Nothing turns out like you expect, I thought, and there was nobody to tell you. Ashes, Walter said, the ashes of your own hopes. Why he said it, I'll never know, but I had them now and I had humiliated him too. And Ifor. *He* knew. You can't disguise a sexual failure, however much you try. We lay apart in silence, and then I thought, perhaps I had finally discovered something at last, some sense in the proprieties. In a different age, I wouldn't have been there at all. I would have believed in propriety, perhaps even in virtue. I might even have been afraid of a vengeful God. Whatever I believed, anything that kept me away from this silence would have been merciful. Because from it, this silence, there was no going back.

Neither of us could speak. I tried to take his hand but it was cold and limp. *He did not want me to touch him.* I tried to move him towards me again but he resisted. My knee touched his, he moved it away.

'Don't rub it in,' I said. 'I'm human too. Honest...' I sounded like a little girl. I should fail more often.

He said nothing.

As well as my own self-disgust, I felt an irrational hatred for almost everything I had read or seen which dealt with experiences of this kind. In a porno world, the lies grow bigger and bigger. The artists are corrupted no less than the public. You never read about the affairs that went off half-cock and fizzled into nothingness. It was love always, or satiation and lust. A wholesome perversion might get an airing with a chorus of 'Courage! Courage!' from the reviewers, but for all our voyeurism, we learned nothing special from that either. Our ignorance multiplied and our feelings shrunk. I doubted if I would ever feel more sorry for anyone than Ifor then, or as guilty. But there was, or might have been, a wholesome me somewhere, I was finding that out, the beach girl that never was.

Then I heard him sniffle. I switched a light on. He was crying and shocked, the lines on his face imprinted there as if he had aged in seconds.

'Oh, don't,' I said. 'Darling, please... It's my fault. We're fools to each other.'

He looked at the floor.

'It's Hilda,' he said.

'*Hilda?*'

'My wife.'

It was a bit late to think of her now, I thought, but I didn't say anything.

Then he looked at me stonily, not seeing me but a reflection of himself, his object. *That was what I was, his object*.

'She's in the other room,' he said furtively. 'She's cut her throat.'

I stared at him. At first, I thought; he's telling me something he fears. Like a child again. Every man I ever met was a child. He's telling me something awful to prepare me for something else, something bad, but less awful. If she was in the house, it was bad enough.

'Where is she?' I said disbelievingly.

He nodded at the wall, then looked away from me.

I looked at my clothes, didn't know whether to dress or not. I didn't believe him. How did he know? He couldn't have seen her, then come back in to me?

But he had. He had... He wasn't going to let anything she did interrupt his life. I couldn't understand it, couldn't believe it of another human being, much less one I knew. Or thought I knew. I didn't think of what I had done.

I put my dress on and went in there. At first I couldn't find the lights, but I smelt her. Then I found the light and saw her, sitting drunkenly on a chair, still alive but weak from all the blood she'd lost. She'd attempted to cut her throat, hadn't made a job of it, and gashed herself with a broken bottle, but in doing it, she'd brought her chin forward, pushing the jugular vein backwards so that it was only the side of her neck she'd cut, a vile gash which she'd have all her life. She was still drunk, the cut had stopped bleeding, but when she moved to look at me, it started again. I'll never forget what she said then, or the way she said it. Nobody would. It was inhuman.

'Excuse me,' she said politely. That was all.

I went back into the other room. He hadn't dressed.

'Get your clothes on,' I said. But he was hopeless. He didn't speak until after I had rung the GP and then only to insist on a private hospital.

I left before the doctor came, walked away in the rain, hitched a lift from a person, then a taxi. She was in no danger, I knew, an elderly drunk who had had a stab at herself, his wife. No one will believe anything about people, I thought. They're too awful. Including me.

When I got home, Rachel had locked the door on me. I banged it, shouted up at her, but she wouldn't answer. I turned away. I felt myself growing smaller all the time. I turned away and looked up at the house. The lights were all out. I knew from the feel of the door that the bolt was drawn and it was no use going round the back. She'd done what she said she was going to do.

I began to walk down the road aimlessly. There was sand in my shoes which I hadn't noticed before and now it was beginning to rain, a fine drizzle increasing all the time. I didn't have a scarf and had dressed in a hurry, leaving my hairclips behind. I was twenty-seven, I thought, twenty-seven and nowhere to go. I had the insane idea of going to Walter, as if he would welcome me out of the rain – as if I could crawl into his bed. Anybody else's, but not his. I had a wilder idea of finding my mother but I didn't know where she lived now, and that was an old wound I'd finally closed myself. So I just wandered and wandered, my hair dripping like rats' tails until finally I came to a phone box. I went in, but who could I phone?

Sooner or later you realise it, when you're really on your own. You have it coming, and there it is, your pale face in a public mirror.

I rang Bryn in the end. The final currency was my insightful thought that he needed me at least until he could get somebody else. Fatal.

As it happened, he'd gone to bed and had had too much to drink to drive anyway. His wife came for me and when I got there, he'd dressed. I told him everything.

'Well,' he said. He had no sympathy. He saw it all from Walter's point of view. 'If you ask me, you've pissed on your chips good and proper.'

'Yes,' I said. This is what life is like. With these expressions and these feelings and these men and these women. And me.

Will nobody in this rotten bloody world ever prepare us for anything?

The last thing Bryn said was that there was no need for me to get up for breakfast, and I knew when he said it that there was a revulsion in his mind at the idea of me being there with his children. He didn't say it, but I sensed it.

Finally, you know everything about yourself. It isn't pleasant.

Vera gave me a drink.

She said, 'Perhaps it would be better if Walter didn't know?'

'He'll have to know,' I said. I felt smashed. It was sentimental to think I'd had my experience, that one day I'd look back on it. There are things you can't get over – ever. You can recover, but you can't get over them completely. Living is avoiding traps, not creating them.

'Well, don't do anything silly yourself,' Vera said.

I must have had a look about me. I had come full circle, I thought. First Walter, and then me. Now we were in the same category apparently.

No one ever knows the obvious things until it is too late.

Platitudes matter, I'd found that out.

CHAPTER TWELVE

WALTER

His face was grave and curious, a little moustache bristling above his upper lip, head peering down at me above the white gear and the mask which he'd let slip to speak to me, the surgeon-in-chief. Himself!

'Well?'

I couldn't speak. My back was open. I had this drip set and they'd made a mess of the last one so that there was blood all over the smock which I still wore. A pair of tubes wound out of my side down to a bottle on the floor. There was a clock or something in the bottle. It kept ticking. Tick tock.

'Well?' he said again.

I thought he meant, how did I feel? Like one of those women who've been violated by a Congolese regiment, I thought. Speak? I couldn't get a word out. There was still stuff at the back of my throat, my lips were dry and my throat scraped, substances clogging it. Perhaps it was a rubber solution back there? I couldn't feel pain in one place, it came in waves like a double-decker bus coming forward slowly every minute, inching over me, soft tyres, hard bus. It was like being held in a vice, slow pain, an ache in my eyes, hard balls of pain behind them and in my side, jagged holes where the tubes entered into me. Consciousness, what was that? Being aware of pain. After the waves, stab wounds: jabs.

I tried to frame a sentence. One sentence... I'd seen pictures of raped women showing their bruised thighs to reporters after some outrage. They were lucky.

The Theatre Sister came in with a grin.

'He's being a baby.'

I tried to frame some terrible curse. Where did they get her from?

The surgeon looked at the bottle under the bed.

'Is that blood or debris?'

Charming, I thought. You'd think they were having me for tea.

He looked at me again, found an ophthalmoscope, tried to get a look at my eye.

I shifted, closed my eyes. I could do that. It was fantastic. Thank Christ for eyelids!

'Your eye, Walter?' he said again.

I wanted to be facetious. Damned familiar, what? But oh, the pain! Inch by inch, it crept along again, slow, buckling rubber truncheons expanding as they came, beating up my body. I knew there'd been a big cut. Forty-nine stitches. They didn't mention the muscles. Another con. If I had muscles, they felt like they'd fallen out of bed and left me behind, hanging on nerve ends. My arms... I was like a man lying on stumps.

I couldn't get a word out. I groaned.

'Aaaaaargh.'

'There he goes again,' the Theatre Sister said plaintively. 'All the time.'

I'd stuff a red hot poker up her, I thought. Up her, in her, and through her, then take it out, and belt it up again. Pubic hairs, she'd have to wear a wig there!

'Doctor's talking to you Walter,' she said. 'Come on, boy.'

I was dribbling suddenly, gouts of it, the stuff, debris or whatever. Rachel ought to have been there, but she'd have analysed it for nicotine. Always a moral to be found.

'How is your eye?' the doctor said patiently.

People talking to you in the post-op. I'd never go to a zoo again, I thought. Never. My back felt like it was falling off. Leprosy, the galloping kind. Did I have ribs left? Yes, they'd prised them open. With a jemmy, Mush said. They put clamps there and fiddled about inside. Snip-snip through the clamps. Perhaps they'd left the clamps inside as well. Something was lying in there. Cotton wool and clamps?

The pump kept on ticking. I could smell myself, my interior. Barber shop stuff. And they still had cotton wool up one nostril. What a nose, I thought! Perhaps they had given me a good going over, *all over*. 'Rough him up a bit, he talks too much.' You think like this. Science is what they do, not what you get done to you as a human being.

Violated. If I was rich, I wouldn't move without solicitors.

I'd have them everywhere, heavies and hoods, briefcases by the bed, dictaphones, microphones, the works. And what was the phrase, my favourite? 'Such redress as I am entitled to in law.' That gets 'em. Even in here. 'He's being a baby...' *When I couldn't speak?* I wanted five Quintin Hoggs on that, jammed in the room and all getting at her; and if that didn't work, the SS, rubber clubs, fingernail stuff – the lot!

'Now then, Walter,' she said. 'If you won't answer, we'll have to lift you up.'

She came in between him and me, and bent over to grasp my shoulders. It was another pincer grasp, a rod going through me, right through me – heart, liver and lungs, or whatever I had left. I tried to grab her. My finger moved an inch, but the thought was there.

She held a bowl to my lips. Now she put on a sweet little Welsh voice for the surgeon.

'Come on, Walter. Spit, my beauty. Expectorate, my Prince!'

I'd see them in chains in adjoining cages, I thought. Once a year, the entire profession ought to be put on the streets to beg. Barefoot in the rain. Why? Because that's unreasonable too.

'Open his mouth,' he said.

She put a spoon handle in my mouth. I knew it wasn't disinfected. Couldn't be. I'd have it in an envelope if I could.

'Quintin, they keep it lying about there, I swear. Jump on it! It's not sterile!' You've got to jump on every little thing. Beat them at their own game.

She prised my teeth open.

'Nasty,' she said.

I'd have her, I would. They'd come from Belgium to see what I did to her. It would go down in the annals of violation, brother, and after her torso, I start on the extremities, including her ears. I'd find a way. Right down to the toenails.

She used the spoon like a navvy with a drill. It hammered against my teeth. I gasped. She got a blob of something out, then scooped it into the bowl. It must have been sizeable because they both looked at it while I was gasping.

'Splendid,' the surgeon said.

Then he brought the ophthalmoscope up again. The white light. So I shut my eyes.

'I'll keep them open with a matchstick,' she said.

'You...' I said. 'You...' I couldn't get any more out.

She laughed, all teeth.

'There,' she said.

Can you see, Walter? he said.

I looked at her. I'd remember her. I'd never seen her before, but I'd remember her. *Expectorate, my Prince...* I couldn't think what I'd do to her, it was too exhausting.

'Your eye?' the surgeon said patiently.

'Oh, piss off,' I said finally. Then a speech: 'There's nothing wrong with my eye, you soft git. What have you done to my bastard back?'

Actual words. Amen to the dying, enter the kingdom of the living.

They laughed. Laughed! *Mark it, Quintin. It's actionable.* And that was it finally. You get obsessional about one thing, and remove it with another. But Joey was gone, vanished as quickly as he had come. I could see. *See!* And they didn't have a clue why, I swear. Not a clue. They mumbled about the allergy, removing the source, but do they know? Never in a million years. It's guesswork. They'll try anything, then give it a reason. They're very good at reasons – after. Pathology is the only safe branch of medicine. There, the mistakes are unimportant by themselves.

But not my back. They'd cocked that up for sure. He was tickled to death about my eye. I'd had no bronchoscope, nothing that tilted me over in case of further haemorrhages, they'd been that careful, but he went out with an expression on his face like a kid that said, 'Look, no hands!' The eye bit had worked.

'You can see out of it, Walter?' she said smiling.

'I can see you all right.'

He'd had another look through the peeper before he left. He'd said, 'The floaters are gone. As dramatically as that.'

They don't realise a thing. 'What about my bastard back?'

'Oh, that's normal,' he said.

See what I mean? Normal … I didn't have a back, just a mass of puss, bones sticking through and these tubes. They grated against my raw flesh and bare organs. I'd never drink again. They'd grated my liver to a cinder. I could feel it, like a football. And jagged. Jagged! Oh, words, they're not enough. I was ripped open and left like that. I felt like something on a fishmonger's stall, dead, but still giving a sporty twitch now and again. She wouldn't leave me alone.

'You've got to put up with it, Walter. All that debris…'

'Over you,' I said.

'Oh, there's nasty. I didn't think you were like that. Sexy, I thought.'

She caught hold of me by the ribs again. The ribs... They were on fire already.

'Now come on, lovely. If your eye's all right, we can put a bronchoscope down you now.'

'You try,' I said.

'Up with it, my sweet.'

When she squeezed, I vomited it up, the cotton wool and the clamps – lumps. Clinical medicine. They did better with a barrel of tar.

I'd wet the bed in the process and now she had to change the sheet.

'I might have guessed with you,' she said.

('Quintin, I want it all read out.')

She had the top sheet off, rubbing it against the tubes. She tickled the toes of my feet as she did so. She might have used a hammer.

'You cow...'

'You've got nice feet,' she said. 'Tell a lot by the feet. You've looked after your feet then?'

I didn't say anything. She worked the other sheet from under me, gave my buttocks a pinch. It was assault all right. And battery thrown in, in my condition. When she got the new sheet on, she put the white socks on me again. I must have kicked them off. Then she gave my John a look, raised her eyebrows, then picked up the debris bowl again.

'Oh Christ,' I said. 'No.'

'You've got to.'

'Please…'

'Pull yourself together,' she said. 'There was a fella up here yesterday that shaved himself the moment he woke up.'

'Propaganda.'

'Now then, cough.'

'I can't.'

'I'll make you. Cough!'

'I can't.'

'Cough!'

'No.' I said.

She came for my ribs again, squeezed. I couldn't lift a finger, couldn't even turn away. When she squeezed, it was torture. I would like to have died right then.

'You've only had the top segment removed,' she said. 'What if it was the whole lung?'

What can you do?

'You see that bell?' she said. There was one beside the bed which I couldn't reach.

'I can't reach it.'

'You'll have to if you want me.'

Then she went away. 'Drugs, Quintin? Why no drugs? At this very moment, why no drugs? If it was the Duke of Thing, the bastard would be smashed.'

But I opened my eye again. They were quite right. The floaters were gone. I could see. If I ever walked again…

I must have slept then, because when I woke up, she wasn't there. They must have kept her for the abrasive stuff. Now there was a coloured nurse with a voice like honey and big, deep, operatic eyes. She stroked my forehead.

'Give us a kiss,' I said.

She didn't say anything, just went on stroking and looking at me.

Perhaps I was dead and she had a thing about bodies? Perhaps they'd taken my legs off to reduce the flow of blood to the eye? Perhaps I was hideously deformed? I didn't know. She went on stroking and staring and I went back to sleep before the pain returned. Mush told me later that she was the one who roughed him up. They work shifts, he said, the one I had, her with the gob-bowl, 'Expectorate, my prince!' and the one he had. The Black Mamba, he called her. She jammed his arm between her legs and held it with her knees to get him to cough. From what he remembered immediately, they were neither of them human beings. But dangling on the ends of tubes, we weren't either. All we had were confused memories. Nobody got the evidence.

After two days, they brought me downstairs. The pain did not lessen, not at all. They took the tubes out, watched the smile of relief, then put them back in again. Rough too. And now it was an ache. No hard drugs, only veganin. Veganin... I'd a matchbox full of veganin, saved on good advice and doubled my dose smartly. In addition to being a potential litigant, you have to be a mastermind to get the extras. And crooked as a corkscrew. For two days I dosed myself and tried to lie low when the physiotherapist came. What they call a pain threshold and you call a pain threshold is the difference between cash and credit. I'd travel miles to see a surgeon get his. But when I got downstairs, the Sister said, 'And how is Mr Lacey?'

305

'Marked for life,' I said. 'Scarred by the experience. If you ask me, there is insufficient information before, and inadequate dosages of painkillers afterwards.'

'There's got to be some pain,' she said.

'Why?' I said.

'Your lung has to function.'

'Why haven't they got more anaesthetic then?'

'The problem is to keep you as active as possible.'

'*Active*?'

'Yes,' she said. 'And even if you're only complaining, you're doing something – coming back to life.'

You can't win. Ever. It took me three days to realise that I could see properly, another three to feel better, and in another week, I was anxious to be off. Almost rational again. Almost. When they took the stitches out, I stuck my hand up the staff nurse's tights, got a good grip.

'You hurt me once,' I said. 'That's all.'

'Thanks,' she said. 'I only came into this job for the thrills.'

Perhaps they get used to it. But there was no pain, forty-nine snips, didn't feel a thing.

'Now that is medicine,' I said. 'Thanks,' I said. 'Thanks very much.'

She removed my hand. 'We were waiting for that,' she said.

They wouldn't let me wander the corridors, but I hobbled in to see Mush next door. They did him the day before, half his lung, a good lop. He couldn't take the drugs so well either. He was lying there, pale against the pillows, weaker than me, that bloodless run-over look. He was so pale, he'd make flour look healthy.

'Well, how is it?' I said.

'I'd sooner do a ten stretch.'

'Ten years?'

'Yeah. Lend us a quid, will you?'

'What for?'

'I'm saving up for skis.'

I like the real Cardiff boys. Hard, they are. My kind.

We knew we were all right, because the surgeons didn't come again. But I wanted a squad around me to protect my ribs. I was half-expecting the eye to go again, but it didn't.

Mush said, 'How are we off for fags? Got any?'

'None,' I said. 'I'm giving it up.'

'I'll have to try the cleaners then.'

'Don't,' I said.

'You don't want to listen to them,' he said.

'What if you coughed?' I said. 'Have you thought that?'

But he had to have a fag.

'And visitors tomorrow,' he said. Could I cover the door of his cubicle?

'Cover it?'

'Yes,' he said. His bird was coming. He had to have a bang.

'You've only just got the bloody stitches out,' I said.

Didn't matter. He'd promised himself. And as soon as he could walk, he had a job to do.

'A job?'

'The fridge in the Sister's office,' he said. 'For the special diets.'

'You're going to crack it?' I said.

'The grub,' he said. 'Peaches and that.'

'You be careful,' I said. I was getting to sound like Rachel.

'Nuts,' he said. He'd save me some cream. We were all of us getting better, reverting to type. A hospital was as good a drum as any. He saw himself as a kind of Robin Hood with the peaches and cream, and no doubt was getting his hand in again.

I didn't know what I'd do, and when Connie came at last, red-eyed and heavy-lidded, I knew something was up. As I'd suspected. She started to tell me. The education world, this wife who'd had a go at herself, the general shittiness of weak, inadequate people.

'I don't want to know,' I said. 'Ever.'

'But...'

'Don't expect me to clear your chest, I've got enough on my own.'

'It was...' she began to explain.

I was half out of bed. She stood up.

'Excuse me,' I said. 'I've got a mate next door.'

I heard his bird struggling to get the screens around the window in the door. I felt I ought to go in there and say a few words. He could have had a haemorrhage on the spot.

'What are you doing?' she said.

'Listening,' I said.

But she didn't ask why. She said, 'I quite understand if you don't want to say anything.'

It was like a stranger talking. This is what we had come to. I didn't look at her. I had more time for the nurses, even the rapist in post-op. Now, there was a character. What she did, she did every day, knew what she was doing. I had to give her that. I remembered her looking at my John, a casual curious glance. What would she be like in a party? Nurses though, they'd taught me something. I'd learned to respect them.

'Walter, there's so much to say,' Connie said tearfully.

'I've got used to being without you,' I said, hard.

'Yes,' she said.

'Yes. Nice, was it?' I knew. You always do.

'No,' she said. She looked away.

'Good,' I said. 'Splendid.'

'Are we going to go on like this?'

'You want everything, don't you?'

'We all do,' she said. 'Or we did.'

'*Did* is right.'

'And now?'

'I've got to get out,' I said. 'Of here. Then we'll see.'

'Is your eye all right then?'

'Ask the Sister. She has the details.'

'I expected that.'

'Yes, well,' I said.

Somehow I knew everything without her telling me but I didn't want to dwell on it. It never pays to dwell on things. But I couldn't say much. I'd said too much before, now nothing. There was so much to talk about, so many things to decide, but I didn't want to talk about them now. Without quite knowing why, I wanted her to go. Especially when I heard the signal from next door. Two taps on the wall. All clear. He couldn't have had a haemorrhage.

'Rachel didn't come?' I said.

'No, she didn't think you'd want her to.'

'That's where she's wrong,' I said. I went a bundle on

Rachel suddenly. I'd got used to her face, her sayings, the folklore. We'd talk a lot, or rather, she had. You couldn't discount her, she was there, formidable, concerned, involved. There weren't many people like that any more. They didn't come that strong. I'd never thought of her except as a piece of the furniture and nobody was that. And now she wasn't there, I missed her.

'Tell her, will you?' I said. 'Tell her I missed her.'

'Yes,' Connie said. 'Is there anything you want?'

'Not at the moment,' I said. We were guarded like strangers and I didn't care somehow. Perhaps it was an improvement, my not caring. You have to look out for yourself, I'd learned; you had to walk your own road, be your own man and take whatever was coming to you, not forgetting to duck. I'd never ducked much, I thought, perhaps that was the trouble. But now I'd learned. You learned strange things in strange places, but the important thing was to be open to experience. There was a time when I would have wanted to know why she hadn't come, and would have needed the details, but now I didn't want them, not any of them. I remembered too, that night when I watched the moth flickering to its death around the television set. Dai was alive then, the old collier who did arm exercises every night as he tried to keep his grip on things.

But his grip had gone finally. He had died next to me, choking to death in his own dust-impregnated sputum, his coughing continuous, going on for hours and days until even the oxygen gave him no relief and he could not eat or sleep and the life began to dribble out of him like the

310

current getting lower in a battery. He kept fighting it all the time, gripping the bed rails until the veins stood out on his arms, and his temples and his face were blue with straining, but he would not relax. I would remember every detail of that death all my life, how the sputum came up from his chest and out of his mouth and nostrils, squeezing itself out, a continuous ejaculation of grey clouded mucous that had lain there for years, all the years he worked underground developing a non-classified industrial disease. It was as if the body was finally purifying itself of all the muck which had brought it to a halt before it expired and then lifted him, gasping bolt upright in bed and he was staring across at me, his eyes bulging and bloodshot, but he never squealed, never protested, never moaned. He took what was coming to him, a simple code for a simple man, and although it would have been better if he had protested or quit that industry years ago, the moment he decided to stick it, he stuck it and lived it, his kind of life the best way he could.

That was what we all had to do, I thought. He had taught me that and I was grateful to him. I never saw a man take so much with more dignity and go right to the end without cracking or flinching like he did. Whatever anybody said about where we lived, including what we said ourselves, there were *men* here, men you could be proud of, men to remember, men who made their private marks on you and the world. I didn't know very many of them, but now I was reminded that they were to be found, tucked away here and there, living their own lives in a small way, and usually not helped by anybody except themselves. It was a cheering thought, something I could have talked to her about once, but now I did not have the inclination.

I remembered Dai instead. There was more than her absence between us. In a short time, so much had happened. When I looked at her, I didn't see her so much as a reflection of what I had been, and that I had thought about enough to want to put it behind me as well as I could. But I had no words of comfort either. When there was this kind of strangeness between people, comfort was a luxury I didn't have to give. I had been too near too fierce an experience to talk too much. Most of what I had found to say, was to myself. If I had moaned when the pain came, it didn't worry me. I knew everybody moaned at this time, but now I felt stronger and less involved. It was wrong to dote on people, wrong to simper, wrong to be reduced to bleeding from the trivial wounds of people's tongues, or their lousy cheating. If you had inadequacies, you should put them right, not describe them, and if you couldn't put them right, you should cover up, and move in another direction. You should never shrink from the legwork, I thought. It was a useful analogy.

So I didn't say much to her. I didn't have it in me to say.

'See you,' I said when she left. No more than that. Perhaps she'd get over it, whatever it was that she had done to herself, perhaps we would start again, but it would be a long time, I knew. Perhaps too long. I had got harder myself, harder and clearer most of the time, especially when I thought about myself and us. I had been a wet, I thought. Too harmless, too doting, falling into the victim's role like a dunce automatically treading his way to the back of the class. You think of yourself as this kind of person and you become it. Accept too much, and you go under. Of course, I still had that old, wry part of myself that slipped out as it had done in post-op, but that wouldn't come again easily. As every day went by, I was growing stronger. Already the wound was beginning to itch, a good sign, they said. In a week or two, I'd be out in the grounds, in two more discharged. I had it all in front of me. Some of us are lucky, I thought. And then I had a further terrible thought, more frightening than any I had had before.

We were lucky because we could always walk away.

I wouldn't go there straight from hospital, I decided. There was a convalescent home where they gave you a week to adjust yourself. Mush was going because he had nowhere else to go. The way things were, I didn't think I had either. And I didn't feel any obligation to tell her either. I had left too many places for everybody's convenience except my own.

CHAPTER THIRTEEN

CONNIE

When the day came for his discharge from the convalescent home, he didn't want either of us to pick him up. He'd promised himself a pint with this new associate, he said. Mush, he called him. Then he'd come home in a taxi. They were already sneaking out for pints in the afternoons, both of them a rarity since surgery wasn't much practised in the treatment of tubercle now. They were like old soldiers together, Rachel said. And a lot else besides.

She said not to expect him to say much, not for weeks. I thought she was exaggerating, but she remembered the boys standing on the square in groups after the first war, not saying anything, just gazing into space. She said there was distance in their eyes.

I didn't understand what she meant. It wasn't very clear. She went on. It wasn't that they'd seen too much, but perhaps they were debating their right to look at anything again. Experience can do that to you, Rachel said, being suddenly removed from the known experience, having to learn to run before they could walk, and when they returned, there was a hesitancy to their walking as if they were not quite sure. It was an impression she had formed, that was all.

I didn't know. We waited for Walter together, not saying much, a change. It seemed to me that you recover from everything by taking a stance. Not that I'd recovered, but I'd taken a stance. I was there, wasn't I? I'd said my piece, even if he hadn't listened. I told him everything finally. I didn't expect forgiveness, anything so naive. Nothing could alter the horror of my own feelings, that poor besotted woman, but I had come in at the end of her life, not the beginning. Ifor was no more pathetic at the end of the affair than he was at the beginning either. Facts are facts. Ifor, his hopelessness, his real aura of dismay, finally reached me, but so did my own. I was sad, but you can stay feeling guilty only for so long.

More than anything, it was Bryn who queered me with myself, I thought. I had to put it some way, his revulsion at seeing me with his children. It was unfair, irrational, but there in his eyes for me to see. I would have thought he was more humane than that. I had gone to him in need, but he didn't really care. Perhaps that's what we have to learn. Very few of us care about each other. Rachel's generation did, ours don't, that's the difference. We retreat into little worlds of our own making, and when those worlds crumble, we have to hide ourselves, our insignificance. Ifor had done that, and brought his world crashing about his ears. Perhaps it was the final experience. Now he would age gracefully, attend her at bridge, find the little courtesies he'd previously ignored. Ultimately, he would be a companion and think of me as old men think of young girls, savouring their bodies, imagining their affection, holding little fragments of memory close to them in their dotage. Despite everything, he had used me, indulging a wild and temporary dream which very nearly ended in disaster but did not. I'd no doubt he'd pick up the pieces.

But would I?

Rachel said that everybody's life was bits and pieces. Some people had to pick themselves up off the floor more than most, that was all. She remained optimistic, hopeful, loving and caring. She'd taken a shine to Walter. He was her golden boy now. I was mentioned in dispatches as it were, but although she said nothing, my fall from grace was apparent. All I could do was make the best of things. I would have to be patient, even contrite.

Bryn hadn't spoken to me much in school. They must have got wind of the affair in the Ministry because they sent another Inspector out to the school a few weeks later. He was unimpressed. Making do, was one thing, he was sure we were doing our best, but the fact of the matter was that the conception of an ancient school making do in a residual area was undesirable. The sooner we were part of a larger catchment area the better. I suppose he came to see me out of curiosity. He thought the workbenches inadequate, the syllabus pedestrian. Bryn mentioned something about my experience on this panel, but his reaction was caustic. In view of my youth, he didn't feel I had any major contribution to make. He didn't feel it at all desirable that adolescent boys were principally in the charge of a woman and trusted that arrangements would be made accordingly. He didn't care much for Bryn either. The sooner we were part of a fully comprehensive scheme the better. When I attempted to challenge some of his assumptions, he said that he had no doubt I had a contribution to make, however small. His name was Rees, and science was his speciality.

'Well,' Bryn said. 'Heels together, thumbs to the seams of your trousers. That's that then.'

'Yes,' I said. It was extraordinary that everything had changed so quickly. Bryn had asked for a new roof on one of the outbuildings, but they said they were going to pull the school down and rebuild elsewhere. We were on the way out, it seemed, and although they would no doubt transfer me when the time came to move, I knew that I would apply elsewhere. There was a distance between Bryn and me now. People hate intimacies finally. They bring you no closer together, merely reveal weaknesses that you both wish weren't there. Confidences shouldn't take place at all, much less pleas for help.

And there remained Walter. Try as I would, I could see no golden future. Physically, he was getting better all the time. He was nearly thirteen stone for one thing, and needed new clothes. He would buy them himself, he said. He didn't want me to go with him or do anything for him.

Of course, I thought there would be digs at me, if not insults, but with that optimism you have, I had a hope for something different. Nobody wants to stay miserable or guilty. But there had never been an even tenor of feeling between us, just acceptance and sex. If he had felt anything, it was sentiment at the idea of being married, or having a girl beside him. There was always his romanticising, but it was so coupled with his failures that it was difficult to know what did go on in his mind. He reacted, that was all, I thought; reacted to whatever the situation that faced him. He never created anything. He clutched at me as a drowning man might clutch at a plank for support in the water. Now that he was rescued from that victimised part of himself, perhaps he would not need me in any role.

I did not know. Waiting there, I thought of my life and all the relationships I had never had. It was a sad catalogue. There was no one else in my adult life except Rachel and Walter. Both thought the less of me now, and if at first I did not care, I began to realise the smallness of my contribution to their lives. I used them both, as Walter had suspected. There had always been this suspicion in his mind, us using him, but now it was amply confirmed, especially where I was concerned. He was harder, more bruised. He did not look at me when he spoke to me. By contrast, when he spoke of Rachel, he was loving and caring. She had got through to him finally where I had failed.

I began to think of things I might do for him. Perhaps we should go into some kind of business together, something small and local which left us time to ourselves. There were things to talk about. If we weren't to have a family ourselves, we might think of adopting children. It was time we grew up. Immediately, we might have a holiday. But I checked myself. My thoughts might have done for somebody else's life. There was already a note in them that sounded like the advice column in a women's magazine. Of course, we ought to go away together to get to know each other again, all that. But if it was right for Walter, a warm, affectionate feeling on that easy-going basis, it wasn't right for me. Although I hoped so, in myself, I knew otherwise. You always know. There is no second chance for caring, either you care with that intensity which is the luck of people with real feelings, or you manage. His phrase again.

And when he came, it was in his eyes, on his face, his stance, stamped across him like a slogan. He had found something in himself and it didn't include me.

He wouldn't sit down and he kept the taxi waiting. He had just come for his things. As soon as he came in, he asked Rachel to go upstairs. He'd see her on the way out, he said.

'On the way out?' she said. She sounded old and querulous.

'Yes,' he said. That was what he had come about, his departure.

She didn't know what to say, where to look.

He held the door firmly open for her.

She must have recognised something new there because she didn't argue, just left.

I looked into his face, his eyes, and the most terrible thing was the kindness in them. He'd been bitter in hospital, bitter and hurt, but now he was so far removed from me that he was sorry. Sorry for me...

'It's always hard,' he said. 'Always. They tell me,' he said. He grinned self-consciously.

I wanted to hold him, move to him, but I could not. If I did, he would have pushed me away. I stared at him, realising it. Every experience becomes a little unreal in your mind on recall. Your mind selects, things get exaggerated. But I knew that I would not forget any of this moment.

'It's not as if we've made a real go of it at any time, is it? It's not just when I was in hospital, not that, or any one thing. It's just that I don't want to live off you any more. Or with you either.'

I wanted to scream, beg, plead, just to preserve one illusion, one hope, but I could not.

'I thought I'd be too soft to say it,' he said, still with that half-embarrassed grin.

'What?'

'Too bloody soft, you know?'

'No,' I said.

'To have to go through this.'

Then I thought, he's teaching me a lesson. Although I showed nothing, I felt hysterical. I was like a little girl again. Oh, not somebody else leaving me?

'It hasn't worked out and you were the first to see it,' he said.

'No,' I started to say.

But he wasn't listening. He'd said what he had come to say.

He turned to the bedroom to get something, then looked again at me. 'Oh, come on. In two days, it'll be like it always has been. Thank God we haven't got any kids.'

I stared at him, the finality of it dawning upon me. Then he went into the bedroom.

'Bloody shoes,' he said, grumbling away. 'That's all I've come for. Nothing else fits.'

I heard him take down a suitcase and fill it with shoes. Even then I thought, I can do something, say something, but it was no use. Whatever I did, we had nothing between us. I had known it all along but now it was final and every part of me that cried out for some last minute succour was a waste. He was right.

He came out of the bedroom carrying the suitcase. It hadn't taken him a minute to find all he wanted.

'I don't know how I'm going to tell Rachel,' he said. He was talking to me as if I were a witness.

I felt bitter suddenly, hating him. 'She'll get over it.'

'Yeah,' he said. 'She's got over quite a few things.'

I felt myself panic. You can be married to somebody for six years and they leave in an afternoon. It isn't reasonable.

'Aren't I...' I began.

'Yes?'

'Aren't you going to kiss me?'

He grinned. 'You know where that would lead to, and anyway, I'm still stinking of tablets. I'll see you,' he said. 'In a calmer moment.'

I had never seen him so calm.

'You're teaching me a lesson, aren't you?' I said.

'Is that what you hope?'

'Yes, Walter. Yes.'

'I was afraid of that.'

'What?'

'That's why I decided not to come back at all.'

'*You bastard!*' I said then.

'Oh, come off it,' he said levelly. He turned to go. 'I'll give Rachel my address.'

Perhaps he wanted a scene, to see me crawl, or perhaps he meant it, really meant it. I didn't know then. I had parted from him before without regrets, I remembered, and now it was his turn.

'All right. If that's the way you want it,' I said. It was so trite, so awful, worse than anything that had ever happened to me. Anything at all.

'That's the way it is,' he said. Then he went out, shutting the door behind him. I noticed he still held himself very carefully, hunching the shoulder where they'd operated. I heard him drop the suitcase on the front doorstep, call to the taxi driver, and then go upstairs to Rachel. He spent longer with her than he did with me. Then he came downstairs at a run, hesitated in the hallway.

'So long then,' he called from the doorway.

I found a voice.

'Goodbye Walter.'

He closed the door behind him and I listened to the taxi drive off, still standing rooted to the spot as I had before I first took him into hospital all those months ago. Rachel began to cry upstairs but I did not. He always said he used to leave nicely and without hard feelings. It was his speciality, leaving people.

It seemed an age before I sat down, and when I did, my weariness was total. He did not need me, and the hardest thing of all to accept was my unimportance, my loneliness, just being me.

Foreword by Rachel Trezise

Rachel Trezise was born in the Rhondda Valley in 1978. *In and Out of the Goldfish Bowl* was a winner of the Orange Futures Prize. *Fresh Apples*, her collection of stories, was published to critical acclaim and short-listed for the Dylan Thomas Award. Her work has been translated into German and Italian.

Cover image by Ernest Zobole

Ernest Zobole (1927 – 1999) was one of Wales' most innovative and challenging painters. He took as his lifelong theme the places and people of his native Rhondda whose landscape he re-interpreted through startling imagery and use of colour. His work is collected by institutions and individuals worldwide.

LIBRARY OF WALES

The Library of Wales is a Welsh Assembly Government project designed to ensure that all of the rich and extensive literature of Wales which has been written in English will now be made available to readers in and beyond Wales. Sustaining this wider literary heritage is understood by the Welsh Assembly Government to be a key component in creating and disseminating an ongoing sense of modern Welsh culture and history for the future Wales which is now emerging from contemporary society. Through these texts, until now unavailable or out-of-print or merely forgotten, the Library of Wales will bring back into play the voices and actions of the human experience that has made us, in all our complexity, a Welsh people.

The Library of Wales will include prose as well as poetry, essays as well as fiction, anthologies as well as memoirs, drama as well as journalism. It will complement the names and texts that are already in the public domain and seek to include the best of Welsh writing in English, as well as to showcase what has been unjustly neglected. No boundaries will limit the ambition of the Library of Wales to open up the borders that have denied some of our best writers a presence in a future Wales. The Library of Wales has been created with that Wales in mind: a young country not afraid to remember what it might yet become.

Dai Smith
Raymond Williams Chair in the Cultural History of Wales
University of Wales, Swansea

LIBRARY OF WALES
FUNDED BY

Llywodraeth Cynulliad Cymru
Welsh Assembly Government

CYNGOR LLYFRAU CYMRU
WELSH BOOKS COUNCIL

LIBRARY OF WALES

WRITING FOR THE WORLD

Dannie ABSE

Ash on a Young Man's Sleeve

Ron BERRY

So Long, Hector Bebb

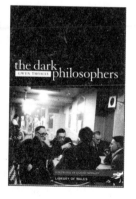

Gwyn THOMAS

The Dark Philosophers

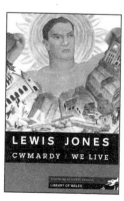

Lewis JONES

Cwmardy & We Live

www.libraryofwales.org

Alun LEWIS

In the Green Tree

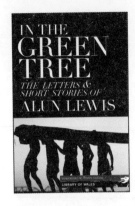

Alun RICHARDS

Home to an Empty House

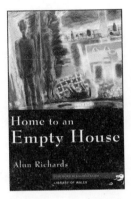

Raymond WILLIAMS

Border Country

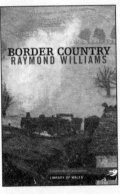

Emyr HUMPHREYS

A Man's Estate

Margiad EVANS

Country Dance

enquiries@libraryofwales.org